Vale of Tears

a&b

Vale of Tears

A Bradecote
and Catchpoll Mystery

SARAH HAWKSWOOD

Allison & Busby Limited
11 Wardour Mews
London W1F 8AN
allisonandbusby.com

First published in Great Britain by Allison & Busby in 2019.
This paperback edition published by Allison & Busby in 2020.

Copyright © 2019 by SARAH HAWKSWOOD

A CIP catalogue record for this book is available from
the British Library.

First Edition

ISBN 978-0-7490-2404-8

Typeset in 11/16 pt Adobe Garamond Pro by
Allison & Busby Ltd.

The paper used for this Allison & Busby publication
has been produced from trees that have been legally sourced
from well-managed and credibly certified forests.

Printed and bound by
CPI Group (UK) Ltd, Croydon, CR0 4YY

For H. J. B.

Chapter One

April 1144

The rider in the green jerkin knew the way well. He had travelled this route often enough not to admire the spring beauty of the Vale of Evesham, and, on this occasion, to let his mind wander to darker things; to think upon his sister. He shook his head, and his horse snorted as if in agreement with his thoughts.

Poor Edith, dead and buried without even a babe to her name. For all that the family had been proud of her marrying nobility, what good had it done the wench? None that he could see. His brother and their mother had been all in favour of it four years back, and crowed like dunghill cocks at their good fortune. He was only grateful now that Mother had not lived to see her only daughter shrouded and buried. Not that he had seen it either. Her lord was so ashamed of his lowly relatives, though not his wife's looks or dowry, that he held them at arm's length even at her death. News had only reached Evesham weeks later, when he had sent his steward with dues for some abbey land, and sent him also to announce her demise. The steward had said his lord grieved mightily, and that was the reason for him not coming in person, but all the lord need have done was send immediately to Evesham and they, her brothers, would have been there at her obsequies. Overwrought by grief? It sounded most unlikely. Her lord had always seemed aloof with her on those rare times Edith had received her relatives.

The man sighed heavily. He was rather more soft-hearted than those to whom he sold horses would ever have imagined. Edith, he thought, had deserved better, and a fine hall and rich hangings did not make up for a cold-hearted husband, and near estrangement from her own kin. How much better it would have been for her to marry Edric Corviser, and live out her days in the happy town bustle within which she had grown up. Perhaps she would have died as soon, but at least not haunted by the constraints of being 'my lady', nor of loving a man unworthy of her devotion. He should have listened to her more attentively at their last meeting, assuaged those womanly fears of hers, so that at least she would have departed this life unencumbered by doubts. Poor Edith, foolish Edith. To fall like that, on steps she knew well, must have meant her mind was elsewhere. Perhaps those worries had overset her. In which case, the lordly husband shouldered some blame. Yet, when brother had confronted husband, the man had looked down his noble nose and told his brother-in-law that he was a fool, and an offensive one at that, and if he so much as stepped upon his lands again he would have his men-at-arms teach him a lesson he would not forget and send him back to Evesham with lash marks that all would see. The rider fumed. He would put any profit from his next two sales for the monks at the abbey to say Masses for his sister's soul, and her hard-hearted lord would live to regret how he had mistreated her, and her folk.

A chaffinch sang lustily on the bough of a crab apple. This first week after Easter 1144 fell at the beginning of April, and the male bird was in full courtship plumage, the slate grey of his head contrasting with the deep, rosy pink of his breast. The blossom was as yet mostly buds, but the first early flowers dared any frost to do its worst upon them. Primroses still adorned bank and spinney, and the green freshness of unfurled leaf and new grass was almost too much to assimilate. The glories of nature passed by at the pace of his trotting horse, whose ears flicked back and forth as a blackbird pinked in a hedgerow. He came shortly to the junction with another track. A rider approached and turned a neatish chestnut cob to take the same route. The rider, who wore his woollen cap at a jaunty angle, and seemed very pleased with the day, nodded in a vaguely amicable way, but said nothing for some time. They passed through the village with its broad greensward in its centre, and continued towards the river. Only as they approached the wooden bridge over the Avon did the happy man attempt to strike up a conversation. He complimented his new-found companion on his handsome horse.

'Ah, now I can see as you are a man who knows his horseflesh, friend. Well up to your weight, and good haunches to him, has your beast. I'll vouch he keeps a good pace all day and does not flag. My old fellow is not as impressive-looking, of course, but has stamina, and that counts for a lot, you'll agree?'

The green-jerkined man nodded in a non-committal way.

'You'll be heading up to Stratford, perhaps? I am only going as far as Welford myself.' The happy man seemed to look forward to the company.

The other rider murmured about heading south into Gloucestershire. This gregarious stranger seemed mightily keen to talk, and clearly took no notice that the responses were brief. He had returned to the subject of the horse again, and was extolling its good points when the cob jibbed suddenly. The man patted its neck placatingly, and heaved a sigh.

'There, and I hoped the beast would have the sense not to play up with yours beside it.' The rider shook his head. 'I do not know why, but he has a dread of crossing water. I end up leading him every time, and cursing him roundly, especially when it means fording, though in all other respects he is a good horse.' He dismounted, and rubbed the cob's soft nose affectionately.

In truth, the animal did not look too distressed, but out of courtesy the man in the green jerkin also got off his horse, puffing slightly, for he was round of cheek and belly, and began to lead his own beast. The Avon was visible through the cracks between the boards. It passed beneath them, augmented by spring rains, but flowing clear and steady, with pike lurking in the sluggish margins among the weed and reeds for unwary prey. The horses clattered slowly over the wooden planks as the riders talked, and then, had anyone been looking, something strange happened. The rider of the cob stepped in front of the man in the green jerkin and turned to face him. A moment later the man in the green jerkin sank to his knees, but was hauled upright and tipped into the wet welcome of the river. Without so much as looking over the low rails, the other man mounted the cob, took the riderless horse by the bridle, and trotted back the way he had come.

The undershot wheel turned steadily, relentlessly, unhurried as always, belying the bustle within the mill as the wheat was ground between the great querns, and the flour slid down the chutes to the sacks beneath. Martin, the miller's son, and Ulf the apprentice, watched them fill and lifted them away before they overflowed. Neither lad numbered more than thirteen years, but the labour gave them muscled arms and shoulders sturdier than their fellows in the village, excepting the blacksmith's boy. Their faces were dusty white with the flour, and they coughed occasionally. Speech was a waste of breath, and brought only more coughing, so they worked in silence, each waiting eagerly for the cry of the miller above that the last sacks of grain had gone in for the morning's grinding. Come noon they were able to ease their shoulders, and enjoy the fresh, clear air outside in the sunshine, while they lounged on the grass and took bread for their hunger, and small beer to wet dusty young throats. Then they could break their unwilling silence, and be their age.

They relaxed in the gentle April warmth, though the breeze had a bite to it still, reminding them that this was spring and weeks yet from summer. It was Ulf who first noticed the body in the leat, thankfully before it caught in the wheel. A dead sheep had done so over the winter and been messy enough. He scrambled to his feet, pointing, and sending Martin running for his father and a stout pole. Wulstan the Miller did not doubt the boy, for he was pale, wide-eyed, and gabbling.

'Nay, slow down, lad, or else I'll not catch a word.'

'A body, Father, a body in the leat. Come quick afore it is taken by the wheel.'

'A beast you mean? A calf or—'

'A man, honest, a man. Come.' Martin tugged his father's sleeve, though the miller needed no prompting.

Ulf had grabbed as large a stick as he could wield, and was trying to delay the progress of the corpse, with a modicum of success, though the force of the water in the narrow leat meant he was struggling. The body floated face down, the arms outstretched, the fingers white and puffy. It had been a man, clearly, and yet it was no longer a man but a grotesque parody of one. Wulstan brought a rake pole that they used to pull clogging weed from the channel, and between the lad and his master, the corpse was prodded into reach. The miller knelt and hauled the waterlogged body from the stream, needing all his considerable strength to pull it clear, and rolled it onto the grass to stare at the sky. Ulf cried out an oath and turned away, retching. The white, oedematous flesh had provided food for fish on its journey down river, and the face was ragged and unsightly. Wulstan crossed himself.

'God have mercy. Best fetch the reeve, Martin. And Father Jerome.' He shook his head. 'It is ill folk will think of me for taking him out, but there was no choice once he was in the leat.'

'Father?'

'The Hundred pays a fine for any man dead by violence who is not proved English, son. It is called the murdrum fine, and King William imposed it upon us, lest we kill his men from Normandy. Not that I have seen more than a half-dozen men in my life as I would think foreign by speech or garb. No, these days it is really a tax, and a way to show the lords are "better" folk.'

'Then cast him into the river proper again, Father, if you doubt he met his death by accident.'

'Tempting, Martin, but this was a man. How would you feel if your kin were put back, aye, perhaps time and again, and kept from holy ground for the sake of such a risk? No, off you go, and tell nobody else on the way, mind.'

The boy ran, glad not to have to look at the ravaged face any more. He wanted to show he was made of sterner stuff than Ulf, but his gorge had threatened to rise, even so. He did not hear his father address the body, in a hushed whisper.

'May you have drowned by accident, friend, and God have mercy on both you and us.'

The priest was easy enough to find, but the reeve's wife could only say he was off with one of the village men, discussing some dispute over an orphaned lamb, and it was some time before Martin and Father Jerome caught up with him. The villager was most unwilling to see the reeve depart before he had made his position abundantly clear, and several times over, and since Martin could not reveal the reason for his urgent need for the reeve at the mill, it was fortunate that the priest was there to add his authority. Only as the three of them made their way along the Avon bank to the mill could the boy tell of what had turned up in the leat that noontide.

Oswin the Reeve looked grave, and even more so when he saw the body. Martin withdrew, having, he felt, been man enough already. Miller, reeve and priest looked down at the remnants of a middle-aged man, well clothed and booted, with a scrip still at his belt, and coin within it, as a brief investigation revealed.

'The poor man drowned,' sighed the priest, shaking his head. 'So many fail to appreciate the river is not to be treated lightly.'

'Well for sure he was not the victim of a robbery, God be praised,' averred the reeve. 'You only have to look at him to see that. If he fell in and drowned, then we might yet avoid the murdrum fine. Yet what worries me is those good clothes. This was no poor man, not by his garb, and the more chance he was not English.'

'I had no choice, Oswin.' Wulstan sounded apologetic.

'No, that I grant you. Pity it is, though. Ah well, I had best head to Worcester in the morning, and report the corpse. Father, he can be kept in the cool of the church, yes?'

'Of course, though we cannot shroud him until the law has seen him.' Father Jerome sighed again. 'We are blessed to be on the fertile edges of the river, but in its floods and what it brings us, we have to pay for that blessing. Have you a hurdle on which he could be carried, or a handcart?'

'A handcart, yes. And some sacking to cover him decent enough. Wait here, and I will fetch both. Then I suppose we has to wait for the lord Sheriff at Worcester.'

William de Beauchamp, Sheriff of Worcester, had much to occupy him. Lady Day had just passed, and rents and taxes had to be gathered from the tardy and unwilling as the new year commenced. His own manors were in the midst of lambing, and his daughter Maud had been ailing of a fever and given his lady wife sleepless nights of worry, and requests for his immediate presence at Elmley Castle. Beset by myriad calls upon him, he was not a happy man, and when William de Beauchamp was not happy, nor were those who served him.

Serjeant Catchpoll headed the list of unhappy underlings. Since the sheriff of the shire would not go door to door with demands for payments, as usual the task was delegated to the sheriff's serjeant. He did not like being set to the task with grumbling and curses, and he also disliked hunting down those unwilling, or indeed unable, to pay their dues, and regarded it as unworthy of him. For all that the tax-gathering gave Catchpoll his name, it was real crime that interested him – murders, blackmails and thefts, though the sheriff would have told him that not paying tax was stealing from the King and from him too, since he took his pennyworth of shrieval dues. Catchpoll had, therefore, in his turn, delegated a large part of it, this particular spring, to his 'serjeanting apprentice', one flame-headed Walkelin. Trouble was, Walkelin, whilst proving a keen young man, and useful in hunting criminals, had a long way to go in mastering the art of being 'a right miserable bastard', which was a prerequisite for acting as the lord Sheriff's tax gatherer. Catchpoll had tried to teach him to smile in the face of the tales of woe with which he was everywhere presented, and to view with the utmost suspicion the promises to turn up at the castle gates the very next day with the missing monies, but all too often he returned with less than the sum due, and moved to pity by reports of infants who risked starvation, and elderly dames who would be cast into the streets without even a blanket to call their own. Catchpoll shook his head and winced.

'I cannot decide which is worse, young Walkelin, you being so soft in the heart, or soft in the head. Half Worcester must know by now that they have but to show you a mite with big blue eyes and a trembling lip, and claim they went to bed hungry the last three nights, and you will be waiving their dues.'

'But what about the Widow Saddler, then, Serjeant? She said as you had turned a blind eye these two springs past to her shortfall. Was she telling untruths?'

'Ah.' Catchpoll paused. Widow Saddler had five brats under the age of seven, and her husband's business had gone to a cousin who considered kinship was all about taking, and nothing to do with giving. She worked hard, plying her neat stitches in bridles as before, but the cousin gave her nothing but a lean-to he rented as part of the property and expected her to stump up the rent money for it. 'That,' announced Catchpoll, decisively, 'is exercising serjeant's' – he floundered for the term he wanted – 'discreet-tion, and only to be used by serjeants with long years of experience. Besides, you'll find I shake that nithing who runs Aelfraed Saddler's business for the extra.'

He sent Walkelin back to chasing up the lagging taxpayers with a stiffened resolve.

Oswin, the reeve of Fladbury, reported first, as was right and proper, to his overlord, the Prior of Worcester, since Fladbury was held by the priory. The Benedictine shook his head in sorrow, promised prayers for the dead man, and sent the reeve on to the lord Sheriff.

'But what of the murdrum fine, Father Prior, if we cannot find a name and prove him English?'

'We can but pray also that the fine is not levied. It is a grievous burden on the Hundred, for sure. But be positive. Were this man not English, surely he would have been remarked upon if lost? And he drowned, remember. Unless it was proved someone pushed him into the river, drowning is an accident.'

'I hope so Father Prior, I do heartily. Wulstan had no choice but to take the body from the water, or else it would have been caught in the water wheel and been mangled, as well as perhaps causing damage to the mill.'

'Oh indeed, he did right. This poor man needs now his name and decent burial with kin to mourn him. But even if that proves impossible, the Good Lord knows him already, and we will pray for his soul as fervently. Now go and inform the lord Sheriff, and hand the business over to the law.'

Oswin went from priory to castle and sought audience of the lord Sheriff. William de Beauchamp was not, however, available, since he was meeting a delegation of the Worcester burgesses, and Oswin had to make do with the sheriff's serjeant. In truth, he found it far easier dealing with a man of his own rank and language, with whom he could discuss the matter frankly. At the conclusion he was given leave by Catchpoll to return home, with the assurance that the lord Sheriff would be told swiftly of the matter, and that most probably Fladbury would see the sheriff's men in the next day or so.

It was several hours later that Catchpoll repeated the tale to his superior, who had had an irritating afternoon with the town worthies.

'A body from the river! Well, like as not it is a drowning from somewhere. Nothing that I need investigate in person.' He growled, and pursed his lips.

'But the report said the body was well dressed, in a green jerkin with fine decoration, and good boots too, my lord.'

'You mean the body might be someone of note?' De Beauchamp eyed Serjeant Catchpoll with suspicion. 'If you are trying to worm your way out of a journey to Fladbury, Serjeant, you are out of luck.'

'Me, my lord? A journey to Fladbury sounds far more interesting than another day making myself the most unpopular man in Worcester, my lord.'

'I thought you had your man Walkelin doing that, you old fox.'

'Ah yes, but he is not yet experienced enough to do it alone for long.'

'And I also thought that at this season it was I who was the most unpopular man in Worcester.' The sheriff grinned, wryly.

'The mantle of your unpopularity spreads wide, my lord,' responded Catchpoll, his lips twitching. He thought he could judge his superior's mood well enough to jest.

William de Beauchamp laughed out loud.

'"Mantle of unpopularity". I like that, Catchpoll. Well, you can creep from under it and head for Fladbury in the morning. And as for the status of the corpse, you can go through Bradecote and tell my undersheriff he can stop tupping that new wife of his and abandon a husband's duties for shrieval ones. He can inspect the body with you, and take any declarations on identity, noble or otherwise.'

'And if it is murder, my lord?'

'You'll bring me the killer, dead or bound, or have very good reasons why not. I trust you not to fail me, Catchpoll.'

'Thank you, my lord.' Catchpoll was in fact less than grateful for the burden laid upon him, but judged that at least if he failed, the undersheriff would share the blame. 'And Walkelin?'

'Oh, take him with you. I don't want a job half-done here, and him maundering about looking lost without your guidance. He shows promise, I give him that, but he has a lot yet to learn.'

Chapter Two

Catchpoll rode into the manor at Bradecote on a loose rein, mid morning on the following day, with Walkelin still chuckling over what the lord Sheriff had said about his newly-wed undersheriff. The serjeant thought Walkelin would do well to be reminded that Hugh Bradecote was not at the top of the chain of command. They got a nod of recognition from the man-at-arms who was honing a knife on a whetstone. Walkelin rather hoped that he would follow Serjeant Catchpoll within, but he was told to walk the horses, since, with luck, the undersheriff would be at home, and they would be able to set off without delay.

Christina Bradecote was sat in the solar, bouncing a gurgling baby of just over seven months on her lap. It was a natural enough scene, and the look of love upon her face would not have been different had she given birth to him. She was his mother now, and if she dreamt of a child of Hugh Bradecote's getting, stirring within her, she had already given her mother-love to baby Gilbert, and prayed for the soul of the woman that bore him. Ela Bradecote had been cold and still within hours of his birth, God grant her peace. Ela might have carried him, reasoned Christina, but it was she would raise him, Hugh's son, now 'their' son, and his first attempts at speech would be directed at her just as surely as if she had passed through travail with him.

She looked up as Catchpoll was ushered in, and smiled.

'Serjeant Catchpoll. Ah, do not tell me! You are here to drag my lord from my side, shame on you.' She pouted, but a dimple peeped. He thought how well she looked, how openly happy. 'He is gone out with the steward this morning, but I expect him to return by noon.'

'Sheriff's business, my lady, so I say as the shame is the lord Sheriff's.' Catchpoll gave his death's head grin. 'And I will wait in the hall, if I may. No wish to disturb you and the babe.' He nodded at the infant, who was now blowing bubbles, and still gurgling.

'He has grown well, since you saw him last, has he not?' Christina sounded mother-proud.

'Aye, he has that. And has teeth, I see.'

'Oh yes, as the wet nurse keeps muttering about.' She sighed. Nobody knew just how much she regretted that she could not nurse him herself, how strong the urge flooded through her when she cradled him, but instinct was not enough. So, when he clamoured for food, it was Aldith whose scent and succour brought peace to the hall. 'But wait here, and tell me of anything interesting that has happened in Worcester.'

It was idle enough chatter, but passed the time until the long stride of Hugh Bradecote was heard crossing the hall. He opened the door, and entered, shaking the wet of a sharp April shower from his hair.

'Catchpoll, you come with orders, no doubt. I saw Walkelin in the bailey, taking shelter from the rain.' He nodded at the grizzled serjeant, and indicated a seat, then gave his wife a bright, and intimate, smile. If the lady Bradecote looked radiantly happy, her lord looked almost smug. Little over two months after they were wed, the novelty of marriage had clearly not begun to dull into the everyday.

'My lord, the lord Sheriff has had word from Fladbury of a body fetched up in the mill leat, and the corpse has to be viewed and decided upon. God alone knows where it has come down from, and how many times it has been cast back, quiet like, like a tiddler, by those afraid to be penalised for it, but there.'

'And the sheriff wants me as well, to look at a drowned body?' Bradecote looked surprised, and not a little annoyed. Was the sheriff just 'reminding' him of his shrieval duties?

'Oh aye, I thought you'd not be impressed, my lord. But this body is not just some villager who thought he would look at his reflection in the water one night whilst ale-sodden, and tumbled in. This corpse has no name, but he has got a fine set of clothes, according to report. The Hundred is keen to find out who he might be to avoid the murdrum fine, if he is English that is. And if he is a better class of corpse, well, the lord Sheriff thought a better class of sheriff's man ought to take a look.' Catchpoll did not grin, quite, but the eyes danced.

'But even if he isn't English, a drowning is not always a murder. Accidents happen all the time.'

'Indeed, my lord, and that is one of the things we are going

22

to look at. Most folk don't study the dead as we do. They see a body in the water and say "Ah, he drowned", unless there is an arrow through his neck or his head is missing. And these people want us to say he drowned in an accident. But you and I know a man can drown, or can be drowned, and if there are signs—'

'So I cannot get out of this, can I?' Bradecote interrupted, with a groan.

'No, my lord,' replied Catchpoll, cheerily.

'I do not see why you should be dismayed, my lord.' Christina was trying not to smile at his reluctance. 'It sounds but a simple task. Go and see this body, decide on how he died, and return home.'

'And if it was murder after all?'

'Then you will solve it. I have every faith in you, in you both.' She beamed at her husband, and then at Catchpoll.

'Thank you, my lady. The lord Sheriff said much the same, but somehow it sounded more of a command and less of a compliment.'

'We will eat, and then be about the business. We can reach Fladbury by evening, easily enough. Go and fetch in young Walkelin.'

'And I will send for food and ale.' Christina called the nurse, who had been dozing in a corner, to take the baby, and would have followed Catchpoll from the chamber, had not her husband detained her by taking her arm. 'My lord?'

'You understand I want to go and to return swiftly?' He spoke softly.

'Of course.' She smiled fondly at his concern, and her voice dropped. 'I know that you will not be away longer than is needful, but your mind must be upon the task, remember, not wandering back here beneath the bedclothes.' She blushed, but her eyes were bold. 'I shall see to it that your manor runs well in your absence, and keep your bed warm ready for your return.' Her finger stroked down his slightly stubbled cheek and across his lips. 'Now, my lord, a wife's duties also include hospitality, so let me go and arrange for bread and a good cheese to set before you, Serjeant Catchpoll, and the ever hungry Walkelin.'

A little over an hour later, Hugh Bradecote mounted his big-boned grey, and with a nod to his lady, led the trio of sheriff's men out of the courtyard at a brisk trot. He had parted more privately from her with an embrace that was both a farewell and a reminder of his passion for her, and she could watch him depart with what appeared upon the surface as almost regal coolness, however loth she was within to see him leave. He was the undersheriff of Worcester, and duty was duty. It was what had first brought him to her, and she accepted that it would also be what frequently took him away from her. All she asked of heaven was that he always came back.

The sheriff's men arrived in Fladbury as the afternoon cooled to evening, and went first to the house of Oswin the Reeve. His wife was quite overcome at the presence of the undersheriff in her humble home, and her nerves sought relief in chatter, which was as voluble as it was inconsequential. Bradecote cast the reeve a look which spoke of the need for a simple exchange of information, and so Oswin ushered them, as soon as he could, to the church, wherein the body lay by the font.

'You need me to remain, my lord?' He sounded none too willing.

'I would rather you fetched the priest, and then the miller and his lads that found him, if you would, Master Reeve.'

'Aye, that would be best. I'll not be long.' He eyed the covered body with distaste, and made his escape.

Catchpoll and Bradecote exchanged looks. The undersheriff nodded, and Catchpoll lifted the old blanket that covered the body. They did not expect it to be a pretty sight, but then they had seen bodies before that had not met a peaceful end in their beds. The serjeant sucked his teeth, speculatively.

'Been in the water some time afore they got him out. Makes things more difficult for us, of course, both to find out what happened and where.' He pursed his lips. 'Did you drown, my well-dressed friend?'

Walkelin frowned.

'If he came from the water, Serjeant . . .'

'That just proves where he was, not where he had been, nor yet what happened. You help me get his clothes off him, young Walkelin.' The younger man pulled a face. 'No point in being sight-sick, lad. It is just a body.'

'But it is a bit . . . ripe, Serjeant.'

'Then best we do it now, before it gets any worse. Come on.'

They took the garments carefully, piece by piece, and Bradecote inspected them for any signs that might help them. The green jerkin was well made and had intricate stitching. The undershirt was fine linen and his boots were not long worn. The sound of footsteps on the stone flags made them turn. The priest had entered. He looked sombre, and nodded at the undersheriff. Catchpoll resumed his inspection of the naked torso, and screwed

25

up his eyes. The flesh was white and swollen from the water it had taken into the tissues, though where the clothing had covered it there was less disfigurement from fish biting.

'Go on, Catchpoll, tell me what you think you can see.' Bradecote studied his serjeant as carefully as the serjeant studied the corpse.

'Well, if you look careful like, I think you can see a thin mark, just here, up by the rib. There is no sign of blood of course, and the swelling of the flesh makes it hard to see. But I think a narrow blade entered here, a dagger most like. If it was long enough it would kill fast, into the heart.' Catchpoll pressed his thumbs either side of the faint mark, and the skin did part slightly.

'Is it enough to prove an unlawful death? It seems such a small wound.' Father Jerome peered, reluctant but wondering.

'Size of wound is not everything, Father.'

'No, but will it be believed?' Walkelin asked. 'You said yourself that folk will be wanting death by drowning, since a murder would bring the threat of the murdrum fine.'

'What they want and what they get is not up to them, or us. It is up to the law. This man died by another's hand.' The serjeant was firm.

'Is it just possible that he could have taken his own life, Catchpoll?' Bradecote would prefer it not to be a killing but . . .

'Well, I doubt a man would stab himself, and right by the river. Most folk that kill themselves want to be found, want to show how they were driven to the deed by circumstance or persons they knew. Remaining unknown is not often their choice. Also, a man might cut his own throat, but this is not a common wound to inflict upon oneself. No, you can be sure this man did not die by his own hand.'

The door of the church creaked open, and the miller, his son and apprentice entered cautiously. The priest instinctively placed himself between them and the pale body, and Hugh Bradecote stepped forward.

'You called for us?' Wulstan asked. 'I am Wulstan, miller of Fladbury, and this is my son, Martin, and my apprentice, Ulf. They first saw the body in the leat.'

The boys nodded.

'When was this?' Bradecote smiled reassuringly at the youths.

'Day before yesterday, about noontide, my lord,' volunteered Ulf. 'We only came out of the mill then, to eat. It was in the leat, about a hundred paces from the wheel, floating. When it entered, we could not say.'

'Understood. Thank you.'

'My lord, I took him out the water, but I have seen things that have been fresh in and those that have not, and he was not. There is no saying where he comes from, nor if this was his first landfall, if you get me.' Wulstan was sombre.

'Unwanted, and thrown back – aye, that is likely,' muttered Catchpoll.

'But I did right, to get him out, the drowned man?' Wulstan needed official commendation. 'Besides the fact he would have got caught on my wheel.'

'You did right, but the man did not drown.'

'But you can see—'

'We can see that he took a blade beneath the ribs, and he did not get that off some Avon pike.' Catchpoll saw the anguish on the miller's face. 'It is sorry I am for it to be so, but we now have even more reason to seek out his identity, for this man was killed by intent.'

'You will find out who he is, my lord?' It was almost a plea. Wulstan was imagining the opprobrium of his neighbours and looked to Hugh Bradecote to rescue him and them from the consequences of his good deed.

'Oh, I would expect to find out – and think of it, Master Miller. There are far more Englishmen than "foreign" in the shire. Personally, since I was born here, have never left the shores of England, and nor did my father before me, I think of myself as English, whatever the bloodlines may prove.'

'Fair enough, my lord, but 'tis those bloodlines that count, and for such purposes you are tainted foreign, however much you gainsay it.'

'There's no cause to berate the lord Undersheriff.' Catchpoll was wary of his superior's dignity, however much in agreement he might be with the man.

'It is all right, Serjeant. Master Miller was stating a fact, and we deal in facts, as you often tell me. The fact we need next is where this man entered the river, and where he came from before he did so. If he had been in the river some three or four days, how far might he have come?'

'Avon is flowing nicely, my lord. If he was midstream it might be he came from Warwickshire, easy enough, but then if he got into the shallows for a bit and lingered, so to say, he might only have come from below Evesham, even.'

'My lord, where he came into the river might be upstream of where he lived anyways,' announced Walkelin, thoughtfully. 'We do not know where he was heading.'

'And we do not know of anyone being cried as missing as yet. That worries me, so it does.' Catchpoll grimaced. 'If a man goes off for the day and does not return, his nearest and dearest make a fuss.'

'Then perhaps he lived alone, or else his "nearest and dearest" did not expect him back for some days, Catchpoll.'

'Or at all,' piped up Martin, becoming interested.

'Or at all, my lad. Well spotted.' Catchpoll nodded at the boy, approvingly.

'We can say as he is not from about Fladbury, for anyone that grand would be well known hereabouts.'

'Which means we look in bigger pools, if he is a bigger fish.' Bradecote smiled slightly. 'Such a man as this might not stand out so much in a town, a town like Evesham. Catchpoll, I am sending you across by the nearest ferryman to work up to Evesham on the far bank, and find out if our man was known or fetched up there in the last few days. Walkelin and I will take this bank and we meet in Evesham tomorrow afternoon. Father, I want the body sent to the abbey at Evesham. Can you arrange for a cart or burden-beast to get it there, but not before noon? I would prefer us to be there first and speak to Abbot Reginald.'

'Of course, my lord.'

'And for tonight?' Catchpoll was wondering.

'I can offer you hospitality, my lord.' Wulstan offered. 'The wife would be pleased to feed you, and there is space enough in the mill.'

Bradecote smiled, though his heart sank at the thought of a night upon the mill floor, rather than snuggled up to his warm, soft wife. Mistress Miller also proved to be a cook who believed in quantity rather than quality. As the undersheriff later whispered to Catchpoll, as they lay wrapped in their blankets and on the mill floor upon as many spare sacks as the miller could muster, his heart had not sunk as deep as the leaden dumplings that the lady of the house had fished up from the greasy depths of her pottage.

'If you hear a strange thump in the night, Catchpoll, it is my insides, trying to move the foul things.'

'They were not so bad, surely, my lord,' whispered Walkelin, from the corner. 'They were filling enough.'

'Filling, perhaps, but so would a lump of iron be filling, and I do not recommend that,' griped the undersheriff. 'Now let us try and get some sleep. And if you snore, I shall kick you, Serjeant.'

Serjeant Catchpoll did not snore, but none of the three men slept well. Bradecote's digestion was disordered, Catchpoll's bones disliked the hard floor, and Walkelin woke with a nightmare in which he was being eaten alive by a huge, talking fish. Dawn saw them stifling yawns and rolling their blankets, keen to shake the mill dust from their boots, and indeed their hair. Catchpoll told Walkelin that he now had a good disguise for his memorable red mop.

They thanked the miller with polite lies, and in admiration of his stomach's hardiness. Walkelin also murmured about his sore ears, but Catchpoll just grinned.

'Now that marks you as a man unwed, young Walkelin. A married man could tell you that after a while a husband learns to "not hear" the majority of what his good woman says. The art is hearing the important parts and always seeming to be attending. It is a bit like the way your nose gets used to a smell and then does not smell it, even if you are a fuller or a tanner. All down to experience, of course, and that you only get with,' he grinned his sepulchral, thin-lipped smile, 'experience.'

'And when you have finished giving Walkelin the benefit of your many years' "experience", Catchpoll, we will bid you farewell and see you tonight in Evesham, at the abbey guest hall. I know you will say we could sleep across the river at the castle, but I had to do service there two years back, and it is a draughty hole of a place that de Beauchamp has erected purely for defence, and seems to have carpenters working on it all hours of the day and night. I tell you, after a month there my head ached all the time. Right, you have more chance of finding news, I grant, for there are no hamlets at the water's edge on the north bank, but we may find fishermen who use it often enough.'

'I'll try at Charlton for any who have been down by the river, but Hampton might be a better chance. The ferryman at least might have seen something, if I can get him to admit as much. He's an observant old bird, like a heron – quiet, but knows his river, of course. I have come across him before, Kenelm the Ferryman.'

'Until tonight, then,' Bradecote wheeled his grey to the left, 'and good hunting, Catchpoll.'

The trio split up. The undersheriff and serjeant's apprentice made their way along the northern riverbank, stopping at every individual they met, whether a man mending a coracle or a lad fishing for minnows. They all looked blankly at the sheriff's men, shaking their heads and denying any knowledge of a body in the river.

'I had no real hopes, though the bend here means the river is slower and there is more chance of the body getting caught up, but from here to Evesham the bend puts the slower current with Serjeant Catchpoll. Hampton ferry could be key.'

Charlton gave Catchpoll as little success as his superior and junior. The villagers were dismissive. If there had been a body in the Avon, well, bodies floated downstream, so why should anyone take note of it? They had seen nothing. Catchpoll was torn between understanding and irritation. They were simple folk with a simple view of the world, and crime did not occur to them, unless it happened to them or theirs, and in a small village, everyone knew their neighbour's business so well that opportunity for crime was very limited. The reeve was keen to recount how there had been a murder in the village in his father's time, when a man had killed his wife for infidelity, but since those days the nearest thing they had to crimes were the odd defamatory comment or the emptying of an eel basket. The serjeant moved on along the bank to Hampton.

Hampton ferry had been worked by father and son for several generations. Some even laughed and said that Kenelm had been conceived on it. Kenelm merely shrugged. What people thought was their business, as long as it did not interfere with the ferry. He saw Catchpoll approaching, and gave him a slow nod.

'Good day to you, Ferryman. The trade plies well?'

'Well enough, Serjeant, well enough.'

'There's been a body washed into the leat at Fladbury. Man in a green jerkin. I was wondering where he went in, see, and thought to myself, there's none keeps an eye on the Avon in these reaches more than Kenelm the Ferryman.'

The ferryman did not bat an eyelid at the compliment.

'And?'

'And so I am asking, if you saw anything green and man-sized pass by here.'

'Friendly, or official?'

'I prefers friendly, but if I don't get the answers I wants, then it will be official.'

The ferryman permitted himself a twinkle in his heron-grey eyes.

'In a friendly way, and in no part saying as the thing ever got nigh a bank, you understand, there was something large and green-clad, I might have noticed a-ways downstream about four days back. Now, I isn't saying it was a corpse, just it was large and green and floating, and I am not talking of a lily pad.'

'That's fair enough, Ferryman. Much obliged.' Catchpoll nodded in acknowledgement. 'And now you can do me another good turn.'

'Which is?'

'Ferry me across to Evesham. Here's coin for your pains.'

The ferryman smiled, and in almost companionable silence, the two men, and Catchpoll's mount, crossed the Avon.

Chapter Three

Hugh Bradecote and Walkelin entered Evesham a little before noontide, and shortly before the corpse, which was well shrouded, then covered with a blanket and laid in the hired cart. The days in the river had done it no favours, and Catchpoll had decided that slung across a mule it would attract the flies that the spring warmth was hatching, and give off foul odours if it was sun-warmed. The town was all bustle as they passed through and headed for the abbey, where they might find a cool chapel for the body, and, since it was the hub of the community, might even find someone who would recognise it, or know of a missing man. The abbey church would draw any wishful of laying a plea before heaven, even if they had offered prayers in their parish. The sheriff's men would also find bed and board, and after the poor fare they had experienced the night before, the abbey kitchens would produce an infinitely more palatable meal.

Brother Porter opened the gates, and directed them to the prior, who would arrange matters over the disposition of the body. Thereafter Hugh Bradecote went to see the abbot, both out of courtesy and to find out how best to discover the identity of the cadaver. There was still a slim chance that it had come from further upstream, but it was a very unlikely possibility. Walkelin awaited the corpse, and then Serjeant Catchpoll.

Abbot Reginald was a spare man with a tonsure ringed with silvery hair, and a quiet manner that concealed a firm and decisive character. He frowned at the sins of his fellow men, but was not in any way surprised at them. He offered hospitality to both the living and the dead, and suggested that the brothers, both lay and choir monks, should view the body.

'Many are from the town and its neighbouring manors, and have kin hereabouts, and from all walks of life.'

'It is not pleasant viewing, Father. The body was in the Avon some days, and the fish . . .'

'The body is destined for corruption in this world, my son, and the brothers should not be overcome by its frailty. I take it you think it still recognisable?'

'Yes. I would say any who knew him well would know him still.'

'Then they will file past at the end of None.'

'Perhaps better after Terce, if they are eating, Father.'

'Ah, I see, yes. You may have the right of it, my lord Bradecote. After Terce then it shall be, and they will add him to their prayers, whether named or not, at Vespers. You say the poor man was stabbed, so there is no chance that it was an accident?'

'If any used the blade in self-defence, one wonders why they did not come forth and tell what happened straight away.'

'Hmmm. Your faith – in the law, that is – is perhaps stronger than other men's. If it were self-defence but the man who struck home was of inferior rank . . .'

'The law makes no difference in rank, Father.' Hugh Bradecote spoke almost severely, and the abbot smiled, a little wryly.

'I am heartened to hear it from your lips, and doubt not that you hold it so, but there are others whose application of the law is not so even-handed. Experience often tells the weak and unimportant that they are ignored.'

Bradecote frowned. What the churchman said held truth. It was not right, but it was true.

'Had they come to me, then . . . But it does admit the possibility of self-defence. I would say, however, it is far more likely to be a case of murder.'

'Alas, yes.' Abbot Reginald sighed and nodded. 'And finding out the identity of the victim is the starting point for your hunt for the culprit.'

'You do not object, Father, in assisting, though it ends in a judgement and death?'

'The judgement of man is but nothing compared to the Judgement of God, and I do not see it as wrong that evil-doers face the former before the latter. We will give what help we can.'

'Thank you, Father.' Hugh Bradecote smiled, and the cleric mirrored the expression.

'As I recall, it was you who rescued the archbishop's envoy and our brothers in Christ before Candlemas. We prayed for their delivery when we heard of their taking, and it is pleasing to meet the instrument of their release. God guided your steps then, and may He do so now.'

'Amen to that, Father.'

The Benedictines dutifully filed before the body as it lay upon a bier in the mortuary chapel, at the end of Terce. Most crossed themselves; a few with weaker stomachs also put hand to mouth. One by one they shook their heads at the undersheriff as they left. Bradecote had given up, when the penultimate monk gasped, and made a small cry. The sheriff's men were instantly alert.

'You recognise him, Brother?' Bradecote tried not to sound excited.

'Yes, my lord. He is kindred of mine. His name is – was – Walter Horsweard. He has – had,' the monk became flustered, 'horses for hire and sale.'

'And has he close family, a wife, a mother or—'

'He has a wife, my lord, and a brother also. What grief to the brother, since it is barely over a month since their sister died. I was commiserating with Walter over that but two weeks since.'

'Yet he has not been reported missing? No worries have been raised in the town?' Serjeant Catchpoll sounded disapproving.

'Ah,' the Benedictine turned to face him, 'but he was often about the shire and beyond, purchasing animals for sale. If he has gone away, why should any remark upon him until after he is due home?'

'True enough. Thank you, Brother, for your help.' The undersheriff smiled dismissal, and the little monk went away, to be consoled by his brothers, and secure in the knowledge that his kinsman would have their prayers.

'I am sorry, my lord, that I did not recognise the body, for I am certain Master Horsweard has come to services here over the years, but alas, whilst every soul is known unto God, they are not known to me.' Abbot Reginald left the shrieval trio to their deliberations.

'Well, that is a start, my lord,' remarked Walkelin, with a remarkable degree of cheeriness for their location. 'So now we go and see the brother and the wife.'

'The widow, Walkelin. So wipe the smile off your face first.'

'Yes, my lord, of course, right away.'

Amicia Horsweard was not quite what any of the sheriff's men had expected, having viewed the body of her late husband. She was a vibrant, chestnut-haired woman in her early twenties, decidedly curvaceous, and with near violet 'come hither' eyes. It was as much as Catchpoll could do not to whistle through his yellowing teeth at the sight of her, and Walkelin's jaw dropped quite openly. Only Hugh Bradecote remained unmoved, but then his head was only turned by a certain dark-haired lady residing in his hall and sleeping in his bed.

'Who would have thought the sly old dog would have a piece as fancy as that,' muttered Catchpoll, under his breath. 'Interesting.'

'Interesting as in you like the idea of speaking with her, or for what it means to the murder?' enquired Bradecote, wryly.

'To the death, of course,' grinned Catchpoll. 'If she had been his age and homely, well it might be that she would play him false, but far less likely. I mean, does a wife like her sit at home with her embroidery, when her man goes away? And even if she does, are there men scrabbling at her door to see how she sets her stitches? There'd be plenty would be keen to offer succour if she pricked her finger, I am thinking.'

'Keener still to prick—'

'Thank you, Walkelin. We don't need your views, not while your tongue is near hanging out. Shame on you, with you worming your way into the affections of that Welsh wench in the castle kitchens. Have you got her to stir you yet, like a good pottage?' Catchpoll gave a bark of laughter.

'When you have both finished, perhaps we might make progress with the matter in hand?' Bradecote tried to sound as sarcastic as William de Beauchamp would have done, but a muscle twitched at the corner of his mouth and ruined the effect.

They approached the young woman, sombre-faced.

'Mistress Horsweard?'

She turned, and her eyes were instantly appraising. Whore's eyes, thought Catchpoll, who had seen her type many times, unconsciously assessing how much, and how much fun she might manage to get from the encounter.

'I am Mistress Horsweard, yes.' The voice was pitched low, and she smiled slowly.

'Might we speak with you privately, Mistress?' Hugh Bradecote found it slightly off-putting, watching this woman play off tricks she must use day in, day out, yet knowing he was about to change her life.

She looked a little surprised, and his serious tone made her frown, drawing together her prettily arched brows. She nodded and led the way into the front chamber of Walter Horsweard's messuage, her hips swinging naturally. Catchpoll noted several men let their eyes feast over her retreating rear. There would be men keen to replace Walter, even if they had not cuckolded him.

The chamber was quite dim, and the lustre of her hair diminished as it was deprived of the life of sunlight. She folded her hands before her, in a gesture that was acquiescent, and calm.

'My lord?' His garb and speech made her assumption easy enough.

'Mistress, when did you last see your husband?'

'Walter? Why, it must be a day less than a week since. He is gone into Gloucestershire to purchase horses. I can tell you nothing of the business, my lord, and if there is any question of the ownership of any beast—'

'No, no. Nothing of that sort, Mistress Horsweard. I am afraid I have bad news for you. Your husband met with . . . an accident. He has been found dead in the Avon.'

She regarded him blankly for a moment. If it was an act, then Bradecote thought it a good one.

'Dead?' She pouted like a child deprived of a treat, and the frown deepened. She took a deep breath, and Walkelin's eyes drifted from her face to the heaving bosom without thinking. 'Was he ale-ripe?'

'That we cannot say, Mistress,' volunteered Serjeant Catchpoll, 'but we can say that if he was, it did not cause his death.'

'But if he drowned?'

'He did not drown.'

'You said he was found in the river. And I know he could

40

paddle out of his depth, for he was used to the river from childhood. So he must have been . . .'

'He was put in the river dead, most like, or senseless at the very least. He was stabbed, probably into the heart, if the blade was long enough.' Catchpoll did not make it easy. He wanted to see how she reacted to stark truth. Bradecote shot him a swift glance. If they misread her, and she had been a loving and faithful wife, this was harsh.

Amicia Horsweard paled, her eyes became bigger in the milk-white face, and her hands gripped one to the other as if for support.

'You are saying he was killed by intent, was murdered?'

'Yes, Mistress, we are. I am sorry for it, but that is truth.' Bradecote tempered the cold fact with a touch of sympathy in his tone. 'So we need to know of anyone here in Evesham who had any cause, real or invented, to wish him dead.'

'Wish him dead?' she echoed, softly, and crossed herself. 'He was successful. That is not always popular, but to seek a man's death for it – no, surely not.'

Bradecote thought her genuine enough, but Catchpoll's eyes were narrow.

'So you think none would want him dead for his horse dealing, but there are more reasons than trade to want a rival cold and buried, Mistress.' He had not quite suggested that she might be a very good reason to remove Walter Horsweard, but it hung in the air, nevertheless. Catchpoll was certain that she closed herself off from that moment. Perhaps she had not been involved in any plan, but he would swear she had very good cause to know names they should investigate.

'Perhaps,' she suggested, tentatively, 'you might look to my husband's brother, Will. They were at odds before he departed – on his travels, I mean,' she coloured at her choice of words, 'but I could not be sure over what. He will inherit the business, for sure.'

Bradecote did not ask if there were heirs of Walter Horsweard's body. If she had children there was neither sound nor sign of them within, and even if there was only an infant at her skirts, a mother would be keen to tell the law that they had a claim of inheritance. Catchpoll was more interested in the speed with which she had offered up a suspect, but only after she had been made a link to the death. If she had simply disliked her brother-in-law she could have mentioned him as soon as they had asked for anyone with a reason to seek Walter's death.

'What time of day did your husband leave Evesham, Mistress?' Walkelin had found his tongue at last.

'And where will we find, er, Will Horsweard?' added Catchpoll.

'Right here.'

The sheriff's men turned as one, to see who stood in the doorway behind them. They beheld a man of little more than the average height, but with noticeably stooping shoulders, and as he stepped into the chamber, a pronounced limp. After the ravages of the Avon, they could not tell if this man's face resembled his brother's. He might be younger in years, but permanent discomfort had etched lines into the face, and aged it.

'Will Horsweard, we have news of your brother, and it is not good news.' Hugh Bradecote stated the fact simply.

'And you are?'

'Hugh Bradecote, Undersheriff of Worcester.'

'Then tell me this bad news, my lord.' His voice was rasping, as if his throat was sore.

Even as Bradecote opened his mouth to speak, Amicia took a great, gulping sob, and began to weep, loudly. It did not take this to tell Will Horsweard his brother was dead, for he reasoned no undersheriff would come to see him if it were not a death or an arrest for a capital crime, and the sheriff's men ferreting for information.

'Your brother was found in the mill leat at Fladbury, Master Horsweard, with the signs of a knife wound that killed him. We want to find out who killed him, and why.'

'And where,' added Walkelin, doggedly. To Walkelin's steady mind the finding of the 'where' opened unknown paths for investigation. There was always the chance that the body was taken some distance to go into the river, but if that was so, why not bury the man out of view, where he might not be discovered at all, as opposed to the river where a corpse, though not uncommon, would be bound to come ashore somewhere and be the object of interest to the law.

Will Horsweard cast his sister-in-law a look that Catchpoll thought largely disgust. So he did not think her the grieving sort either, did he?

'He was a decent man,' declared Will, heavily. 'Have you the body that we might bury as he is due?'

'We have,' confirmed Catchpoll, 'and though he has been identified to us, we would like you also to say it is Walter Horsweard.'

'Is that not my duty?' asked Amicia, sniffing now that nobody was paying her attention.

'Might be better if his brother did it.' Bradecote did not think the body suitable for a woman's viewing, whether she was grief-stricken or not. His look to Will Horsweard spoke volumes.

'Aye, you keep yourself here and make arrangements for a wake feast, Sister, and leave that part to blood kin.' Again the unspoken animosity prickled in the air.

'The body lies at the abbey. One of the brethren identified it. He said as he was kindred.' Catchpoll was so alert to every nuance of this pair that his hair almost stood upon end.

'That'll be our mother's sister's son, Wilfrid. If he has vouched for it being Walter, then there is no doubt of it, but I'll come just the same, and collect the body also.'

'You'll have to make presentiment of Englishness, while you are about it,' Catchpoll declared.

'Aye, or the souls that took him from the Avon will pay for the "privilege",' nodded Will Horsweard.

'Then come with us now, Master Horsweard, and the deeds can be done and the burial arranged.' Bradecote looked at the widow. 'And we will leave you to your arrangements, Mistress.' He nodded, part acknowledgement, part dismissal, since he felt he controlled what was going on.

Out in the spring sunshine, so at odds with the funereal gloom within, Bradecote gave Catchpoll a look, and engaged Horsweard in conversation, whilst the serjeant grabbed Walkelin by the arm and spoke to him in an urgent whisper.

'You make yourself as invisible as that mop of yours permits, and watch the widow. She may set about the arrangements as directed, but if she has a lover, aye, or more than one, you can

44

be sure she will run to him first. So you watches, and follows, and keeps note of all you see and all you hear. Meet back at the abbey guest hall when you're done.'

Walkelin nodded, his young face serious. With a pat on the arm, Catchpoll went to follow the slow pace of the halting Will Horsweard, noting how hard it was for the long-legged undersheriff to keep step.

The newly declared Widow Horsweard did nothing for a few minutes, beyond sitting heavily upon a stool and closing her eyes. It was not in prayer. As Bradecote had foreseen, her world was turned upside down in an instant, and comprehending it seemed all but impossible. The stables, the messuage, would go to Limping Will, and she would find herself unwelcome in what had been her home these three years past. Well, she would not miss it, but to return to her now widowed mother, to be lectured and moaned at for not giving Walter a son and making her position secure, was something she sought to avoid. After all, Walter had never got a child off his first wife either, so why should she be blamed? Yet even if things went as she hoped, there was a period of mourning, and that meant a time here, treated as an incubus, or in her mother's house, belaboured. She must make decisions, and not about what fare to offer at Walter Horsweard's wake.

When she emerged from her cogitations, it was with her full, bow-curved lips compressed tight with determination. Her first act was, however, simply to change her gown for something sombre. If word had begun to spread in the town, it would be best not to look frivolous or disrespectful. Then she

45

slipped from the house, head down, modesty personified, and threaded her way through the streets to a house in Colestrete, and knocked upon the door. She looked left and right, but saw nobody. Walkelin, his hair stuffed under a wool-felt cap that his mother had given him and which he loathed, but for which he saw a good use, had turned his back and was apparently studying a tray of belt buckles. The door was opened, he could not see by whom, and she disappeared within.

'Good, solid work, master, and each one different.' The vendor smiled encouragingly at Walkelin.

'I am sure,' replied Walkelin. 'Do you have something suitable for an older dame, not like the comely wench that just set foot in her house, over there.'

'Comely we—?' The man looked puzzled and then laughed. 'Comely, aye, master, but that weren't her home, for sure. That is the house of Robert the Coppersmith' – he dropped his voice to a throaty whisper, and gave a conspiratorial wink – 'who is better known as Robert "*Hengestgehangod*".' He gesticulated with his hands, and Walkelin fought the rising blush.

'You mean he's . . . you know, like a stallion?'

'A fine figure of manhood, indeed he is. Known for his, er, size and stamina ever since his voice broke. You understand, young master, in a town with a river, like Evesham, and where the lads all play in the water, such things are noticed. And to be honest, you would be hard pressed not to notice Robert's "assets", even if he did not make sure they were common knowledge. Unfair it is, really, that some should be so endowed when others are lacking, but there. It is God's work, a man's form, so we must not complain.'

'And that is not his wife?' Walkelin sounded suitably curious.

'He buried her two autumns past, poor woman. There's some say as he wore her out . . . eh, but in truth she coughed blood, God rest her soul. That "comely wench" is Mistress Horsweard, whose husband is often from home, and when he is there cannot provide for all her needs, if you catch me.' He sighed. 'Not that there wouldn't be a queue of Evesham men willing to do her justice, given half a chance. Pity it is I am happily married.' He sounded regretful of the fact.

'But that is adultery.' Walkelin could not keep the shocked disapproval from his voice. 'What if the lusty coppersmith gets her with child? And if you know of this, surely word travels like a flame through straw? The husband must know.'

'I dare say Walter would not worry overmuch, if it gave a son to keep his brother from the business in time, and he is not a man to think too hard about what his woman does in his absence. Best that way, I think you'll agree.'

'He must surely hate his brother, if that is the case.'

'Hatred? Perhaps not, but there is no brotherly love between them, I am thinking. Walter's brother is crippled in body, and Walter treats him as if crippled in mind, which he surely is not. Rankles, that does, and makes Will a bitter man. So, if a son lies in Walter's crib, whether he seeded it or not, he would not be too worried.'

'But to share her favours . . .'

'You are not married, are you, master?' He grinned.

'No.' Walkelin blushed.

'Ah, that'll explain it, then. You see, a husband like Walter Horsweard, a mature man with a young, beautiful, and hungry

47

wife, can be one with ears, or one without. If he has ears, he must be prepared for a fight, often and often, and have a miserable spouse in his bed. If he has no ears, he enjoys peace at home, a willing wife when needed, and his friends know when to keep their tongues still.'

Walkelin blinked at this pragmatic attitude.

'Better to share and enjoy them yourself, than not receive them except unwillingly and with ear-grief all the while. No, some might mock Walter Horsweard as a cuckold, but I say he is a wise man.' The seller of buckles nodded at his own wisdom, and then changed the subject. 'Now, a buckle for an older lady. Your lady mother, master?'

The price of a small buckle seemed worth it to Walkelin, for all the information gained, and he hoped that the undersheriff might make a contribution to the outlay of two silver pennies.

Chapter Four

'Well, spit it out, young Walkelin.' Serjeant Catchpoll gave him a hefty prod in the ribs. 'What, if anything, have you discovered?'

Walkelin had arrived back at the abbey, clearly with news, but not sure how best to express it. He looked rather bashful.

'You were right about the widow, Serjeant. She waited for a bit and then headed to a place in Colestrete, where lives Robert the Coppersmith. I made myself look like just a casual customer with a man selling buckles close by, and he was eager enough to tell me the gossip, though it seems far from idle gossip, from what I could tell.' He paused, and the redness of his cheeks increased.

'You never heard them at it, did you?' Catchpoll looked almost shocked. After all, the woman had only just had the news of her husband's death.

'No, no,' declared Walkelin, hurriedly, 'but the buckle seller seemed to know what all Evesham knows, if you understand me. Mistress Horsweard visits the coppersmith regular, that seems common knowledge.'

'Common enough for her husband to find out, eh?'

'The suggestion is he knew but did not mind. The gossip is that he, Walter, wasn't . . . Perhaps he couldn't, not often . . . And she is young and . . . keen.'

'So he accepted another man frolicking with his wife?' Bradecote did not sound convinced.

'That was what I thought, my lord. It did not sound likely, until the man gave explanation. He said better to have a happy wife who obliged when required, than a miserable, carping one who resented the occasional wifely duty. As such, it makes some sense.'

'Mistress Horsweard therefore picked the coppersmith, or he picked her. He must think himself lucky.'

'According to the neighbour, it might be the other way around. Robert the Coppersmith is renowned for his . . .' Walkelin, caught between embarrassment and the desire to pass on a good joke, gave indication by hand signals.

Catchpoll raised an eyebrow.

'They call him Robert "*Hengestgehangod*",' whispered Walkelin.

Hugh Bradecote's lips twitched, and Catchpoll gave in to mirth. Eventually, wiping his eyes, he told Walkelin to continue.

'Well, she left the coppersmith's in that sort of furtive way that is so obvious you might as well put up banners, but she did not return to her house. She went to another, just outside the abbey walls. I wondered if it was her old home, from when she was a maid.'

'And that would have been many moons ago,' chortled Catchpoll, but did not say more, as Bradecote hushed him with a hand.

'But I do not think it was, for a man came to the door, and they spoke there for several minutes before she entered. Now, as I reckon it, if it had been a brother, and he was too young to be her sire, he would have welcomed her straight in. He held her hands, but for a lover looked very serious. I could not make it out.'

Bradecote rubbed his chin, thoughtfully.

'What manner of building was it, Walkelin? Wealthy or poor-looking?'

'Well kept. Neat. Not the best in the town, but not impoverished at all.'

'Then perhaps she is torn,' suggested Bradecote. 'The coppersmith "hung like a stallion" might keep her warm at night, but would she trust him to be a faithful husband? Perhaps this other man is more dependable, if less exciting. She might be seeing how each reacts when they hear she is without a husband. After all, there are men who like to keep a mistress, but are most reluctant to wed the woman, even if free to do so.'

'That is true enough, my lord.' Catchpoll nodded sagely. 'It might also be that one of them already knew the husband was dead, of course, or she might have gone to one to tell him the body was discovered.'

'But then why go to the other?' Walkelin frowned. 'If she knew of the murder, was involved in its planning, the second visit seems odd.'

'Then how about she thinks that the coppersmith might have done the deed, knowing perhaps she told him when Walter

51

was going away and where he was headed. She goes to him to see his reaction, and thereafter goes to Master Plain-but-loyal to play the unprotected widow.' Bradecote spoke half to himself.

'If he was going into Gloucestershire he would have taken the Hampton ferry or the Bengeworth bridge.' Walkelin was still keen to know the location where the murdered man entered the water.

'Well, it was not the ferry, for the ferryman thinks he saw something green and big enough to be a corpse downstream of his ferry some four days past.' Catchpoll added his information.

'And Colestrete is close by the bridge, if the coppersmith wanted to leave his business a short while to look out for Walter Horsweard passing by.'

'All very well, but the Bengeworth bridge is rather a public place to kill a man. It is overlooked by the castle, and by those at the Evesham end. It would be very risky.' Bradecote could not see so open a killing.

'Thing is, my lord, perhaps there was an opportunity, and the coppersmith had been prepared to follow Horsweard until he was away from folk. A sudden shower would have had few people gazing at the bridge since they would be getting under cover or covering their goods. Suddenly there was a chance, and it meant he could be back with his business without anyone noting his absence.'

Bradecote considered the matter.

'That is possible. I suppose I could ask at the castle, though you would have thought anyone with sense would notice a man being toppled into the river.' He paused, and looked at Catchpoll and Walkelin. 'Of course, he might have killed Horsweard and taken him back to the river.'

'Makes no sense, though. The river always gives back what is cast in, eventually, and there could be no guarantee that it would not turn up on the Hampton bend. A body covered in branches and out of the way, let alone buried, would not be found but by chance.' Catchpoll pulled a face. 'I say as it was someone taking their chance when they could, and casting him into the Avon in a twinkling of an eye, not dragging him back.'

'Would the killer assume that the body would just be seen as a drowning, though, not murder?' Walkelin was concentrating.

'Only if he thought we were idle or brain-addled.' Catchpoll shook his head. 'That wound was not obvious, but nor was it a fluke I found it. Any decent inspection of the body would see it.'

'We are tying ourselves in knots here.' Bradecote ran a hand through his hair. 'Let us eat and rest, and in the morning we will look at this afresh. I think I will go to the castle, and you two can find out as much as possible about the Widow Horsweard and the men in her life.'

'And Will Horsweard also, just to be sure, my lord.'

'Him too, Walkelin. Now, food, and food that will not give me a bellyache all night. Heaven spare me from lead dumplings!'

Fortunately for Hugh Bradecote, the abbey kitchens produced good fare, and as he was the guest of Abbot Reginald, he dined on wood pigeon with wild garlic, pease pudding, and cherries in wine. The contrast with the previous evening was stark. He did not make comment, however, knowing that churchmen could sometimes feel guilt over their regular and sustaining meals. Starvation, even in the hungry months, was not a fear among the cloistered.

Abbot Reginald was an interesting host, a man with a sound religious core, but pragmatic about the world. He had been effectively 'fortifying' the abbey with the construction of a great wall about it. There might not be any Geoffrey de Mandeville in the western counties to desecrate an abbey as had befallen Ramsey, but there was no such thing as security for a wealthy monastery in dangerous times. The abbot's relations with William de Beauchamp were not always amicable, for the abbey lands and those of the sheriff were all too often adjacent and disputes arose, but the abbot judged men as he found them rather than by their overlord, and what he saw, and had indeed heard, of the tall, dark-haired undersheriff, inclined him to trust the man and his word.

'Am I permitted to ask if you have paths that may lead to the killer of Walter Horsweard, my lord Bradecote?' he enquired, after giving thanks for the meal.

'Of course, Father, though I would say they are not clear enough paths as yet to be sure the trail leads to the culprit. We hope to find more tomorrow. I have to go to the castle on the Bengeworth bank, to see if anyone upon watch there saw a man in a green jerkin about a week since, crossing the bridge, or even falling from it.'

'Falling? But if an accident—'

'No, Father. I am not being clear enough. I doubt any watchman would have seen the stabbing from that distance, but perhaps he saw a man fall. I would have hoped he would have reported such a thing but . . .'

'In that place? Forgive me, my lord, but there is little good can be said of Bengeworth Castle. The men that reside within it do so not because it is theirs to hold, but because it is their service time. A few are good, most are idle. Drunkenness and debauchery are more common than duty and diligence.'

'I spent a month there, two years back. In fairness, even to the dutiful, it is not a place to inspire hard work. It is a fortification, not a castle in which to live. It is cold, miserable and rat-infested. I loathed the place, and the other vassals I served with were half the time at each other's throats because of it and ill-temper. It was, forgive me, Father, godforsaken.'

'God forsakes not even the rat-infested,' smiled Abbot Reginald, 'but I understand your sentiment. I will pray you have success, and if we can aid you in any part, be sure we will.'

'Thank you. I can ask no more, and am grateful.'

The morning began with a brisk shower, and none of the sheriff's men wanted to spend the day steaming and damp, so it was not until the monks went to Chapter that they set about their allotted tasks. Walkelin went the short way to the street by the abbey wall to find out what he could about the second man Amicia Horsweard had visited, and Catchpoll took up where Walkelin had left off in finding out all about Robert the Coppersmith.

'Best I go, lad, since you nosing about again might look suspicious, and besides, I am too old to be shocked.' Catchpoll grinned, and winked.

The undersheriff departed with Catchpoll still gently poking fun at Walkelin's inexperience. Any light-heartedness he might have felt dissipated as he crossed the Bengeworth bridge. The castle had a fairly squat stone keep, but the rest of it was wooden palisading and daub and wattle quarters for the men. The only advantage for the lordly was that their accommodation was less cavernous and cold. For some reason the damp clung to the place, and gave it a mouldy smell. Even as he gained admittance, the miserable memories flooded in like the Avon in a flash flood. The serjeant of the guard did not recognise him except by his quality, and was deferential enough, passing him on to the lord currently commanding the garrison. Hugh Bradecote had met him before on service. Odo FitzEimar was an older man, inclined to be cynical and life-weary. He nodded at Bradecote and asked, without any marked enthusiasm, what sheriff's business brought him.

'I heard you had taken de Crespignac's place since last summer. Thankless task, I'll be bound.'

'It has its moments.'

'No doubt. Mind you, if de Beauchamp sends you in his stead, you do not have to report every watch to him, and can be your own man. On the other hand, you have to work with that gallows-faced Serjeant Catchpoll. There's a bastard as was born miserable.'

Since Bradecote had left Catchpoll chuckling, the accusation seemed harsh, but the undersheriff knew Catchpoll relished his 'miserable bastard' reputation, and so concurred.

'He is a good sniffer out of crime, though, and I cannot fault him for diligence.'

'Well, rather you than me, is all I say. Now, what is it that you, my lord Undersheriff, are sniffing out this side of Avon?'

'Murder.'

'Indeed? And how can we help?' Odo was wary now. He did not want his men associated with a murder.

'Only that the murdered man came from Evesham, and left nigh on a week ago to purchase horses in Gloucestershire. He turned up in the mill leat at Fladbury four days past, waterlogged, but with a neat stab wound to his chest. All I am trying to find out is if he crossed at the bridge or not. He wore a distinctive green jerkin, and was middle-aged and a little on the fleshy side. His horse would have been good too. No horse seller rides a breakdown. I want to speak to those who took watch the days about then, to find if any saw a man of that description cross the bridge.'

'Ah.' FitzEimar relaxed. 'I can furnish the men easy enough, but near a week ago? I doubt they recall what they saw yesterday, unless it was carrying a tray of ale beakers. Let me call my serjeant.' He did so, and the serjeant returned. He was a man who could purse his lips as well as Catchpoll, but Bradecote did not see the same spark within him. He did his job and no more, no less. He sniffed, did a mental review of the guard and went away, returning a few minutes later with six men-at-arms, who looked slightly nervous before the undersheriff of the shire.

'These are the men, my lord. Stand up and at least try to look awake, you misbegotten mongrels.'

They shuffled.

'All I seek is information.' Bradecote spoke authoritatively but without force. He needed no claims that were false but given to be the 'right' answer.

He described Walter Horsweard, and let them think. One by one they shook their heads. If only he could be sure that they had been attentive, proving the murdered man did not leave the town as expected was an interesting step forward. He was fairly certain, but could not base everything upon it as fact. He thanked them, and FitzEimar, and returned to the abbey, wondering what, if true, the information told them about the deceased, and the killer. He had nothing to do but wait, and hope his subordinates had had better success.

Walkelin, being unknown in Evesham, did not really mind that his red hair might make him stand out. He had used the time in the abbey to bring out his whittling. He had come to the conclusion that a bit of whittling could always be useful to a sheriff's man, either as a disguise or even as a way of letting him think through a problem. He had produced a couple of simple fish, but he had an innate ability to give even a basic fish a fluidity of shape. He also had a piece to work upon, and knew from experience that children would come to peer at him working. Children, according to the oracle that was Serjeant Catchpoll, could be very observant, and early in life, remarkably truthful. He positioned himself in the street, within twenty paces of the place into which Widow Horsweard had, after some interchange, disappeared. Then he took the small stool he had borrowed from the abbey porter, and sat down to whittle a duck.

It worked. It always worked. Within five minutes a sharp-faced boy of about six edged close to ask him what he was making, and very soon after there were four or five children about him. He had watched them emerge and knew these were local children, so asking what sort of trades were plied along the row of premises was easy enough, and getting the children to point out who lived where followed smoothly. He was priding himself of ascertaining that the dwelling of interest was that of Master John Pinvin who made bridles. Well, there was a connection between the man and the victim, and it probably showed how Master Pinvin met the horse trader's wife. At which point a woman emerged from the house behind him and shooed the children away for being noisy.

'Move on, pedlar, and sell elsewhere.' She looked careworn and tired. 'I have an ailing father within and would have him pass in peace, not straining to hear the words of the priest over the crying of wares.'

'I am sorry, Mistress.' Walkelin's apology was perfectly genuine. 'I could not know. I do not cry for custom, though. Mine is a trade that sells by observing.' He showed her one of the fish. To his horror, she burst into tears. 'Mistress? What is it? How have I upset you?'

'My father is a carpenter by trade, but when we were children, made such things for us. Yet here he is, weaker than a babe, and the priest called for.'

'I will not add to your distress, then.' He paused. 'If he made such things, would he be aware enough to handle one, for they are "seen" best by touch? I would wait here.'

The woman frowned, considering, then nodded.

'If it gives him a moment of happy memory even as all fades, it would be well. Thank you, I will take a fish.'

Walkelin placed the wooden toy in her hand and said nothing. She disappeared within, and he waited. The priest, preceded by a lad of about ten, hurried down the street, and entered the home of the dying man without registering

Walkelin. The lad came out, solemn-faced and with the fish in his hand.

'Mother thanks you, and says Oldfather smiled when he held it.' The lad was upset, but trying to control his emotions. 'The priest is come, and I think it cannot be long now.' His lip trembled.

'It is never easy, lad,' Walkelin patted the boy's shoulder, 'but your oldfather must have had good length of years to see you grow to be strong and heading to manhood. That is a thing to give thanks for.'

The boy nodded, but sniffed. Walkelin was a kind-hearted soul, and had painful memories of losing his own father when he was only a few years older than this youngster. His attention to his task was distracted for a while.

'Has she sent you out? Then wait here with me. Your mother said he made such things as these when she was but a little girl. Would you like to watch me whittling? I am making a duck.'

The boy nodded, and Walkelin sat down again on the stool, with the boy beside him. After a while sniffs gave way to questions, and the questions reminded Walkelin that he too should be asking things. He asked the boy, whose name was Godwin, about Master Pinvin, claiming to have known a man from that village himself.

'Master Pinvin has been here since afore I was born, for he was journeyman to Old Redbeard.' The boy blushed, looking at Walkelin's red hair, but Walkelin just grinned, and the grin encouraged. 'He took the trade when his old master died. He is a quiet man, but friendly enough. I used to go and watch him work sometimes, until . . .'

'Until?'

'Well, Mother got annoyed, and said as I should not go any more.' Godwin looked puzzled. 'I cannot think why.'

'Was this long since?' Walkelin wondered, already surmising.

'No more than last All Souls. I miss watching and talking with him.'

'And I expect he misses an interested lad, if he has no apprentice. Does he live alone?'

'Oh yes. There is a kind lady, very pretty, I have seen visit sometimes. I think she brings some sweetcakes in her little basket and cheers him. I do not tell Mother about it, since when I mentioned it once she clipped me about the ear. I thought the pretty lady very charitable.'

Walkelin had a pretty good idea of her 'charity', but said nothing more about her. Instead, he turned the conversation.

'I suspect his kin are back in Pinvin, though he might visit them.'

'He rarely leaves for longer than it takes to buy foodstuffs. I cannot remember when he last went away even for a morning, let alone overnight.' Godwin paused. 'I like him because of his stillness, I think. You feel settled in his company. I miss our hours together.' He sighed.

Walkelin did not question, but thought perhaps that Godwin's own father was some time dead. The lad had clearly latched onto Master Pinvin as a male influence in his life, a father figure. The worse it was that his grandsire was departing this life.

'I live with my mother, Godwin, just us. Yours will need you more than you know. It is not easy being a man, early in life, but I think you will do well. Being, like Master Pinvin, able to be still, is a good thing.' He looked down at the fish that Godwin had returned to him, picked it up, and handed it to the boy. 'This made your oldfather smile, even at the end. Keep it as a good memory of him, and of what I say. I will not ply my trade in front of a house of mourning. God be with you, lad, and yours.'

With which he rose, picked up his stool, and walked away. Godwin, holding the fish, watched his retreating figure, as the sound of sobbing came from within the house.

Chapter Five

Serjeant Catchpoll, meanwhile, had been pursuing his investigations in his own way. He was not quite anonymous in Evesham, and a few of the less savoury characters in the town behaved with abnormal circumspection when they saw him on the prowl. The majority of the townsfolk, however, carried on as normal. Murder, in his experience, was often committed by people who were not previously of interest to the law, springing from sudden events and situations in which people acted out of emotion. There were planned deaths, but these were more unusual. If Mistress Horsweard or her lovers had taken more than a day to decide to kill her husband, other than in vague words of frustration, he would be surprised. This meant there had to have been something that had changed, and one thing sprang to mind. If the erring wife found herself carrying the lover's child, either the lover wanted her to wed, or she thought husband Walter would not be as forgiving as he was over her seeking mere pleasure elsewhere.

He sucked his uneven teeth. Trouble was, it was mighty difficult to tell with women in the early months. She might know, or might just suspect, but without being at her side to see if she was sickly each day, none who did not know her would be able to tell, excepting perhaps a very experienced wise woman. He pulled a face. He was certainly experienced, and in the ways of criminals quite wise, but the woman bit was beyond him. The answer, therefore, was to speak with women who knew Amicia Horsweard.

Women, in Catchpoll's long experience, were a fount of information, but making the initial contact and getting past their natural reserve with a member of the opposite sex could be tricky. Before he headed to Colestrete, he returned to where the Horsweard home and business stood, and had a stroke of luck. Two women were huddled in gossip, and casting glances at the front door. News of the death must have spread. Catchpoll offered up a silent prayer of thanks for nosiness, and strolled past, catching a few low-voiced words. He halted, nodded to the women, who regarded him suspiciously, and spoke casually.

'Was this where the body they brought to the abbey used to live?' He sounded the semi-curious stranger, and one of the women looked him up and down and then decided she might safely speak to him.

'Might be. And what interest is it to you?'

'Oh, nothing. Just that I brought the cart in from Fladbury.'

This did everything he had hoped. The women's attitude changed on the instant. The curiosity was all on their side.

'They say as he was found drowned in the river,' commented the taller of the two, 'but most of the local men could paddle since they were lads. Blind drunk, I suppose he was. There's men for you. Not that his widow will weep for him.'

'Oh, was he an unpleasant fellow? Beat her, did he?'

The second woman looked pityingly at his ignorance.

'Not as any ever heard. Good enough man, was Walter Horsweard, but that wife of his . . .'

'A shrewish woman, eh, complaining if he came into the house with dirty boots?'

'House proud, her? No fear. The only thing she takes care of is her own appearance, and her a married woman. Shameful it is.'

'I am a married man myself, and I like my wife to tidy her hair for me, brush off the dust from her gown. Shows respect and . . . other things.' Catchpoll forced the hint of a blush, designed to make the women feel they were on the edge of the indiscreet. The taller one stifled a giggle that Catchpoll thought must be the sound of a rat, sneezing.

'Nothing wrong in that, but if she only does it for others . . . Different thing altogether.'

'You mean . . . No, surely he would find out and then beat her soundly, if nothing more?'

'Ah, that is what you might think, but Walter Horsweard was either blind or tolerant, and from how well he picked good horseflesh you would not call him blind. He did not "notice" her traipsing off and returning eye-bright and flushed.'

'Perhaps she had been for a stiff walk?' offered Catchpoll, dangling the bait for a warm response.

'Stiff aye, but not a walk,' cackled the second woman, with a lecherous wink. She jerked her thumb towards Colestrete and the coppersmith's. 'Robert the Coppersmith's was where she has gone these two years past, pretending to bring him patties because he is a "lonely widower". Hah! It wasn't her patties he licked his lips over.'

'Two years? But what if he got her with child?'

'Well he never got poor Alys his wife with child in the ten years of wedlock, nor any other woman out of it, as I heard. So perhaps, however able in one sense, he is not in the other.'

That seemed a good reason to think it unlikely the motive for the killing was Amicia Horsweard carrying a misbegotten child, though not conclusive.

'The coppersmith is a lecherous fellow, eh?'

The taller woman looked prim.

'Never set a hand near me, and if he had I would send him off with my mark on his cheek.'

Catchpoll could well believe that nobody ever wanted to take liberties with her. She was hatchet-faced, in his opinion.

'Ah, but with less virtuous dames perhaps . . . ?'

'Well, not that I watch, you understand, but it is so obvious . . .' The second woman wanted to show her knowledge. 'There was that woman from Hampton, red-haired piece, and then the fair girl he seduced. Witless maid, not that she stayed a maid long. He paid her father off, it is said, for there was an apprentice who would take her even as she was.'

'Don't forget the Widow Chapman. There's one as thought she would catch him as soon as his poor wife died. Would have been a step up in the world for her, of course. But he dropped her like a hot hearthstone as soon as she even hinted at wedlock.'

This was useful background information, but the trouble was it did not make Robert the Coppersmith more likely to have killed Walter Horsweard. Rather it made him far less likely to have done so. Why kill a man if you did not want the complication of the woman then expecting marriage?

'Surprised he has time for his smithing,' observed Catchpoll, lightly, and the women smiled as he went upon his way.

It was not far to Colestrete, but Catchpoll was already processing all he had learnt. It was interesting that neither nosey neighbour had mentioned a second lover, and however bad it was that Amicia Horsweard had taken another man, it would be more than twice as scurrilous if she was known to be spreading her favours even more widely. If they had even a hint of it, the women would have said as much. Either this second man had come into her life very recently, was a kinsman and not a lover, or she thought of him in a different way to her lusty coppersmith. What if she had been lining the other up as a replacement husband, knowing the coppersmith was not the marrying kind? No, that would not work unless Walter had told her he was ailing, but had concealed his ill health from his brother, otherwise Will would have mentioned it when the death had been announced. Not knowing would be odd if he was to inherit. Catchpoll stopped in his tracks. What they had not considered was that Walter Horsweard might have left his assets to another if he and his brother were at odds. It was not like some lordly title, which had to go to next of kin. Walter might just have decided to spite his brother, and what better motive for killing him than the announcement that he was about to declare his will before a churchman that would leave brother Will nothing at all? If a man were dying, it was a positive action at a time when he must feel powerless against fate. It was not the most obvious scenario, but it meant that they should investigate the argument between the brothers before Walter's departure. Will might have offered to go with him a short part of the way, and then seemed to make his peace with his brother, clasp him in a fraternal hug, and drive a sharp knife into his chest. The trouble was that even if Will had not known of it, Amicia ought to have spoken if her husband had suffered from an affliction.

Colestrete was very quiet when Catchpoll wandered past the premises that Walkelin had described to him. Unusually, there were no children playing, no gossiping women outside their homes, no eager purchasers haggling with vendors. Catchpoll sighed. Such times made a serjeant's job more difficult. He did not want to confront Robert the Coppersmith before he had all the background information he could muster.

As if in answer to a serjeant's prayer, a woman emerged from the adjacent dwelling with a blanket, followed by an adolescent girl with a beater. Catchpoll instantly adopted his 'helpful passer-by' mode, and offered to hold one corner of the blanket so that the whole could be held taut in one go. The woman thanked him. She seemed too weary to question the charitable act. Strands of greying hair had escaped from beneath her coif, and her shoulders stooped.

'Extra hands make an easier task, Mistress, eh?' Catchpoll was exuberantly cheerful.

'Indeed, and we thank you.' The woman's voice was thin, like her cheeks.

'Would you rather I did the beating, and let your girl hold the corner? A man has stronger muscles.'

The girl looked slightly sceptical, obviously regarding Serjeant Catchpoll as some aged greybeard. Well, perhaps he looked thus to youth, but the mother thought differently.

'Aye, would be best if you would, friend.' She gave a small, grateful smile. 'I miss a man's strength about the place these days.'

Catchpoll smiled inwardly. He had been right, for he had assessed her as a widow.

'But you must have neighbours who would help in heavy tasks, out of good Christian charity.' Catchpoll sounded every inch the pious good Samaritan.

The girl sniffed dismissively as she exchanged places with him.

'Christian charity is thin round here. You should hear the excuses of the man next door.'

'Quiet, girl. You forget he is our landlord also.'

'He never lets us forget it.' There was a bitterness to the girl's voice, and a tinge of colour to her cheek. Catchpoll put two and two together. Robert the Coppersmith, who was able to attract beautiful women, also liked to feel the power of control. Whatever the rent in silver, Catchpoll would lay odds there was a toll in flesh, even if the girl withheld that knowledge from her careworn mother. He suddenly disliked Robert the Coppersmith. When he was simply a lecherous man it was a matter for his own conscience, but putting pressure upon a girl of perhaps fifteen, that rated as contemptible in Catchpoll's mind.

'Perhaps he is not as fit as I am,' declared Catchpoll, sounding the man still proud of his stamina, whatever years he counted.

'Fit?' the girl snorted. 'Fit enough to beat copper for his trade, and use his cot for more than sleeping every night.'

'Daughter!' The woman sounded shocked, but the girl shrugged.

'Why should we pretend when he flaunts it, Mother? All Evesham knows about our landlord.'

'Should one pity his wife or think her lucky?' grinned Catchpoll, feigning ignorance of his circumstances.

'Oh, he wore his wife out and laid her in earth two years back, not that he kept himself to himself even then.' The girl sneered. 'If any asked, he always said he had a "good appetite" and it was a gift of God. Sacrilege, that is.'

'Sssssssh!' The mother looked agitated, and glanced nervously at the coppersmith's door.

Catchpoll thought he would get good information from the girl if her mother were not present, and began to cough, hoping that the mother would fetch him a beaker to ease his throat of the dust. She might as easily send the girl, but today providence was on the side of the law, and she gave her corner to the girl, bustling indoors to fetch a small beer.

'I take it your mother don't know, then?' Catchpoll had no time to skirt the realities.

'What do you mean?' The girl blushed.

'I have eyes, wench, and years too. Fair enough that you keep it from your mother, but do not tell me you have not seen the inside of your neighbour's chamber when she has not known, and not from your choice.'

70

The girl narrowed her eyes, seeing Catchpoll in a new light. She was suspicious.

'And of what matter is that to you?'

'I'll not tell your mother, but I need to know about Robert the Coppersmith, and swiftly too.' He had no qualms about revealing the name.

'He's an animal. All he wants is women, those he attracts because of his reputation, and in between times . . .' She shuddered. 'The horse trader's wife is his latest and she won't be his last, whatever she may think.'

Serjeant Catchpoll looked grim, and the girl, thinking his thin-lipped snarl was aimed at her, took a step back.

'Nasty piece of work, then, is Master Coppersmith.' Catchpoll meant it. He had no concern over men who took what opportunities were offered, but coercion was a different matter. The man could not even claim it was the only way he could subjugate a wayward body. No, this put Robert the Coppersmith beyond the merely lecherous and into the group Catchpoll mentally lumped together as those he would like to have in a small room to 'question' rather more actively than the undersheriff would think reasonable. In fairness to Bradecote, Catchpoll thought that in a case such as this he might turn a blind eye to a little rough handling. Men who bullied young women, were not even prepared to buy their pleasures, were due a lesson in what it felt like to be powerless and frightened.

'Did the horse trader's wife come here yesterday?' He knew the answer, but it was interesting to see if the girl kept an eye open for what the man was about.

'She did, and agitated she was too.'

'And was he about his trade as usual a week since?'

The girl thought, her sandy brows beetling. 'Not sure. I know one day about then he went out early and did not return until the abbey bell tolled None.'

It was not evidence, but it gave a possibility of being so. It certainly gave Catchpoll enough reason to think that Robert the Coppersmith would be receiving a visit from the sheriff's men in an official capacity. He thanked the girl with a nod, resumed his paroxysm for the benefit of the returning widow, and headed back to the abbey enclave as soon as he had downed his beaker of refreshment.

Hugh Bradecote awaited the return of Walkelin and Catchpoll with the porter by the abbey gate. Brother Porter was Evesham born and bred, and though his abbot would have considered it worthy of confession, he was not above good town gossip. He heard much as the townsfolk passed his gate on the way to church. He shook his head over Walter Horsweard.

'His father, Edbald, was a good, simple man. He had a few ponies for the hiring, and some people paid him for stabling if they had no stables of their own, but aspired to be among the horse-owning folk. Never gave himself airs, did Edbald, but his wife, now there was a woman with ambition. Always wanted a bigger messuage, more servants. You know the sort, my lord. Very worldly, she was, but Edbald just laughed and let her have her way. Now Walter took after his father with his attitude to position, by and large, though he would not take to being treated badly, and was warm enough with his horse trading. Nobody ever sold him a horse older than they claimed, nor one prone to lameness.

'It is his brother, Limping Will, who takes after the distaff, and wants to be a noted burgess in Evesham. Perhaps he sees it as making up in some way for his infirmity. While his mother was alive, they chivvied Walter, did they ever. It was the pair of them who managed to get the daughter of the family, Walter and Will's sister, married off to a man of standing in the shire, all on the weight of her looks and dower, of course. Why else would a lordly man with two manors to his name take a wife of her sort?'

He looked at Bradecote, for a moment, fearing that his unchecked tongue had betrayed him into giving offence, but the undersheriff looked unconcerned. Brother Porter gave a silent prayer of thanks. You never knew how the grander folk stood when it came to their rank.

'Yet it has availed them nothing, the position. Old Mistress Horsweard died the year after Edith wed, and she, poor lady, has followed but under a month since.' He shook his head.

At this point Walkelin strode in, looking pensive.

'Now what has given you cause for a furrowed brow, Walkelin? Something of interest to us?' Bradecote tried to sound more positive than he felt.

'I have information, yes, my lord, but I admit my thoughts were also astray, remembering.'

'Well do not let Serjeant Catchpoll catch you remembering anything that is not relevant to the crime in hand, that is all I will say.'

'Aye, my lord.' Walkelin smiled. 'I shall be most careful.'

Bradecote was conscious of a slight tension. Walkelin was too far removed from him to engage in natural conversation without the presence of Catchpoll as a buffer. Then his words might be taken as to the serjeant and not directly to the undersheriff. Bradecote knew that no such barrier existed now between Catchpoll and himself. In part, the grizzled serjeant had age and experience to set against rank, but it was much more than that now. They understood each other as men, and, he realised with surprise, had a bond of friendship. It had been forged silently over the best part of a year, but in a furnace of hard work and the camaraderie that one found in warriors. Perhaps they were fighting, fighting unlawfulness. It made him shake his head, smiling. Walkelin, watching, wondered what had amused his superior.

'Do we wait until Serjeant Catchpoll arrives before—'

'Before what?' Catchpoll ambled round the corner. 'You were not even thinking of starting without me, were you, young Walkelin?'

'No, Serjeant.'

'Good.' Catchpoll seemed in cheery mood. 'So, what have we discovered this morning, then?'

Bradecote half-expected him to rub his hands together in anticipation of a treat, as if he had been offered apple dumplings in honey.

'You sound as if you have something worth the sharing, Catchpoll.'

'More round-and-about things, my lord, rather than facts or important discoveries.' He sniffed. 'Shall we find somewhere to mull over them?'

Brother Porter, within earshot, tentatively offered the little gatehouse, which was accepted. In the small chamber, undersheriff and serjeant took the small bench, leaving Walkelin to lean against the wall, on the grounds, declared Catchpoll, of youth and rank.

'Right. Let us hear these round-and-about things.' Bradecote saw no point in wasting time.

'I wondered if Mistress Horsweard might be carrying a child, and that fear that her husband might object had set off the idea of murder. To my mind this was not a killing likely to have been long in the planning, so there was a thing that lit the tinder, so to speak.'

'A fair thought, I agree.' Bradecote nodded.

'Aye, but hard to prove. I spoke to women who live hard by the Horsweard messuage. That Mistress Horsweard was viewing the coppersmith's roof beams on a regular basis was, as Walkelin found yesterday, common knowledge, and for at least two years past. The problem, in a sense, is that however lusty, he never got his wife with child in ten years of wedlock, and he was not faithful even then, but no rumour is there of any bastard of his getting. So it makes it very unlikely that she announced that she is going to have to explain a swelling belly to a seedless husband.'

'Unless she carries a child of Master Pinvin's,' commented Walkelin.

'Who?' His superiors looked at him, puzzled.

'That is the man she visited by the abbey wall. He is a bridle-maker, which accounts for how they met. She visits him regular enough for a neighbour woman to think her unchaste.

And yet the little I heard of the man was not what you would expect of a man giving another's wife the benefit of his loins.' Walkelin paused.

'Go on, we're listening,' encouraged Catchpoll.

'I was speaking to a lad, son of the neighbour. He used to visit Master Pinvin and watch him work. He described him as a man of great stillness, and for a child to latch upon that as his description of him, it must be marked.'

'That is a fair observation, and counts for much, but even a "still" sort of man can be knocked from that stillness by a beautiful woman offering her body.' The serjeant gave Walkelin his due.

'But why offer it to him? The man I saw was not so handsome a man, quite ordinary in fact, his hair even a little thin on top.'

Catchpoll scratched his nose, thoughtfully.

'There are occasions when looks are less important, even to a woman who uses her eyes most. And that one does, for I saw the way she looked at you, my lord, the first time we met her.'

Bradecote blushed slightly, and made a choking noise.

'Sometimes a man has more to him than . . .'

'. . . Robert the Coppersmith?' Walkelin grinned. 'That would be difficult.'

Catchpoll regarded him repressively.

'I fear you are thinking overmuch about er, size, over quality. Think on it. Her husband cannot satisfy her. The coppersmith can, but not if she actually sets store on a babe at her breast. And if your eyes glaze like that at the image in your head, I'll tell that Welsh wench of yours,' he admonished. 'Perhaps the bridle-maker has a quality that appeals to her

76

brooding instinct. She sees him as a man who could get her with child, aye, and be a good father to it thereafter. Women can get such feelings.'

'Which brings us back to whether he has got her pregnant.' Bradecote sighed. 'And might explain matters if it is believed Walter Horsweard would have turned a blind eye to a son of another man's getting. She tells the bridle-maker, who is keen to raise the child himself. Walter is in the way. Remove Walter, and wed the widow, even if it means pretending to "adopt" the babe.'

'I am sorry, my lord. It doesn't settle with me.' Walkelin was unsure of putting forward so strong an opinion, but felt it had to be said. 'I have not spoken direct to him, but it sits ill. And,' he added as a clincher, 'the lad could not remember when he as much as left his workshop for a morning.'

'He might have slipped out a while without the boy seeing, and after all, it would not take long to the bridge.' Catchpoll tried to sound more positive, but failed.

'Ah, and that is where I have to add that it seems very unlikely that Walter Horsweard was thrown into the Avon from the bridge.' Bradecote pulled a face, almost worthy of Catchpoll. 'The castle guards are not ideal witnesses, especially after a week, but none recalled seeing a man in a green jerkin either cross the bridge or tumble in. I honestly doubt Walter left Evesham that way.'

'So was he lying to his wife?' Walkelin wondered. 'She said he was going to Gloucestershire.'

'There is a new slant to things.' Catchpoll frowned. 'We have worked solely on someone killing him to get him out of the way to have his widow, but what if he was finding solace elsewhere, and her husband found out.'

'Come on, Catchpoll. You are asking us to believe such a tangled web, and she is,' Bradecote sounded reluctant, 'a beautiful woman.'

'No, my lord. He knows she is unfaithful – accepts it, even – but just as we wondered at her taking the plain bridle-maker as a lover, perhaps Walter sought comfort in a more homely bosom.'

'I think we are lost, in "perhaps".' Bradecote rested his head in his hands, his long fingers combing through his dark hair. 'We need to go back to the facts as known.'

'Walter Horsweard left Evesham about a week ago, on his way to Gloucestershire to buy horses,' Walkelin offered.

'And we fall at the first hurdle, for the only proof of that is that it is what Mistress Horsweard told us.' Catchpoll frowned. 'So that leaves us with Walter Horsweard's body floated past Hampton five days ago, and—'

'But we are pretty sure he did not fall from the Bengeworth bridge, and,' declared Bradecote, 'if he had, then the body is likely to have passed Hampton more than five days ago, assuming he left when we were told.'

'That gets us into assuming again. We do know he was not killed to be robbed. Therefore, that leaves us with several options.' Catchpoll ticked off his fingers. 'He knew something that someone wanted kept quiet. He had roused someone's anger to killing pitch. He was engaged in shady dealings and a rival had him killed. Someone wanted to take his place. Or there is a madman about who dislikes men in green jerkins. The last is unlikely.'

'I am not convinced any are likely, so far,' grumbled Bradecote. 'However, we have not interviewed Mistress Horsweard's lovers, not put any pressure upon her or his brother. I think we interview all four this afternoon, and if we get to the nub of the matter, I shall offer coin for prayers of thanksgiving in this abbey.'

Chapter Six

Catchpoll told the other two sheriff's men all he had discovered about Robert the Coppersmith. Although he seemed an unlikely suspect for murder in the light of these things, they all agreed it was a good idea to speak with him, and not be gentle either.

'I knows your views well enough, my lord, but this man needs to feel frightened, cocky bastard.'

'Literally,' sniggered Walkelin, and received a playful cuff about the ear from Catchpoll.

'Act your age, and remember you are not a man-at-arms with his brains in his codds, but a serjeanting apprentice with a position to keep up before the general public.'

'Yes, Serjeant.' Walkelin did not seem at all abashed, and kept a grin right until they stood on the doorstep of the coppersmith's in Colestrete. He hammered in an official manner upon it, and stood aside to let Serjeant Catchpoll and the undersheriff take position. Robert the Coppersmith opened the door cautiously. Catchpoll stepped over the threshold, pushing the man to one side.

'What . . . ?'

'The lord Bradecote, Undersheriff of the Shire, and I am Serjeant Catchpoll. We want to speak to you, about your goings on.' Catchpoll was intentionally non-specific as to which 'goings on' these might be.

Robert the Coppersmith looked panicky.

'But I—'

'Sit down.' Walkelin pushed him down onto a bench, thereby making him feel vulnerable. That was a trick Catchpoll had taught him.

'You are a nasty piece of work.' Catchpoll, who looked even nastier, snarled at him. 'Can't keep yourself off other men's women, or indeed innocent maids who don't want you pawing them at all. You think it isn't against the law, excepting that of the Church, but look where it leads you.'

'What do you mean?'

'Walter Horsweard.' Bradecote dropped the words like a stone into a pool, and watched the ripple of fear cross the coppersmith's face.

'Murder,' murmured Catchpoll in the man's ear.

'It wasn't me,' gabbled the coppersmith, shaking.

'Prove it.' Bradecote sounded very cold.

'I . . . I . . .' He swallowed convulsively. 'The day he left, Amicia came to me, straight away. She was here until after noontide.'

'So? That is just the morning.' The undersheriff was clearly not impressed.

'Ah, but then I called in the wench.'

'Which wench?'

'I just calls her "Wench". The one from next door.'

Catchpoll could be very swift when he chose. He grabbed the man's arm and twisted it up his back so he half-rose off the bench. The position was uncomfortable, and the muscles began to tremble in the coppersmith's legs, but if he relaxed the shoulder risked dislocation. Bradecote did nothing.

'You do not even bother to find out her name, you mongrel. If I had my way, Robert "*Hengestgehangod*", you would be gelded in public as a warning to others of your ilk.'

'Will she vouch for this?' Bradecote folded his arms.

'Of course she will or—' The man choked, having nearly betrayed himself.

'Fetch her, Walkelin.' Bradecote's command was terse, not, Walkelin knew, for any reason other than to show power to the frightened coppersmith.

'Straight away, my lord.' He sounded efficient, and went out, only then wondering which side the girl lived. He could hardly knock at a door and ask if a daughter of the house was being bedded by the man next door. He groaned, but was then relieved to see a girl with a pail of water heading to the small dwelling on the left. She was pretty, in a bedraggled way, and youthful.

'Maid, I am the lord Sheriff's man. Did you speak with my serjeant, yesterday, a grey-haired man?'

She nodded, wary.

'Then you need to come in here a moment.' He saw her concern. 'You are quite safe, but we have to ask a question of you.'

She approached slowly, and he opened the door wide to let her in, still carrying the pail. At the sight of Catchpoll she looked less scared, and when she saw the fear on the face of Robert the Coppersmith, all her own faded to nothing.

'I am Hugh Bradecote, Undersheriff of Worcester.' Bradecote smiled, and his voice invited confidences. 'Will you give us your name, for your neighbour does not seem to know it.'

The girl looked down at the coppersmith. He was sweating.

'My name, my lord, is Aelswith.'

'Then will you tell us, Aelswith, if this,' he pointed at the coppersmith and paused before adding 'man', 'took you to his bed the afternoon a week ago, after Mistress Horsweard departed. A week past.'

She paused. Part of her wondered whether the truth would help or harm the man she loathed, but in the face of the undersheriff, she spoke the truth.

'My lord, I cannot say for sure which days, for they are often, and as one in misery to me, and the Mistress Horsweard comes many days. But about a week since she came in the forenoon, which is odd, and he,' she pointed at the seated man, 'made me come here in the afternoon. My mother was told he needed the floor sweeping and the place making fresh, but I neither swept nor cleaned.'

Bradecote did not ask what had occurred. Her face spoke volumes.

'Then she gives you good excuse of this crime, Master Coppersmith, and you will remember that, for whatever "debt" you make her pay is as nought from now on. If it comes to the notice of the law that a finger is laid upon this maid,' and he gave her the title generously, 'then you will be arraigned for rape, and you know the penalty.'

The girl stared at Bradecote, then at Catchpoll, as the words sunk in. She was free, but she had also aided this man. Her bosom heaved.

'Never a finger, remember,' she growled, and threw the contents of the pail over the coppersmith's head. She bobbed a curtsey to the undersheriff, and turned on her heel, head held high. Catchpoll let go of the coppersmith's arm and moved to open the door for her. She looked at him.

'It was only water. How I wish it had been a soil bucket.'

Catchpoll nodded, and shut the door behind her.

Robert the Coppersmith was spluttering.

'And I agree with her, for water is too clean for scum like you. Your neck is safe this time, but you curb your lust or it will end in a noose.' Bradecote, noted Catchpoll, was developing a nice line in 'disdainful bastard'. He approved.

Robert the Coppersmith wiped his eyes and gibbered.

'You know,' remarked Walkelin, as the sheriff's men walked down the street, 'I bet that shrank his ardour, in more ways than one.'

John Pinvin was working by the open door of his premises, setting neat stitches in the junction of nose band and cheekpiece, with needle, thread and palm. He only looked up as the shadow of the trio cut out his light. He nodded greeting.

'Are you John of Pinvin, the bridle-maker?' Catchpoll was being official this afternoon.

'I am. Who asks?'

'I do, Hugh Bradecote, Undersheriff of the Shire.' This was to be a double act at least.

Master Pinvin laid down his work and rose to make polite obeisance.

'My lord.'

'We wish to talk with you about Mistress Horsweard, and the death of her husband.'

The bridle-maker looked flustered.

'Best come within, my lord, for fear of ears.'

Bradecote wondered what Amicia Horsweard saw in him. He had the faintest of stoops, and the hair on his pate had shown thin as he bowed. He did not seem lecherous, either.

Pinvin offered the undersheriff his stool, and stood, hands clasped together before him, more as if about to make confession to a priest.

'Mistress Horsweard comes here to you.'

'She does, my lord.'

'And gives herself.'

'Sometimes. Not often. Most times we talk.'

'Talk?' Walkelin sounded amazed. 'A woman like that and you "talk" to her?'

'I do. She is a lonely woman. Her husband is – was – a good man, but does not understand her needs.'

'She needs to talk?'

'She wants to learn, to be useful with her hands.'

Walkelin's mind boggled. Bradecote had to bite his lip at his expression.

'You mean she wants to stitch?'

'Aye, my lord. Her father was a saddler, but died when she was small. I reckon as it is in the blood.'

Bradecote was not convinced by the reasoning, but the man seemed to be telling the truth.

'And now she is widowed?'

'When her mourning is done, then if she will have me, I would wed her.' He made it seem so simple.

'Master Pinvin. She has seen others beside you.'

'Robert "*Hengestgehangod*". Oh, I know about him.'

'And you care not?'

'I care, of course I care, but what can a man like me do about it? Until now, of course. She is angered by his attitude. Well, mine was none so brave yesterday, but I am determined now. I will stand by her if she needs me.'

'I think she may sooner than you think, for her brother-in-law has the property now, and there is no love lost between them.'

'Then if she comes, I will take her in.'

'And did you assist her coming?' Catchpoll queried.

'What do you mean?'

'Did you kill, Walter Horsweard?' Bradecote was not going to be obtuse.

'No, my lord. I am a sinner, but my sins do not extend to killing a man.'

'Though you cuckolded him.'

'I know. Yes, it was wrong, and I know it, but she . . . I would sin for her, with her, but not that sin. On my oath not that.'

Bradecote was inclined to believe the man. He stood before him, calm now he had broached the subject.

'And can you prove that at all?'

'I live alone, my lord. Barring her visits there is none to speak for me. When did Walter Horsweard leave?'

'A week ago.'

'Then,' he shook his head sadly, 'I can do nothing except swear that I did not do this thing. I did not leave here, but to buy bread and onions. I am no cook. She cooks for me sometimes. That is nice. None will remember me, my lord.'

The bridle-maker stood there, sad-faced but very still. Catchpoll saw what the boy had seen, the stillness of the man. He judged characters a lot. Any man could be brought to kill given enough fear or anger or both. John of Pinvin possessed very little of either in his soul. He would almost swear an oath for him. He looked at Bradecote, and shook his head slightly.

'There is one who does, Master Pinvin. The lad Godwin says you rarely leave your premises and he did not see you leave about the time of Walter Horsweard's departure.'

'Ah, he is a good and honest lad. I fear his mother has kept him from me, knowing of Mistress Horsweard's visits. A shame that it is so.'

'Master Pinvin, I would believe your word, but cannot prove it correct, so you will not leave Evesham until we tell you.'

'I have not left Evesham since last Nativity, when I went back to Pinvin to bury my mother, my lord. I will be here.'

The sheriff's men left, and headed to the reason for their interviews, the alluring Amicia Horsweard.

The Widow Horsweard was busy preparing for her husband's wake. She looked suitably solemn and thoughtful, but the cause of this was not her bereavement, but her future. The meeting with Robert the Coppersmith had been as her head told her it would be, and as her heart hoped it would not. He had shrugged at Walter's death, and only shown interest when she had declared the sheriff's men were hunting for a killer. He saw risk to himself and sought to avoid it. His first thought was that she was a fool to have come to him, and then he decided it would be better if Amicia ceased her visits, at least for a while. After all, he thought, there was always the girl next door if he needed anything.

Amicia Horsweard faced facts. Robert, however wonderful a lover, was never going to leap into marriage as he did into bed. She had some harsh words for him, but he just smiled.

'My sweet, do you really think I could not find another to fill your place within days? Evesham has plenty of willing women who would like to find out if what they have heard is true.'

'Was it all just lust, then?'

'Oh yes. I have a lot of lust.'

She had told him what she thought of him, and in uncompromising terms, then left, to seek the more gentle comfort of John Pinvin.

The bridle-maker had opened his door to a woman with tears on her lashes. His instinct was to dry them, and make her comfortable. He had enjoyed her favours occasionally, often enough to be bewitched by even the memory of them, and to wonder at why she offered them to one such as himself, a very ordinary man, but his feelings for her were overwhelmingly those of quiet devotion and a desire to look after her. That she had a husband to do that troubled his conscience, but only when she was not present. He was so unlikely a home-breaker he found it hard to even see himself as the adulterous lover.

He was not so foolish as to want to put his neck into a noose for her, however, and had been nearly as keen as the coppersmith to hang back for a while, although he held out the promise of care 'as soon as this nasty business is over'. It was all Amicia could get from him.

The arrival of the sheriff's men at her door put the seal on a miserable morning. She glared at them, and only reluctantly admitted them into the chamber. In normal circumstances, Walter's coffin would have been there, but Will had thought it best the body be shrouded and coffined at the abbey before being taken to the parish church later in the day for the funeral rites. It might only be April, but after some days, the corpse had a heavy smell of death to it.

'I am busy, my lord, for I have to bury my husband this afternoon. Indeed, it would be better if you returned tomorrow.' She sounded petulant, and Bradecote disliked being told what he should do.

'No, it is better now. If you answer us without dithering, we shall not delay you. You may wish to sit.' His tone commanded, and was not placatory. He was telling her she might sit in her own chamber. She looked at him with an expression of dislike he found far less disconcerting than her appraisal of the day before.

She wavered, then sat, hands once more folded in her lap.

'Ask me the questions then, my lord, and let us be done.'

'You said your husband left a week ago for Gloucestershire to buy horses.'

'Yes, he did.'

'Yet he crossed the Avon neither at Hampton ferry nor by the Bengeworth bridge.'

'I do not understand.' She frowned.

'Nor do we, if he was heading south,' murmured Catchpoll.

'Have you any proof that is where he was going?' Bradecote continued.

'I . . . Perhaps he said so in front of the servants. Wait, Will knew. Mind you, he might as easily deny it just to get me into trouble.'

'And speaking of getting into trouble,' Catchpoll grinned unpleasantly, 'how did your lovers react to the news of your loss?'

She paled, and her eyes widened. She looked from Catchpoll to Bradecote, and saw no way out by playing the poor weak woman act, so she held up her head and answered brazenly.

'Neither welcomed me with open arms.'

'So they did not want Walter dead?'

'Robert certainly did not,' she sneered. 'He prefers his fun without bindings.'

'And this comes as a surprise to you?' Catchpoll raised an eyebrow. 'You believed him devotedly in love, did you? More the fool you. He does not even keep a cold bed when you are not in it.'

She looked angry, shocked. That he was a natural philanderer she could appreciate, but that he bedded other women, whilst also conducting an affair with her, outraged her. Catchpoll was not going to betray the unwilling girl, but smiled as he drew a picture of him filling her place as soon as she left his house.

'He swore to me . . .'

'That sort swear a lot, but at least you have the bridle-maker, eh? Or is he running scared too?'

Her eyes narrowed in dislike.

'That is different. He is simply cautious.'

'Would not want to marry a woman who might have got rid of her first, I suppose,' chipped in Walkelin.

'No!' She looked horrified.

'"No" he wouldn't, or "no" you did not kill Walter?' responded Bradecote, swiftly.

'I did not kill my husband.'

'You betrayed him with other men,' Bradecote pressed home the point, 'and all Evesham seems to have known it. Did you simply not bother to be discreet?'

'You do not understand.'

'Clearly. So explain to us.'

'Walter was a good man, but . . . not a good husband, in private matters. He understood I have . . . needs.'

'Very understanding of him.' Catchpoll sounded cynical. 'So he patted you on the head and told you to trot off to any man who could oblige?'

'I would not leave him, he knew that. And if ever he . . . I made no objection.'

'Generous of a wife, that,' Catchpoll addressed the remark to Walkelin. 'You be guided by that. Only pick a wife who does not raise an objection to lying in your bed with you.'

'Indeed, Serjeant. I will remember that.'

Amicia Horsweard looked from them to Hugh Bradecote.

'Walter was not young. I looked to the future, to possibilities, yes, but I did not want him dead.'

'And might your lovers have?'

'Robert, plainly not, and John Pinvin is a good man, a patient man. If you want someone who might find it better if Walter was dead, ask him?' She pointed past them.

They turned, and saw Will Horsweard standing in the doorway, his face almost puce with anger.

'You remain here until the wake is over, and then you get out, whore! Go to whoever will take you, since they have been taking you often enough while my brother breathed.'

Bradecote thought his attitude not unfair, but said nothing.

'I can see as you might feel aggrieved, Master Horsweard, but perhaps you ought to just tell us why you and your brother were at odds before he left.' Catchpoll sounded very reasonable.

'It was nothing.'

'Tell us this nothing, then,' Bradecote commanded.

'He was bemoaning Edith again.'

'Edith? His first wife?'

'No. Our sister.'

Bradecote suddenly recalled what Brother Porter had said.

'The one you and your mother married off to a lord.'

'It was a good match.' He sounded somehow defensive.

'But?' Catchpoll had caught the tone too.

'She loved him. That is no reason to berate me. And accidents happen. If the man did not take us to his bosom, what of it?'

'Quite. Why did he raise it just before he left?'

'I do not know. He was muttering about how he had failed her, not telling her high-and-mighty husband it was his fault.'

'Whose? Walter's own fault?' Walkelin was confused.

'No, Brian de Nouailles, lord of Harvington.'

Bradecote and Catchpoll exchanged glances. Harvington was a little to the north of Evesham, and not far from the bridge at Offenham. A man might choose to cross the Avon there and then head south if he had been to Harvington.

'Did he say he was going to see de Nouailles?' Bradecote tried not to sound too interested.

'No, but he went on and on about how Edith should have had blood kin at her burying, and how we were fools to think Brian de Nouailles would have anything to do with a horse-trading family after he got the dower and the beauty.'

'So he may have gone there?'

'If he did, he would get no kind reception. He said that the last time, he had been threatened with a whipping.'

'Really not keen on you then, this lord.' Catchpoll was trying not to look again at Bradecote.

'No. If he passed me in the street he would look away.'

It was clear where their next move lay, but Bradecote asked one final question.

'And there was no idea of Walter naming another in your place to inherit?'

'Who? Her?' He pointed at Amicia. 'Blood is thicker than . . . He knew what she is, but like a fool he was content with his lot, meagre as it was.'

'You are just jealous, because I refused your fumblings. Cripple.' She almost spat at him.

There were all the makings of a murderous row, but the sheriff's men were not interested in remaining. If either were found dead in the next few days, they would know whom to arraign, and they had no power to part them. Yet Bradecote felt a sudden responsibility, so he folded his arms and grinned.

'Don't mind us, as long as the blood does not stain our boots.'

The angry pair suddenly remembered his presence and turned to look at him.

'No, carry on. We'll hang the survivor and it will be a quick day's work.'

His cheerfulness defused the situation far more effectively than any command. They both looked at him, lord or not, with open loathing. The smile lengthened.

'I think we have heard all we need here, Serjeant Catchpoll.'

'Yes, my lord. Plenty.' He smiled his death's head grin, and the three sheriff's men left, feeling remarkably cheered at the revealing of a new scent to follow.

Chapter Seven

The sheriff's men ate the evening meal in a state that combined disappointment at the failures in Evesham with relief that they had a new path to tread.

'We leave you tomorrow, Father Abbot,' declared Hugh Bradecote, breaking his bread.

'Have you made an advance, my lord?'

'We think so. Walter Horsweard may have gone to visit Brian de Nouailles at Harvington.'

'Ah.'

'That "ah" sounded significant, Father.'

'Well, you will get a good Christian welcome from the priest at Harvington, Father Paulinus. He was of this House when young.'

'And de Nouailles?'

'I regret that there you may be accorded a less generous welcome. Brian de Nouailles is a difficult man. He has been in dispute with this abbey over a mill he leased, and now claims to own outright, and the land about it. His actions have been . . . less than accommodating. We sent our local steward to him and the poor man was hounded from the village with threats and blows.'

'He was married to Walter Horsweard's sister.'

'He was? Wait now, I do recall he married an Evesham maid, but Horsweard's sister?' He shook his head. 'Is it relevant to the death?'

'I do not know, but if we find Horsweard did go that way we have a greater chance of finding where he died.' The undersheriff did not mention the thought that had occurred to him, which was that if he had not been expected to go north to Harvington, then all the more likely that the killer came from Harvington. The number of people there who would know Horsweard would be limited, let alone have a reason to want him dead. It suddenly looked far more promising.

'I shall pray for your success.' Abbot Reginald gave a small smile.

Bradecote had not been attending for a moment.

'Oh. Er, thank you, Father. The priest at Fladbury, Father Jerome, he is lettered, yes?'

'Oh yes. I admit some country priests forget much of their learning over the years, but I know Father Jerome is not one such.'

'Then might I ask that a note be written and sent with the next guest from your guest hall heading through Fladbury, just to say the murdered man is named and is English.'

'Of course.' Abbot Reginald instantly understood the

importance of such a message. 'It will be a relief, indeed.' The cleric noted the undersheriff's frown. 'My son, even if the murderer eludes you, you have the consolation that the All Highest knows them, and that He will judge them, if they do not repent.'

'That, good Father, is assuredly true, but will not placate the ire of the lord Sheriff, who expects results of a tangible nature, nor give the people faith in the ability of the law to protect them from being victims of violence.'

'Then I shall add a prayer for William de Beauchamp also.'

'And for me?'

'My son, that was already guaranteed.' Abbot Reginald's smile grew, and Hugh Bradecote responded to it.

The three shrieval officers departed shortly after Prime next morning, and Bradecote was conscious of the good wishes that attended them. It was only a few miles north to Harvington, where the manor dominated the village in a brooding way. Hugh Bradecote always thought of his manor as enfolding the village of Bradecote in protection, and thinking of it brought Christina to his mind. He had been resolute in doing as she had commanded, and concentrating upon his duty, not dreaming of her, but the warm glow it gave him to think of her with the baby in her arms was worth a minute's dereliction.

They trotted into the village, and were watched with suspicion by an aged woman on her doorstep, a bemused infant, and a man who lacked a hand.

'They'll be out in the fields, no doubt.' Catchpoll felt the atmosphere also. It made his hackles rise.

The manor gates at Bradecote were more often open in the day, but here the heavy oak shut out the world.

'What price our welcome?' wondered Walkelin.

'We are the lord Sheriff's men, so it matters not,' growled Catchpoll, and hammered upon the gates.

They waited. Eventually the gate swung open a fraction, and a wary eye looked them up and down. It was an eye singular, for the other had the sunken look and blank stare of the blind.

'Your business?' The man sounded grumpy, as if he had been disturbed.

'I am Hugh Bradecote, Undersheriff of Worcester. We are here upon the lord Sheriff's business, and would speak with Brian de Nouailles.'

There was a pause while the man assimilated this information.

'I will see if he wishes to see you.'

'No. You will tell him we wishes to see him, and you will let us inside first,' snarled Catchpoll.

The gates opened with a creaking reluctance.

Bradecote looked about him. It was tidy enough, but forbidding. The hall was on the first floor of a stone building, with a flight of steps leading down, much, he thought, as at Cookhill, where he had first seen Christina. There were men about tasks, a girl carrying a heavy pail of water and leaning to one side to balance herself, but there was no chatter, no laughing, not even loose chickens scratching about in the bailey dirt.

The man from the gate spoke to a thin individual who climbed the steps and disappeared into the hall. A few minutes later a well-dressed, close-bearded man came out. He remained at the top of the steps, looking down.

'What does the undersheriff want to know of me?' Brian de Nouailles had a deep voice, but it had a discordant crack to it, not a mellow rumble.

'We would speak with you, but in private.'

'About what?'

'That, de Nouailles, I will tell you . . . in private.' Hugh Bradecote did not like being treated in such a manner.

De Nouailles shrugged.

'Then best you come in.'

He turned and disappeared into the dark of his hall, leaving the trio to dismount and follow.

'You stay with the horses, Walkelin, and keep your eye on the way out, eh.' Catchpoll had not liked their reception either.

Walkelin nodded.

Their eyes adjusted to the Stygian gloom of the hall. The shutters were mostly closed. Brian de Nouailles did not invite them into his solar, but sat at his high table as if about to decide the fate of a peasant misdemeanour.

'So, we are private. Say what you have to say.' He made no effort to be pleasant.

'We are interested in the movements of your wife's brother, my lord de Nouailles.' It cost Bradecote a lot to be even formally polite.

'I am not, and my wife is dead.' The closed expression grew even more so, in Catchpoll's opinion, shutting them out as firmly as the gates of the manor.

'So we have heard, my lord.' Catchpoll invested the comment with significance, even if, in truth, it meant nothing.

'I buried her little over a month ago, and if I never see her brother again, I will be happy.'

'Then you are in luck, my lord, for they buried Walter Horsweard yesterday,' the serjeant responded, quickly.

De Nouailles' expression did not flicker.

'Then the sheriff's interest in him comes too late.'

'We are interested in who killed him, de Nouailles, and why.' Bradecote's voice had an edge to it.

'Frankly, I do not care. I loved my wife,' de Nouailles' voice wavered for a moment and he paused, but when he continued it was as strong as ever, 'but her family were nothing. When I wed her, I removed her from them. Would you want horse traders, smelling of stables, sitting down to your table as kin, Bradecote?'

'No, but then I did not choose to marry a horse dealer's sister. You did, knowing her background.'

'Edith was different. She was beautiful, in face and heart.' De Nouailles suddenly turned his face away and shielded his eyes with his hand. 'Damn you, cannot you leave a man's grief untouched? You have surely never buried a woman you loved.'

Bradecote could not reply for a moment. He had buried Ela, been cast into a form of grief that robbed him of the power to think and act for a while, stunned by her sudden absence, but he had not loved her. Perhaps he ought to be more accommodating, for grief might make any man turn against the world.

'We have a duty to the law to find who killed Walter Horsweard, that is all, my lord de Nouailles. We know,' and he thought it better to be positive, 'that he came here, and then only that his body turned up in the mill leat at Fladbury

100

several days later, stabbed. We also know you threatened to have him whipped if he came here again. That is not just keeping unwholesome marriage kin at arm's length; that is dislike bordering on hatred. What had he done to rouse it?'

'You root like a hog in beechmast, don't you?' de Nouailles sneered.

'It is my task.' Bradecote did not rise to the bait, though Catchpoll's eyes narrowed.

'Look, I said I would have him lashed to keep him away. He had no more right to call me "brother".'

'He did that?' Catchpoll sounded surprised. He could not imagine Will Horsweard doing so, and nor, by association, Walter.

'Not to my face. He valued his hide that much.' De Nouailles looked Catchpoll up and down, and recognised him for what he was. Some serjeants were, he thought, just naturals, born to the job. Here was one, and he would not be knocked off balance by insult.

'So why threaten him?' Bradecote would not let this drop.

'Oh, for the love of the Virgin, is it not clear? He came here, complaining that he and his brother were not told of Edith's death in time to attend her burial. Well, she was buried as befitted a lady, and no taint of stable was going to attend it, nor was I thinking of them at the time. She was my wife, that was enough. I wanted nothing more to do with the family, the tie was broken. So I threatened him with a whipping. What of it? I did not threaten to kill him.'

'But he came here, one last time. Did you whip him then?'

'No. I saw him, told him in simple terms such as even a man like him might understand that there was no connection

101

between us at all, that he would get no favours from me, nor support, and that if he interfered in my life I would make his so miserable he would wish he lived in the Fens.'

'The Fens?' Bradecote was momentarily thrown.

'Yes. Ever been there? I did once, and I hope never to go again. November it was, boggy, foggy and the air festered in your lungs.'

'Glad you didn't threaten him, then,' murmured Catchpoll.

De Nouailles threw him an angry glance.

'Do you know where he went after he left Harvington?' Bradecote was back on track.

'Neither know nor care. Why should I have asked after his plans?'

There was sense to this, though it helped them not at all.

'And you know of no connection between Horsweard and any of your villagers? No reason any should dislike him?'

'None, to my knowledge. So you have found all you can here and can leave me in peace.'

'We decide when we leave, de Nouailles, and that is not yet.'

'I offer no hospitality.'

'Understood.' Whilst it made matters more difficult at a practical level, Bradecote could not imagine staying under de Nouailles' roof would be pleasant. 'If we need to speak to you, or to your servants, again, we shall.'

Brian de Nouailles frowned. He disliked the idea of the sheriff's man questioning his servants. Then he shrugged.

'Do as you please. My servants are loyal. You can see the door. Use it.' The dismissal was deliberately insolent and insulting. Catchpoll had little personal pride, but accounted the office of sheriff's officer barely below that of the King himself, and ground his teeth. Hugh Bradecote feigned unconcern, though he shared the anger.

'We will, de Nouailles, for leaving, and, if needs be, for entering.'

He then turned and stalked to the door, with Catchpoll in his wake.

'You know,' de Nouailles' voice carried after them, 'I dislike de Beauchamp, who holds the manor next to mine of the abbey, nearly as much as I dislike the monks, and I can see that his minions are as bad.'

The air, even in the bailey, seemed blissfully fresh. Walkelin was holding the horses as instructed, but also engaged in clearly bantering conversation with a servant girl, who scurried away as the thin steward appeared from the kitchens.

'Are we finished, my lord?' asked Walkelin.

'For the time being.' Bradecote gathered his reins and mounted. 'Now we speak to those without these walls, and seek shelter for tonight. I do not really want to return to the abbey at Evesham.'

Had the atmosphere not been so oppressive, Harvington would have been accounted a pleasant village, but its inhabitants were loomed over by their lord, and were wary. Most were in the fields this April morning, but Catchpoll suggested trying the church. Whilst village priests often laboured with their parishioners, they also kept the daytime offices, labouring with prayer. The three men therefore dismounted and tethered their mounts by the little church, which stood at the junction of three trackways, and entered. The windows were small, but the nave was light, for the walls were whitened, and the zigzag pattern over the arch to the tiny chancel was picked out in red ochre. It was a building on which love had been lavished, and the echo of it lingered in the stone. A spare figure in a priest's garb was wielding a broom over the stone floor, with the hiss of a man grooming a horse and keeping the dust from his lungs interspersing with snatches of Latin. He turned as the door closed behind them, and his face welcomed. It was the first smile that they had seen in Harvington.

'Father Paulinus?' Bradecote recalled Abbot Reginald's words, and Catchpoll looked approving. The undersheriff had found out the name of the priest in advance, had he?

'Indeed, my son. You seek me?'

'Well,' Bradecote's face erupted into a grin, 'we seek knowledge, and where better to find it than in the church.'

The priest actually laughed, and set his domestic duty aside, indicating a narrow bench set against the wall of the nave, where the most elderly and infirm were permitted to sit rather than stand for the services.

'No better place indeed, my son. And since you know me, might I know you?'

'I am Hugh Bradecote, the Undersheriff of Worcester, and these are the sheriff's men, Serjeant Catchpoll, and,' he paused, 'Apprentice Serjeant Walkelin.'

Walkelin had never heard himself announced by such an impressive title, and his chest stuck out with pride.

'Goodness! What can the authority of the shire hope to learn here?'

'We seek to find out who killed Walter Horsweard of Evesham, who was brother to the lady of this manor.'

'Walter Horsweard is dead?' The priest looked shocked, and crossed himself. 'God have mercy upon him.'

'You knew him, Father?'

'Not well, you understand, for he came rarely, much to the sorrow of my lady de Nouailles. She was a loving woman, and loved husband and family both, so it gave her great sadness that her lord wished to forget her kin. She spoke of him more than I saw him. But you say he is dead by violence? I saw him, about a week back, alive as we are here. Poor man.'

'He came to see the lord.' Bradecote declared the fact. He did not want Father Paulinus to think he was about to reveal secrets, not that he looked a man to be swayed by threats over justice.

'I believe so, yes. The poor fellow was very aggrieved that he and his brother were not here for the funeral, and . . .' the priest paused and furrowed his brow, 'he felt that blame attached to the lord de Nouailles over his sister's death.'

'But did she not die in an accident?' Bradecote looked perplexed.

'Oh yes. She tripped and fell down the steps before the hall, and broke her neck.'

Hugh Bradecote paled, thinking of how his Christina had tumbled down the steps at Cookhill and lost her baby, just before they had met. It had been a terrible thing, but could so easily have been fatal, and then he would never have met her, never fallen in love, never found the happiness that cocooned him now.

'Then how could her brother blame her husband, unless it was that the steps were in bad repair, and he needed a man to blame?' Catchpoll could read his superior's face, and filled the hesitation.

'No doubt he did want someone to blame. It is human nature to want to rail against something that lives and breathes, Serjeant. But I think it was because he could not see how she tripped on steps she knew so well without distraction.'

Bradecote nodded. Christina had been distracted by the news of her lord's violent death.

'Did he know of any distraction?' Catchpoll probed.

'He knew she was troubled in mind and heart, and her lord was the cause of it.'

'Seeking entertainment elsewhere, was he?' Catchpoll offered.

'Seeki—unfaithful? Oh no! I am sure that was not so. She adored her husband, and I am convinced he was equally attached to her.' Father Paulinus sounded hopeful more than certain.

'You are unsure, Father?' Bradecote had caught the doubt.

'Brian de Nouailles is not a man who shows his emotions, not his tender ones. His anger is another matter, of course.' Father Paulinus sighed. 'He is not a man in whom love of his fellows is strong. But to marry one not of his standing shows how taken he was with the lady's beauty, and she was very, very fair. Even a man who has put aside the lusts of the flesh would recognise that.' He smiled. 'A vision, you might say, and as sweet of temper as of face. He was intensely proud of her looks, however much he hid her origins, and since her death has

106

been shut within his manor, and even more uncharitable than normal. His servants fear even to be in a chamber with him. I have prayed for him, but I doubt he prays for himself, for God to give him consolation. My lady de Nouailles was very pious, and though her days were short upon the earth I am cheered by the expectation that she will be welcomed in glory, and stand among the blessed.'

The priest's simple and total faith shone from his face.

'Do you know of any in this village who might have had reason to dislike, or even know, Walter Horsweard, outside the manor?'

'None, my lord. Herluin the Turner sold him a good pear-wood bowl last All Souls, but otherwise I doubt any others had even exchanged words with him.'

Bradecote sighed, and Catchpoll sucked his teeth.

'I fear in this case the Church has not given the enlightenment you seek.' The priest sighed.

'Our path is often not clear until the last, Father. However, it means we have not finished our enquiries here.'

Father Paulinus smiled.

'Ah, and let me make a guess. You have not been offered the manor roof over your good heads.'

'Quite correct, Father.'

'Then you have a choice. You may return to Evesham or you may accept my hospitality.'

'I doubt that will put you in the good grace of the lord of the manor.' Bradecote gave him a wry smile.

'Ah, but my Lord in heaven is more important, and His example was always to be charitable.'

'Then we accept with thanks, Father.'

'I ought to say, before you leap at my generosity, that the Good Lord did not bless me with cooking skills. I can make bread as hard as the quern the flour was ground with, but he did bless me with good parishioners, who do not wish to see me waste away from poor fare. I give my provisions to several good women of the village, who then make more when they bake bread, or make a pie.' What he did not say was that he gave far more than was needed and thereby assisted two widows with children, and an indigent old woman. 'I will have fresh-baked crusty bread, an eel pie, as I have been told, and ale or cider, if you would care to share my simple abode.'

'Your generosity is welcome to us, and we will return before dusk. Our hunting must take us first to the bridge at Offenham, for it seems likely that the murdered man headed that way when he left here, for he was meant to be going into Gloucestershire, yet did not cross in Evesham.'

'My house is obvious, being next door to the house of God, so you will not need directions to find it upon your return, even if the light is fading.' His smile was a benediction, and they left subtly buoyed by it.

'My lord, does it occur to you de Nouailles might have had a good reason to kill Horsweard, or have him killed?' Catchpoll mounted, and glanced at his superior.

'You mean if he feared Horsweard telling all he met that he was responsible for his wife's death? The only thing against that was that she fell, and if he had pushed her you cannot tell me such a thing would not creep from under the stone of secrecy.' Bradecote frowned.

'If Horsweard harangued him over it, and he was in foul temper, he would not think of the sense. A man who could snap easily, that is what I would say he is.'

'True enough, Catchpoll. But if so, I would think he would be so angry he would want to do the deed himself, and I cannot see him chasing after . . . Unless he killed him then and there and had the body cast into the river.'

'That would have not been from the bridge my lord,' reasoned Walkelin, 'but the nearest quiet spot, flowing but not overlooked.'

'Walkelin is right about that. Mayhap looking at this bridge and asking the villagers will get us nowhere. But such is our duty.' Catchpoll had the 'resigned and long-suffering serjeant' expression on his face.

Bradecote broke into a canter.

'Let us get it over with, then. Come on.'

Chapter Eight

It was but a short ride to Offenham, across the bridge from which they still hoped Walter Horsweard had been cast into the Avon. They came to the slightly rickety wooden structure and dismounted to cross slowly, Catchpoll with his head down, scanning every plank and rail in case something was left that might indicate a struggle or a man's weight striking heavily. The wood was grey with weathering, and showed knocks here and there, but Catchpoll wanted something comparatively fresh. About a third of the way across he halted, handed his reins to Walkelin, and crouched to view the rail, grunting at the creaking of his knees.

'You know, I think this is new. There is a split in this section, look. If I press it, you can see it is not sound. A man's weight, a good-size man such as Walter Horsweard, being flipped over it would do this. The weight was only there a moment before going beyond, so the rail did not smash, but it is damaged.'

'But not something we could prove.' Bradecote was regretful.

'No, my lord, not prove, but it tells us, pretty surely, we are on the right track.'

'What we need is a nice bit of real evidence,' announced Walkelin.

'I knew we brought him along for something,' remarked Catchpoll, caustically. 'It was to state the obvious to us.'

'I meant a nice bit of evidence like a strand of green wool, pulled from a jerkin. One,' Walkelin paused for effect and reached just beyond where Catchpoll had discovered the damage, 'like this.'

He took the fibre from the splinter of oak on which it had become trapped. Catchpoll regarded him with a mixture of pride and disinterest, lest his eagle-eyed success led to him thinking he was clever.

'Now that,' declared Bradecote, unashamedly admiring, 'is a very good find.'

'Thank you, my lord.'

'Not proof beyond all possible doubt, of course, since it is possible that the thread and break are not connected, or from another person's clothing, but I grant it makes it very, very likely. Well done, Walkelin. You spotted it before me there.' Catchpoll's tone made it clear that he would undoubtedly have spotted the thread in the next few moments.

Walkelin was unabashed, and grinned.

'So we are nigh on certain Horsweard fell into the river here, whether killed here or ashore. Even if here, there would be little blood and almost no chance of finding a trace now.' Hugh Bradecote sighed.

'I say here simply because you would have to ask why out this far on the bridge if the killer was just dumping the body. The flow is good enough ten yards back at least.'

'And the bridge would not carry many abreast, so the murderer was probably alone,' Walkelin chipped in.

'A reasonable assumption.' Bradecote was thinking ahead. 'So that means we can finally discount suspects in Evesham unless they followed Horsweard to his angry meeting with de Nouailles, then killed him here and got back to Evesham without anyone knowing they had been missing for at least a whole morning or afternoon.'

'Which then means that the lord of Harvington assumes the place of chief suspect. I have no problem with that, my lord.' Catchpoll nodded.

'The thing is,' Walkelin sighed, 'how in the Lady's name do we prove it by evidence, let alone getting him to confess it?'

'That is our next hurdle.' Hugh Bradecote rubbed his chin. 'I am not convinced that being annoyed at Horsweard bleating on about his blame for the wife's death would have driven him to murder, and him chasing after the man would have been too obvious.'

'Not unless he did kill her,' murmured Catchpoll.

'We agreed pushing her is unlikely, surely?' Walkelin looked from undersheriff to serjeant.

'That is only the most obvious way.'

'Meaning Catchpoll?'

'If the good lady was given strong drink beforehand, or made sleepy with poppy juice.'

'Well, where would he obtain the latter? And if he got

her drunk, the servants would have seen, or smelt it on her.'
Bradecote thought it unlikely.

'Then we find out if it was him who picked her up with her neck broke. If he did, who is to say she was really dead at that point and not just in a swoon. He could carry her to her chamber and break her neck before any saw a change in her.' Catchpoll tried not to sound as if clutching at straws, but failed.

'And this, the man who adored his beautiful wife?'

'The man who seems to have done so, my lord. She was distressed over him, and if not him being wayward with other women, you have to ask what made her unhappy?'

'We may discover more from Father Paulinus, tonight. But first we will go and ask in Offenham in case any saw something suspicious on this bridge the day Walter Horsweard died.'

They completed their crossing, and trotted into Offenham.

Here too the inhabitants were mostly out in the fields, and the three men took a detour to speak with them along their strips of ridge and furrow. They asked first for the steward, and a florid-faced woman pointed a begrimed finger to the edge of the pease field.

'Over there, my lord,' she announced, taking in Bradecote's demeanour and garb. 'Alcuin, the abbey's steward.'

'And have you seen the lord of Harvington in the village about a week ago, or on the bridge?' asked Walkelin, following up.

'Him?' The woman crossed herself. 'The saints be praised, no. When he comes he brings trouble, to us and to poor Alcuin. You ask him about the lord of Harvington, and he will keep you hard by for long enough for me to milk both my goats.'

113

Alcuin the Steward was younger than most in his position, perhaps thirty, no more. He was young enough to be keen, and Abbot Reginald, who was his overlord, would have given the undersheriff a glowing testimonial as to his hard work and abilities. He frowned at the mention of Brian de Nouailles.

'You will not get a good word from me about him, that is for sure. I was sent to him, on behalf of the abbey, about the mill.'

'Offenham mill?'

'No, no. You see, the abbey has land the other side of Avon. Has had for hundreds of years, odd gifts and such. There are a tidy few acres of good land a bit below Harvington mill. Now, in the time of the lord de Nouailles' father, the Harvington mill had a big fire. It was scarce more than charcoal. It would take time to rebuild, and the abbey had been thinking of putting a mill on the other bank to us. It had got to the stage of a leat being cut and the first timbers going up, but then something went awry. It might have been a flood. I am too young to recall. Whatever it was, the project was left unfinished. De Nouailles' father offered to finish the mill on condition that, having put in the work, he might have free tenure of it, and the land, for two dozen years. This meant Harvington got a mill quickly, and then he rebuilt the original so there were two. It gave good trade with villages lacking a mill. Made de Nouailles a rich man. The lease was up last year, but the new lord claims the agreement was different. He says it was granted for a hundred years, because his father paid good coin also. There is nothing of this in the abbey accounts. He has produced some document to prove his case, but I say as what is a piece of vellum that only he has? The abbey accounts are good for decades, so the fact that this one thing is not there . . . Well, I do not trust de Nouailles, and I do trust the abbey.'

'So he did not take to your visit?' Bradecote already knew the answer.

'You might say that. He threatened to set his hound on me and had me thrown down the steps of his hall, with the admonition that he would do the same if the Abbot of Evesham came in person. Lucky I was not to break every bone in my body. As it was, I could not lift as much as a hoe for nigh on a week, and my poor wife had to rub me near all over with some salve her mother invented.' There was just a hint in his voice that that part was less unpleasant, but then, he was a man in his prime.

'Dangerous steps they have at Harvington's manor house,' murmured Catchpoll.

Alcuin raised an eyebrow.

'You have heard of that, then? Poor lady. Only came across her a couple of times, for de Nouailles kept her close, but I never heard aught of her that was not good, and she looked like, oh, a vision. How she managed, wed to a hell-hound like him, I do not know. Perhaps he drove her to throw herself down them to escape.' The steward shook his head.

'Can you tell us if you saw de Nouailles on or by the bridge, about a week back?' Bradecote thought it best to get back to the evidence as well as background.

'He rarely comes this way, and glad I am of it. I was not near the river, for my strips are more inland, but you might ask Brictric. He fishes most days, but today is helping his brother over yonder.' Alcuin pointed to a pair of figures a couple of hundred yards distant.

'Thank you for your help, Master Steward.'

'Glad I am to help, my lord.'

They trudged across the clinging soil to where two middle-aged men had halted their labours and were obviously discussing the strangers. Catchpoll introduced himself and asked which was the fisherman.

'That'll be me,' the older man, who had thinning hair, and a missing front tooth, admitted.

'We were wondering if you saw aught amiss on the bridge about a week since. Some argument perhaps? Two men? One in a green jerkin?'

The fisherman frowned with the exertion of memory.

'Green jerkin, you say? I saw a man dressed so, and another with him, briefly. My net got tangled see, so I was looking to sort it. When I looked up, they must have crossed, for I could not see them.'

'Did you recognise either?' Catchpoll sounded casual, but Bradecote could see the glitter in his eyes.

'Too far away for that.'

'What about the man not in green? Was he taller or shorter than the man in the jerkin? Clean-shaven or bearded?' Walkelin could not contain his interest, and earned a warning frown from his serjeant.

'I would say shorter. He was not a tall man. He rode a stocky chestnut and had some covering on his head – a cap, I suppose. I saw no beard. They were both leading their mounts. That is all I can tell you.'

'What part of the day was it?' Bradecote did not think it vital, but every scrap might help.

116

'Ah, that I can say. It was early in the afternoon, for sure it was, for after I cleared my net, I made a good catch and took it home well before sunset, cleaned and ready to cook over the fire.'

'Mighty useful you have been. May you catch a big fish next time you take out your net.' With which 'blessing' Catchpoll nodded, and the sheriff's men headed back to their mounts, grazing at the field boundary.

'And we are one step closer to catching our big fish,' announced Walkelin, looking very pleased with the afternoon's investigations. 'Also with eel pie and ale to look forward to.'

'Ah yes, Walkelin of the ever-empty stomach. Heaven protect us from famine, or you will be eating the lord Bradecote's horse when he is not looking.' Catchpoll grinned, and winked at the undersheriff, who laughed.

'I will make sure I count the legs before mounting.' Then he halted, and his face froze. 'The horse. We have not asked ourselves what happened to the horse. Sweet Jesu! Walkelin, run back and ask the fisher if he can recall any details of Horsweard's mount. That will be a start, and as soon as we can, I am sending you back into Evesham to get a full description from Will Horsweard.'

His voice held a mixture of excitement and self-blame. Walkelin set off at pace.

'The blame lies as much with me, my lord.' Catchpoll frowned. 'I should have picked up on that from the first. I suppose we were so busy haring after the widow's lovers it did not register, not within the town, but by heaven, it should have.' He shook his head at his own failing.

When Walkelin returned, breathless, he could only report that the horse was bay or dark brown.

Father Paulinus was leaving the church after saying Vespers when the three horsemen trotted into Harvington. He thought they looked contented with their day, and raised a hand in greeting.

'You come in good time, my lord. Your efforts have been rewarded?' He smiled up at them.

'We do think we have made progress. Almost certainly, Walter Horsweard was killed upon the bridge by Offenham. He was seen upon it, and then . . . not seen.' Bradecote smiled back.

The priest crossed himself and sighed.

'Such evil as men do, and yet we were made in the image of God. How we are fallen.'

'We can but do our best as we see it, though we are all indeed fallen, Father.'

'Indeed so. Now, as to your mounts, I have no stable myself, but there is room where the plough oxen are stalled, and I keep my mule, and I have arranged for them to be sheltered there. I will show you the place.'

He led them to a building, and was quite surprised that Hugh Bradecote remained to see his own horse comfortable, rather than merely commanding Walkelin to see to it for him. He therefore went home alone, and the widow who had made the pie came and fussed, knowing it would be fed to so high-and-mighty a figure as the lord Undersheriff. By the time they entered the priest's house, there was an enticing smell from the hearth, mingling with the smell of warm herbed bread.

118

'We are very grateful for your hospitality, Father.' Bradecote was conscious that in his generosity, Father Paulinus risked the anger of Brian de Nouailles.

'Oh no, please. I need no gratitude. Indeed, it is Widow Fisher here who deserves thanks, for it is she who has given us good fare.'

The widow blushed and curtseyed, and murmured so quietly that her words were lost. Bradecote thanked her and declared, in perfect truth, that her cooking made their mouths water with its delicious smells. Thinking back to what they had endured at Fladbury Mill, he only hoped the taste was as good as the promise. When the meal was served, they discovered that the odours did indeed not lie, and it was a very contented and replete threesome who sat about the priest's fire as the evening shadows crept into every corner.

'We spoke to the Steward of Offenham, Father. He has had good cause to dislike Brian de Nouailles. He says he was thrown down the hall steps when he came on Abbot Reginald's business.'

'Ah, the mill, you must mean he came about the mill.' Father Paulinus shook his head. 'I have known Father Abbot many years, for I took my vows in Evesham before being called to minister to my flock of souls, and I knew him before he was head of the house. He is a good and honest man. Now, you may say that of course he is, simply because he is a monk, but I am not so blinded by the cloister that I do not see some who are tonsured as being less than holy. It happens, even within a House of monks.

'I recall that the old lord, Judhael de Nouailles, made

agreement with the abbey about the mill that had never been finished, the one opposite to Offenham, when his own burnt down. It came before Chapter. The details I forgot, for what interest had I in such things, as a young man full of religious zeal? It all seemed a bit too worldly to think of it. Ah, I was very young in wisdom. Anyway, I do not know what was agreed, but am sure that if Abbot Reginald swears no document exists but for the one leasing the mill for two dozen years, then it is true.'

'Brian de Nouailles contests that. Yet how can he do so if there is a document?' Bradecote frowned.

'He has another, dated some months later, and though the abbey denies its existence, he has stated he will not give up the mill. He says they have to prove his document false, and how can they do that?'

'Can he read?' Catchpoll wondered out loud.

'No, that he cannot, but he got a clerk to read it for him.' Father Paulinus sighed. 'He said he would not trust me because I was of that House of Benedictines and monks looked after their own. He only had what he says his father told him of the agreement, until it was read out to him. And there is another coincidence. About four months since, a man I had not seen in nigh on a score of years came through the village. He was in some need, poor fellow. Once he had been a Brother of Evesham, but there had been some problem, after I left to come here, and he left the order. He told me there had been accusations from one brother, which he was unable to refute except by one man's word against the other, and the other brother had been believed. Since that time, he took work as he could, scribing for any who paid him. He asked if the lord might have employment for him,

120

and at most times that would have been unlikely. Yet he came just when Brian de Nouailles did need a man to read the vellum for him. Thomas was accorded more courtesy than most who enter the manor, at the first.'

'At the first?'

The priest sighed and looked sorrowful.

'Alas that he came here. I do not know what it was, as I said, that made Thomas leave the cloister, but I fear now it was dealings with a woman. You see, he saw the lady de Nouailles, and his mind was turned by her beauty. The evils of lust poisoned him, and he . . .' He paused.

'And?'

'The lord came home from hunting and found Thomas in the solar, attempting to force his . . . attentions upon the lady.'

'Nothing was said to the lord Sheriff.' Catchpoll sounded surprised.

'There was no need. It was dealt with. The lord of Harvington has right of *infangentheof* here. Thomas was caught with the lady's gold and amber brooch in his hand, so the lord hanged him from his walls immediately, as a thief. It was terrible, but the law has long accepted justice in the moment, and you can see why Brian de Nouailles reacted as he did, even if the law would want the case to be a plea of the King. He spared his wife the ignominy of making presentiment before a court, and there was no doubt to the guilt. The punishment was no different.'

'Was the lady harmed?' Bradecote asked.

'In body, not so as one saw. But I think her spirit was sore afflicted. It made her sad and nervous, poor lady. I think she blamed herself, because her beauty had driven Thomas to succumb to wrong.'

'Father,' Catchpoll frowned, 'I must ask. Is there any possibility that the lady de Nouailles was so distressed by what had happened that she brought about her own end?'

'None.' The answer came swiftly. 'She could not have been buried in holy ground else.'

Bradecote and Catchpoll exchanged glances. The priest was sincere, but he was a good, generous man, and they could not see him keeping a woman he had described in glowing terms for her piety from a grave in consecrated earth without irrefutable evidence that she had taken her own life.

'We understand that, Father,' murmured Hugh Bradecote, 'but Serjeant Catchpoll is right. We needed to ask. The most godly can be driven to commit the sin of self-slaughter if their minds are overwhelmed. I have sometimes thought it is the madness that commits the deed, not the person themselves.'

Father Paulinus considered the undersheriff's words.

'I have no reason, none, to say she did anything but slip upon a step. You speak such thoughts as I would account true, but the Church is strict upon this, whatever feelings an individual might have. If there is doubt, I have given the deceased the benefit of it in my time, but if there is none there is nothing I can do but pray for them, and see them buried outside the churchyard boundary. In the lady de Nouailles' case, though I know she was troubled and distressed, I never doubted at all. You see she blamed her own looks, but her concern was for her husband. She loved him totally, and, with little understanding of the law or theology, feared that his reaction would be seen as murder, if not by the King's Justice, then in the eyes of God, because he hanged Thomas in anger.'

'She told you this?'

'Not exactly, but she asked about the judgement of those that judged, and said that her lord was not a man given to considering his actions, and also he had been very angry with Thomas the Clerk. Had she said these things in confession, I could not tell you of them, my lord, you must know that. The sanctity of confession is not broken by death. I am telling you what is the only reading I can make of her comments to me, outside of the confessional.'

'Is there anything that she did say, which we may not know?'

'I cannot tell you that. I am sorry.' The priest shook his head. 'You must think me obstructive, my lord, but I answer to a higher authority even than the law.'

With which the law had to be content, though it might wonder. Indeed, whilst Walkelin slept soundly, both Bradecote and Catchpoll lay in the darkness, considering permutations, trying to make disparate facts into a cohesive whole, and one in which Brian de Nouailles was central.

Chapter Nine

The morning brought the opportunity for the sheriff's men to discuss their nocturnal cogitations. Father Paulinus went to say the first office of the day, and then to feed his fowls. Catchpoll, Bradecote and a bleary Walkelin sat in the warm dimness of the little dwelling. There was a silence, almost as if they had commenced with prayer.

'So.'

'So, my lord?' Walkelin was perplexed.

'So, indeed. What the lord Bradecote means, Walkelin, is what did yestereve tell us in the solving of the murder?' Catchpoll's smile of understanding was broadened by the knowledge that Walkelin was half a step behind in thought.

'Which murder?' Walkelin enquired, and before his head could be bitten off by his serjeant, qualified his question. 'I mean, are we still only investigating the murder of Walter Horsweard, or are we also investigating the death of the lady de Nouailles?'

Catchpoll's features relaxed from the growl that had been forming.

'Technically, we still have but one murder, but if there is a second, it sort of explains the first.' Catchpoll pulled a 'thinking' face. 'We could not see a motive for de Nouailles wanting Horsweard dead, as opposed to sent packing. Well, if the horse dealer was accusing him of murder, and especially if he had grounds, then if he *had* killed the wife there would be good reason for him to kill the brother-in-law if he threatened him.'

'There are a lot of "ifs". You are saying, then, that de Nouailles' act as the grieving husband is all show, and he did not love her?' Bradecote was undecided on this matter.

'Well love and hatred are close bedfellows. One can become the other very swiftly.' Catchpoll gave a look that spoke of many years' experience of this occurring.

'So he stopped loving her because . . . ?' Walkelin looked confused.

'He could not bear the thought that she had been sullied by the clerk, perhaps. We have only the report that she did not show evidence of harm. So there were no bruises visible.' Catchpoll shrugged. 'That does not mean much. What if the clerk was found to be doing the deed? The noble lord reacts out of instinct, and then does not want to be shamed by his wife's shame. That festers. He does not want to touch her, and having taken out his ire upon the clerk, he starts to blame her for not putting up a better resistance, perhaps even imagines she did not resist at all.'

'If she had met the man by consent, she would have confessed, and the priest, though he would not tell us of it,

125

would not wax so lyrical about her virtues.' Bradecote was staring at the red embers of the fire.

'I said "imagines", my lord. I doubt the lady was anything but a good and virtuous dame.'

'That is all well and good, Serjeant Catchpoll, but if de Nouailles killed his wife by pushing her down the steps, why are there no witnesses?' Walkelin did not look convinced.

'Ah, young Walkelin, who is to say there are no witnesses? It might be that we simply have not found them yet. If de Nouailles is feared, it might yet be a secret, for all we thought otherwise.'

'Feared enough to keep murder secret?' Walkelin sounded dubious.

'Did you see the man with one hand as we entered the village yesterday? What odds he suffered de Nouailles' summary justice for a misdemeanour?'

'If – and I stress this "if" – you are right, Catchpoll, we need to speak to the manor underlings, and without their lord looking on, or within earshot of any who might report their words for the sake of favour.' Bradecote sounded as if this was an almost impossible feat to achieve.

'Well, there's ways and means, my lord. What we need, primarily, is a diversion.' Catchpoll grinned, slowly, his eyes fixed upon his superior. 'De Nouailles will not be watching his minions if he is busy fending off questions from the only one here with rank to demand being seen. Meanwhile I speak to the steward, who will no doubt keep things close, and young Walkelin,' he gazed at his apprentice serjeant benignly, 'puts his ferreting skills to use, starting with that wench he was giving the bright eye to yesterday.'

'I wasn't, Serjeant. I was just making myself agreeable. You said it was important to get close to those who might have information.'

'She looked like she wouldn't mind getting mighty close to you, and I am not so sure you would remember the questions if she did.'

'I know my duty, Serjeant.' Walkelin blushed, but stuck out his chest and gave a fair approximation of a virtuous sheriff's officer.

'I am sure you do, Walkelin,' Bradecote intervened, his voice serious but with a wry smile on his face, 'and I am sure you had no other motives but duty.'

Catchpoll guffawed, then grinned, but his smile faded as he considered what needed to be discovered.

'The thing is, lad, that you are more likely to find out information than we are. Make yourself agreeable, not just with the wench, but any you can, while you can.'

'Which means a delay in sending you to Evesham to get the description of the horse, but this chance may not come again. Oh, and Catchpoll, what do you suggest I ask that will occupy de Nouailles, but keep him from setting his hound on me?' Bradecote raised an eyebrow.

'I reckon as you are safe from teeth marks, my lord, however little he likes your presence, and whatever you ask. Rank is rank, after all.'

'My only real concern is how long I can act as this diversion without him guessing it is but air. Do not let yourself get dragged into mere rambling about his harsh treatment, Walkelin. Listen, but steer the conversation also.'

'I will do that, my lord, as best I can.' Walkelin felt the burden of responsibility upon his shoulders, but was rather excited by it.

'Best we make a start then.' The undersheriff got up, and they went about their task as Father Paulinus returned, brushing dirt from his habit. 'We shall almost certainly trespass upon your hospitality again tonight, Father.'

'No trespass, my lord. You are very welcome.' The priest smiled.

The gatekeeper seemed even less keen to admit them than the day before, and his hostility was obvious. It seemed to spring less from a devotion to his lord than idleness, but Catchpoll decided that any conversation with him would be a waste of breath, and made no effort to be amiable.

'If he wants to be curmudgeonly, he'll find I do it better,' mumbled Catchpoll, hawking, and then spitting into the dirt. 'And here comes Longshanks the Steward.'

The steward was stony-faced, and his greeting frosty. Catchpoll countered it by being at his most cheery and affable, which took the man by surprise.

'Good morrow to you, Master Steward. Yes, we are back again, and in your way, no doubt of it. But the lord Undersheriff has more questions for your lord, and where he goes, we go too, so here we are, under your feet.'

Catchpoll being convivial was almost more worrying than him being morose. He clapped the steward upon the back and began propelling him towards the hall steps. Hugh Bradecote followed them, and Walkelin veered off to lounge by the door of the kitchens, as though he were no longer on duty.

The hall was still gloomy and shuttered, and there was a smell of stale ale to it that Bradecote guessed the lady de Nouailles would never have countenanced. His Christina would have had the shutters opened, the rushes changed, and herbs scattered. It spoke of the lack of a woman. This, he thought, could have been himself, his hall, except his had a babe within it, demanding, but making one look forward not back. He felt sympathy for Brian de Nouailles, sympathy that withered when the man emerged from his solar. He looked sullen, as if he had lost himself to wine the previous night and was paying for it now. That happened, but there was also a glint in the eyes that might be masked, were he not too over-hung to disguise it. Bradecote had seen that before, in men who enjoyed inflicting pain in others. If his lady had roused him to jealousy or dislike, he pitied her.

'Back again, my lord. I ask myself why?' Brian de Nouailles snarled.

'I am glad you are in the mood for questions, de Nouailles, for I have several.' Bradecote tried the same cheerful manner as Catchpoll. 'When we were here yesterday, you did not mention the circumstances of your wife's death.'

'It has nothing to do with Horsweard's death, and I told you I did not wish to discuss it.' He nodded curt dismissal to his steward, and Catchpoll withdrew also, content that the lord Bradecote had opened the questioning by placing de Nouailles off balance.

'So you did, but I do.'

'Then you are in for disappointment, Bradecote.'

'I can ask all day. To start with, why was the lady de Nouailles in a state of low spirits and worry?'

'How do I know? Women are like that sometimes. If you were married you—'

'I am married. I have also lost a wife. Do not keep claiming "You cannot understand". Was she upset after the affair with the clerk?' Bradecote chose his words carefully.

'Affair?' De Nouailles scowled.

'When he tried to be familiar with her, and you hanged him . . . for theft.'

'I had the right.' The scowl deepened.

'I did not say that you did not. Did he actually lay hands upon her, or were you timely?'

'It is none of your business, and the lady is dead.'

'She is, which is why I ask.' Bradecote did not enjoy such a line of questioning, but it was needful. 'She was buried in holy ground, so the Church saw no reason to think she took her own life.' He kept Father Paulinus's name out of specifics.

'Of course she did not.'

'Yet she slipped on the steps of her own hall. Were they wet and slippery?'

'Not especially.'

'You see, that is what puzzles me. The lady falls on steps she could have descended with her eyes shut.'

'Such things happen every day. Have you never tripped in your own hall?' growled de Nouailles.

'Yes, but mostly when my mind was elsewhere. So if she was not worried . . .'

'I did not say she was not worried.'

'Oh no, you did not, did you. You just gave me no reason why she was.' Bradecote's tone was not friendly.

'No doubt what happened was a shock to her, as it would be to any lady.'

'Enough to distract her, weeks later? A great shock.'

'What are you saying, Bradecote?' The lord of Harvington was losing his temper.

'If no actual assault took place, her reaction seems excessive. If she slipped.'

'If . . . ?' De Nouailles' fists clenched. 'It was an accident.'

'Were you there? Did you see her fall?'

'Yes. I tried to grab her arm, but the sleeve of her gown simply tore in my hand.' De Nouailles shut his eyes. 'There was nothing I could do. When I picked her up she was limp. Her neck was broken. For God's sake, Bradecote, leave this now.'

Hugh Bradecote was unwilling to push further. There was room for doubt, but only that, and he needed corroboration. A lot would depend upon what Catchpoll, and more likely, Walkelin, could discover from the lowlier inhabitants of Harvington manor.

Walkelin was in fact doing a very good job of not being the sheriff's man. He had poked his head around the door of the kitchen in time to see a motherly woman lifting a heavy iron cook pot from scouring.

'Might I take that for you, Mistress?'

Walkelin, the helpful young man, stepped swiftly forward and lifted the heavy pot. The woman eyed him with approbation, and just a touch of reminiscence for when men like that wanted to help her out of a desire to gain her favours, not just an extra portion of pottage.

'There now. I wish as I had help like you about every day, young man. Who might you be?'

'Oh, I am the man-at-arms come along with the lord Undersheriff and his serjeant,' he declared airily, demoting himself. 'You know how it is when you are just left hanging about until someone expects you to be there, prepared for anything and looking as if you know what is going on, but you don't.'

'Indeed. Them that has power leaves us ordinary folk in the dark, often as not. It is like when the lord demands a meal when he returns unexpected, and is angry that it is thrown together from what I can find in the store and has hung long enough and a bit more.'

'You look like a dame who is rarely caught out, Mistress.'

She coloured, and murmured that he was like all men, out for what he could get. He grinned, and gave her a smile and a slow wink.

'Ah, Mistress, see, rarely caught out.' He paused. 'Must be different round here, without a lady in the hall.'

The woman sighed and shook her head.

'Poor lady, and her so lovely. Had a lot to learn in some ways, when she wed.' Her voice dropped as if imparting details of an unfortunate blemish. 'She wasn't born to it, see. Mind you, I do not begrudge her, and she never enjoyed it, for she was lonely, excepting when he was with her.'

'He?'

'The lord. You can see just why he was so smitten with her, but why she adored him, only heaven knows. But to be fair, she was the one person he never struck, nor rarely threatened with the lash. He is a hard man, our lord, and unfair, but his lady softened him. He even smiled when with her.'

This was clearly not a common sight, and Walkelin could believe it from the little he had seen of him.

'So what happened to her?'

'It was an awful accident. I think something had upset her, for she came out of the hall in tears, weeping, and him trying to soothe her, right behind. Then all of a sudden, she was falling, and though he grabbed at her arm she tumbled over and over to the bottom of the steps.'

'You saw this?'

'Well, only the end. I was told the start of it by the others. I came out at the shout from the lord. He was at the bottom of the steps, holding her, rocking her like a babe he was, and weeping pitiful. Never thought I would feel sorrow for the man, but I did then. He carried her back to the solar and would not let even the priest within for hours. Since then he has been dangerous. That is the only word for him. Three servants have been flogged, and after the lady's brother came last, he beat the steward for not keeping him from his hall.'

'He beat his own steward, for that?' Walkelin shook his head. 'Hard man, indeed. Must have hated the lady's brother, though.'

'No love lost between them, that is for sure. And Master Horsweard, him that is her brother, seems a nice enough man. He only lost his temper with the lord Brian, which is not wise.'

The woman had clearly not heard of the horse trader's death. It might mean nothing, and yet such news should spread as flames through kindling. De Nouailles, and perhaps his steward, if he had heard of it within the hall, were keeping the knowledge of the murder to themselves. That was odd. Well, Walkelin thought it time that it was known. It could lead to interesting talk.

'But did you not know, Mistress, that it is because of Walter Horsweard that the lord Undersheriff is here?'

He had her interest.

'It is?'

'Yes, for he has been killed, and his body found floating in the Avon. Looks like he was killed crossing the bridge by Offenham, after visiting here.'

'Lord have mercy upon us and him!' Her hands flew to her mouth. 'What is the world a-coming to, that is what I wonder?'

Walkelin murmured agreement. He hoped his superiors would commend his letting the information about Horsweard's death be known. If the killer was here, let him know that the law knew when, where and how, and was closer therefore, to who.

'We live in bad times,' the good woman shook her head, 'what with lords and king and empress all fighting. It means evil flourishes. Poor Master Horsweard must have looked a tidy prize to some cut-throat. Always came here well dressed. In his best, I expect, so as not to make the lord Brian look down his nose more. What a good thing that Aelfric was not—'

'And is the preparation begun for the meal, woman?'

The steward loomed in the doorway, Catchpoll just behind, and giving Walkelin a vaguely apologetic grimace.

'In a trice, Master Steward, never you fear.' The cook gave Walkelin a swift, twisted smile, and looked the steward in the eye. 'The young man just gave me a hand with the pot. Best you all leave me to my work.'

The steward eyed Walkelin suspiciously, but Walkelin smiled the vacuous smile of one who never thought for himself and was content to be told how to do every menial task.

'There is no cause for sheriff's men to swarm all over the manor,' grumbled the steward.

'I would not call our Walkelin a swarm. Harmless enough, and about as bright as my horse. He gets underfoot, but no more. Come along, Walkelin, and leave the cook to her work.' Catchpoll spoke as to an idiot.

'Yes, Serjeant,' responded Walkelin, looking as dim as possible.

The steward remained in the kitchen, clearly signalling that he would not have anyone speak with the sheriff's men out of his earshot. Catchpoll 'herded' Walkelin into the courtyard, keeping up the impression that he was a brainless minion with a flow of basic instructions. Beneath his breath he grumbled.

'Tried my best, Walkelin, but he grew mighty suspicious, and was close as an oyster. Any luck?'

'Cook was useful. Missed the maid, though.'

'Fair enough.' Catchpoll raised his voice again. 'You wait out here, lad, while I see if the lord Bradecote is ready to depart.'

Walkelin stood still in the middle of the bailey, and Catchpoll went back up the steps to the hall. He heard de Nouailles' voice, with its hoarse, jarring note, before reaching the half-open door. He did not sound in good humour.

'You cannot trust the Church, Bradecote. Oh, not upon scripture, but the Church as landowner, as a lord. They purse their lips and fold their hands, and pretend to holiness, but they grasp and cheat like any merchant.'

'Well, my holdings march by abbey lands but—'

'Then beware, lest they encroach.'

'But it is not the fault of their steward sent on their behalf. Evesham sent the Steward of Offenham, and, by all accounts, he suffered assault.'

'Hmm. "By all accounts" means the peasant himself and that old fox in Evesham? Well, if you take their word for it, that is up to you. I deny any mistreatment.'

'I—' Bradecote halted as Catchpoll entered, and his relief was patent to one who knew him well.

'Beg pardon, my lord, but I was wondering if you would be needing the man-at-arms and myself again this forenoon?' Catchpoll sounded unusually deferential, and Hugh Bradecote noted the reference to 'the man-at-arms'.

'Er, yes, I wish to ride to the bridge again, Serjeant Catchpoll, but my discussion with the lord de Nouailles is at an end, so you may accompany me.' It all sounded very like a mummers' play to the undersheriff, but he hoped de Nouailles was too busy seething about the Abbot of Evesham to notice. He turned back to Brian de Nouailles. 'I am sure we will have further words, my lord, at some point.' He nodded, indicating he had said all that he wished, and turned to leave, with de Nouailles sensing something, but being unsure what it might be.

Only as they mounted and trotted out of the bailey did Bradecote heave a sigh of relief. They did not look back, and even if they had they could not have seen the figure watching them from the narrow window, high in the gatehouse.

'I hope that was worth it. Any luck, Walkelin?'

'I did not meet the servant girl, my lord, but the cook had

some interesting things to say, in a sort of sideways way. I did not think that—' Walkelin halted, for the serving wench was at the doorway of a cott, and bearing a large basket of washing. 'My lord, might I have permission to dismount and—'

'Yes.' Bradecote's voice matched his for urgency. 'Dismount and give us your reins. We will take ourselves off, and you assist the washmaid. We meet back at the priest's.'

Walkelin vaulted from the saddle, almost threw his horse's reins over its head and handed them to Catchpoll. The riders turned aside and cantered away, leaving Walkelin to amble towards the girl with the washing, who was still talking to the woman at the door.

'Coming along nicely, is our Walkelin, my lord. You should have seen him playing stupid in the manor. Did it a treat he did, and now he sees a chance and takes it. One day he'll be a good serjeant, mark my words.'

Chapter Ten

It was about twenty minutes later that Walkelin strolled nonchalantly towards the church, concealing whatever excitement he felt at having been the major instrument of detection for the morning, and having had to exercise his own discretion. He felt it showed the confidence of the undersheriff and, more importantly to him, Serjeant Catchpoll, in his abilities. He found both with beakers of cider, seated on the bench before the priest's dwelling, and looking as casual as he did.

'Here comes Walkelin of the honeyed tongue, eh?' grinned Catchpoll, raising his beaker. 'How far did you get with the maid, then?'

'Back to the manor gates, Serjeant,' replied Walkelin, instantly.

'Right. You can stop playing dim as December dusk, and tell us what you found from both her and the cook. Best we do it inside. Come along.' He jerked his head towards the door.

In the privacy within, Walkelin reviewed what he had asked and heard.

'I helped the cook with a heavy pot, and treated her like one of my aunts; just a bit cheeky, but respectful all the same. She lapped it up. First of all, I got her talking about the lady de Nouailles. She said much as the good Father Paulinus. The lady was sweet of face and manner, and, she said, lonely in her position. But she stressed she was devoted to her lord, and thought him softened by her. She also said he never raised a hand to her, as he did oftentimes to others, and shouted less. She said since her death he has been "dangerous", and that was her word. She also said that the lady died in an accident, though she actually only saw the end, as de Nouailles shouted, but she clearly got the details from another, for she said the lady came from the hall, weeping, with her lord behind her. She slipped, and he made a grab for her arm.'

'That part, at least, de Nouailles told me, but nothing of weeping,' interjected Bradecote.

'Aye, well the cook saw him at the bottom of the steps, with his wife in his arms, and weeping himself. She said her neck was broke, but I do not know if that is what she heard rather than saw. De Nouailles carried her back and apparently would not let even the priest into the solar for some hours, but stayed alone with the corpse, distraught.'

'Mayhap that was so, but there are opportunities there, my lord.' Catchpoll sounded grim.

'I can see them, Catchpoll.' The undersheriff dragged a hand through his hair. 'If she was not actually dead, but merely knocked senseless, all he had to do was bewail that she was dead, carry her indoors and break her neck or simply suffocate her, in the solar. They might appear different to us, but after a few hours, and with him visibly distressed to distract . . . Yes, he could have killed her easily enough, even if he did not engineer the fall, and it was an accident in part.'

'That is what I thought, my lord.' Walkelin wished to continue his narrative. 'I then spoke of the lady's brother. The cook was clear he and de Nouailles did not get on, but talked of him in the present, for she had no idea he was dead. Came as a shock to her, it did.'

'Did it indeed, Walkelin? Well, there's a thing.' Catchpoll raised an eyebrow.

'I took it upon myself to tell the woman that he was murdered, and was found in the river, but had gone in at the bridge after leaving here. I thought it might prove useful if it became the topic on the lips of all, and if the killer is in the manor, they will know we know more about the death. I did right?'

'You did right, Walkelin.' Catchpoll did not wait for Bradecote to answer, which drew a frown from the undersheriff, though he did not interrupt.

'That was almost when you arrived with the steward, Serjeant, but as he came in she said something else, something that was cut off short as if the steward was very keen she should say nothing more.'

'What did she say?'

'I kept her words in my head exact, my lord. She said, "What a good thing that Aelfric was not . . ." And then halted.' Walkelin paused, mulling over the scene. 'It might be nothing, and yet somehow I think it has a meaning.'

'Might be almost anything, as you say, but it would be useful to speak to this Aelfric and find out what or where he was not, that afternoon.' Catchpoll sucked his teeth.

'Which is where the maid with the washing comes in, my lord,' declared Walkelin, with aplomb. His superiors stared at him in surprise and expectation.

'She does?' Bradecote found his voice.

'Yes, my lord. I got talking to her, casually enough, about missing her in the kitchens, and how the cook had spoken of the lady de Nouailles' death. She told me that she had seen the accident herself. Her version tallies with that of the cook, and I dare say it was she who told her of the start of it. She confirms that the lady was agitated, weeping, even fending off her lord, who was trying to take her arm. That was when she fell.'

'No hint of her being pushed, though?' Bradecote was concentrating, imagining the scene.

'None, my lord. The girl thinks she fell because she was off balance, pushing him away, and because she was distressed. She said the lord almost fell after her, so swift was he, but too late. The lady was in a crumpled heap at the bottom of the steps. He picked her up into his arms, wailed, and buried his face in her hair. Everyone present held back. He stayed there, rocking, some minutes, then carried her up the steps and into the hall. All she knows thereafter is that not even the priest or steward was given access to the solar for hours after, and since then he has been like, she says, "a soul in torment". I think her a bit fanciful about that.'

'What had he said to distress her so, I wonder?' murmured Catchpoll to himself.

'And what did she tell you about Aelfric?' enquired Bradecote.

'Ah yes, my lord, I got on to Walter Horsweard's visits. It seems he visited a week or so before the lady died, and was closeted with her some hours. The wench says the lady had been pale and hollow-eyed from the time of the attack by Thomas the Clerk, but she said she never saw her walking stiffly, as if bruised or harmed. Anyway, Horsweard returned a few weeks after the lady's death, and in anger. He called the lord some names for not letting her kin know of her death or letting them be at her burial. That was public. Then they argued in private some time before Horsweard left in a hurry, with the lord threatening to have him whipped if he came to the manor again.' Walkelin frowned a moment. 'It is my belief he, de Nouailles, likes seeing a good whipping.' He sniffed. 'The girl was clearly surprised when Horsweard returned after that, again a week or so later. She saw him, in that green jerkin, and the steward let him into the hall, after a short interchange between them. The steward did not want Horsweard causing a commotion in the bailey. He had been yelling about how he owed it to his sister, and it was de Nouailles' fault. He was in the hall a while, then came out alone, mounted his horse and left, grim-faced. De Nouailles did not this time follow with threats.'

'And where does Aelfric come into this story?'

'He doesn't, according to the girl. But that is not saying as he is not important to us. I told her how Horsweard died. She was wide-eyed and caught by interest mixed with a little fear. I told her the cook had said that it was fortunate Aelfric had not gone the same way, guessing, I admit. She nodded. Seems Aelfric is the steward's nephew. Thinks a lot of himself, according to her. But he was sent off to one of his lord's Warwickshire manors that day.'

'Which probably means he gooses her when he thinks he can get away with it,' interposed Catchpoll, sagely.

'Er . . . Yes, well . . . That day, de Nouailles sent Aelfric off to one of his other holdings to the north, and then on to a manor of his in Warwickshire. The maid did not know which one. She said that Aelfric is a young man keen to show his lord he is even more his man than his uncle, Steward Leofwine. He has not returned. I thought that interesting.'

'You are right there, Walkelin. Did she say what he was wearing?'

'That was my last question, my lord, as we reached the gates.' Walkelin looked glum. 'There she failed me. She could not recall what he was wearing. She did say, though, that he rides a chestnut horse, a stocky one.'

'That is something. It is certainly very suspicious. Pity about no knowledge of a cap, but it is enough to take further. It would be even more useful to find out where Aelfric was sent, and indeed if he went there.'

'I doubt we will find any information from within the manor itself now. That steward is going to see to it all know not to speak with us.' Catchpoll was thoughtful.

'But Father Paulinus could tell us about Aelfric, and perhaps even if he often wears a cap.' Walkelin was more optimistic.

'Trouble is, this time of year, a man would be sensible enough wearing a cap if going on a journey.' Catchpoll sucked his teeth.

Father Paulinus entered, carrying a small sack, and looked questioningly at the sheriff's men.

'It seems my prayers for divine aid have not been heard. You look quite cast down. Has your hunt lost the scent all of a sudden?'

'Not exactly, Father. We know where to sniff, but there are so many scents they become muddled, and now we think we cannot cast about there again.' Catchpoll grimaced.

'Ah. The manor is not a place where talk is free; a very closed place it is.'

'Father, can you tell us about the people within it? Not de Nouailles, but the ordinary folk, to give us a picture.' Hugh Bradecote did not like deceiving the kindly cleric, but he thought asking him to tell them which were most likely to have committed murder would not get a response. 'And is it true that de Nouailles would not let even you into the solar to pray over the body of his wife until sometime after the accident?'

'That is true enough. I was called for straight away, though it was a while before I was found. When I got there, Leofwine, the steward, he was in quite a fuss, for the solar door had been barred from inside. I think he feared the lord had taken his own life to lie cold with his wife. But saints be praised he did eventually let us in.'

'And the lady? Was she cold?' Catchpoll queried.

'Not cold, but cool.' The priest sighed. 'I look upon death often. I see it defeated by faith. Dying can be hard; death is easy. She had departed the body some time since. He had closed her eyes but not laid her as for burial, but on her side, her hands, as if in prayer, beneath her cheek, her body slightly curled up. His first words were that she was sleeping, though I know he knew otherwise than his heart told him.'

144

'I told him we must prepare her for sleep until resurrection, for the stiffness was beginning. He was reluctant, and would let none but himself touch her.'

'Her neck was broken.'

'I did not touch her, as I say, but it seemed so. When he moved her, it did not look quite as usual, if you understand.'

'Yes, we understand, Father.' Bradecote spoke gently. 'But on to the living. Tell us about the manor folk who put up with Brian de Nouailles' foul temper.'

Father Paulinus managed a small smile, and then started.

'Oh, but first I must send these to Nesta, who has offered to cook tonight as the Widow Thorn has her youngest teething and fractious. One of my flock is adept with a slingshot. He got two wood pigeon for me. It is two between three, but . . .'

'Between four, Father.'

'Oh no, I will content myself with pottage. Now, if you will wait . . .'

'Tell me where to deliver them, Father, and I will take them,' offered Walkelin, holding out his hand.

The priest smiled his thanks and gave directions. Walkelin went out, but returned only a very few minutes later, breathing slightly fast, having obviously run upon his errand. Father Paulinus was talking about Leofwine, the steward.

'His father and his father's father were steward before him. If anyone understands Brian de Nouailles, other than his late wife, it is Leofwine, and he does his best to guard his lord from things that would anger him. A devoted and loyal retainer, better than de Nouailles deserves, is the steward, though like master, like man in some ways. A hard man is Leofwine.'

'Will his own son succeed him as steward?' Bradecote had a good idea of the answer, but thought it an easy progression to Aelfric.

'Alas no. His wife and babe died years back, and he never wed again. I think that is what set him upon his course to be without the softer feelings of a man. He has a nephew, though, and is preparing him for the service.' Father Paulinus frowned. 'As a man of God I should be in charity with all, but Aelfric, for that is his name, is hard to like, for he is cold without need. Leofwine lost much, and coped by turning in upon himself, but Aelfric has never had misfortune to make him as he is. When he looks at you it is as if he sees stone not flesh. He has no feelings for others, I fear. Even his uncle he seems to tolerate rather than respect. Brian de Nouailles is not a good man, and his passions are too strong, but Aelfric lacks any passion at all.'

'We have not seen him,' commented Catchpoll.

'No. He is away. Sometimes the lord sends him with messages to his other holdings in Warwickshire, though usually he returns in a few days. I have not seen him at Mass for over a week now. I hope he has not suffered an accident upon the road.'

'I suppose he is tall and lanky, like his uncle,' remarked Walkelin, glancing at Catchpoll, whose eyes narrowed in approval.

'No, no. He takes after his father, who was even a little shorter than most.'

Asking about headwear seemed a little too pointed, so Walkelin asked no more questions about Aelfric, and let the priest describe his other parishioners within the manor. They were of no interest to them as individuals, but it built a picture of the atmosphere within. Bradecote found it totally alien to that of his own manor.

Father Paulinus went to say the noontide office, and the sheriff's men stood in the little church to hear it, thinking it a courtesy, and because thinking actually did become clear with the Latin cadences in the background. The three men took different paths of thought, but this was good, since it prevented them becoming focussed upon one thing only. They emerged into the sunlight, blinking slightly, and the priest went to labour among his flock. The showery April sky had resolved into an expanse of cloudless blue, and only the crisp bite in the breeze reminded them of the month.

'My lord, may I ask a question?' Walkelin was frowning, and it was not to shield his eyes from the brightness.

'Asking questions is part of your job, Walkelin. Ask away.'

'What are we investigating most, the murder of Walter Horsweard, or the death of the lady de Nouailles, which is not definitely a killing? We seems to have lots of pieces, but they come from different pots, so to speak, and it muddles me, sorting them.'

'We are . . .' Bradecote looked at Catchpoll, realising it had become a knot.

'Walter Horsweard was murdered. We are hunting his killer. The killer comes from here, without doubt, unless it was a passing madman, and such would kill others, not just one man and carry on blameless through life. Most folk here did not know Horsweard. The only one with even dislike of him was de Nouailles. If de Nouailles did not kill him himself, and he does not fit the description of the killer, then he ordered it. We therefore have to find out why he wanted Horsweard dead. Obvious answer is that Horsweard threatened to tell everyone he had murdered his wife.'

'Are we sure he did, though? He might have, but might just as easily be the distraught husband he claims to be?' Bradecote muttered. 'The more I hear, the more he sounds a nasty piece of work who happened to love his beautiful and adoring wife. Yes,' he raised his hand as Catchpoll opened his mouth to speak, 'I know you will say his behaviour was odd at her death, but if he did kill her as she lay unconscious, there was plenty of time before the priest arrived. Locking everyone outside for hours, laying her as he did, sits better as the man lost in grief.' Bradecote shook his head. 'I no longer think he killed her, but he did have Horsweard killed, and we have no motive left at all.' He rubbed his chin in thought.

'I think,' announced Catchpoll, 'that we have got too dizzied by this place, by everything in it. It is like swimming in a cook pot; you keep banging your head on the side. As Walkelin says, we have pieces, but perhaps we are putting them together wrong.'

'Then we have to try and separate them again, look at each, and make a new "pot"?'

'That is what I am thinking, my lord. Why not head to the river, by that mill de Nouailles is so keen to keep, and think away from the village and manor? And we need to ask Father Paulinus if he can tell us how many manors de Nouailles has in Warwickshire.'

'We forgot that, yes. Walkelin, you find the good Father,

and ask him how many, and where. Meet us by the mill on the bank opposite Offenham.'

'Yes, my lord.'

He left, glad to be doing something. His head ached with thinking. He found Father Paulinus, habit kirtled up halfway to his knees to avoid the damp soil, giving thanks for the sprouting of green along his strips in the wheat field to the north of the manor. Father Paulinus was a man who tended his crops with prayer as well as labour. It did not take long to find out what the priest knew of de Nouailles' Warwickshire holdings, and Walkelin set off, skirting the village, to find the lord Undersheriff and Serjeant Catchpoll. He did not expect to find the servant girl whose washing he had carried.

The mill that Judhael de Nouailles had built from the abandoned construction planned by Evesham Abbey was well made and neatly kept. Bradecote and Catchpoll did not enter, but stopped short to sit themselves upon the warmed verdure, which gave off the smell of new-sprung grass and lifted their spirits. The Avon flowed past them, ignoring the troubles of men, and Catchpoll had to fight off the urge to think with his eyes shut.

The two men set out the facts that were known, the things that were probably true, and the things they just felt were true.

'Trouble is, when you throw them together, they falls naturally into the shape we made of them, my lord.'

'Which means we are either missing vital parts, which turn it into something else, like the lip that makes a jug, or we—' Bradecote stopped as a horse came towards them at some speed. He recognised de Nouailles, and the man's expression was not the usual disagreeable, but positively thunderous. He vaulted from his horse even before it had been hauled to a halt, and confronted Bradecote, chest heaving.

'So this is the benefit of law is it?' he yelled. 'You come to a peaceful manor, accuse me of killing my beloved wife, and presumably also her brother, since you are so interested in his demise, and while you are here one of my servants is brutally murdered. Fine protection the law is, Bradecote.'

'Murdered?' Bradecote looked stunned. 'Who? How?'

'A wench from my kitchens. I do not recall the name, and how is easy. She was raped and strangled in a field not five hundred paces from the manor gates. She has been carried back on a hurdle.' He sneered at the undersheriff. 'But do not be concerned, for we have the killer.'

'You have?' Bradecote was still trying to get to grips with the news.

'Yes indeed, for it was your man that did it!'

Chapter Eleven

'That cannot be true.' Bradecote shook his head.

'You just do not want it to be true. He was found by the body, and he was seen plying her with his false words but an hour beforehand.' De Nouailles almost spat the words.

'He was speaking to her upon my express instruction, if it was the wench who brought washing in to the manor before noon.'

'And he found the body. That is no crime.' Catchpoll shrugged.

'Then why did he admit it? Answer me that.'

'You are saying Walkelin admitted rape and murder?' Catchpoll could not keep the incredulity from his voice.

'He was heard to say, by my steward, who found him kneeling by the corpse, "It is my fault she is dead". What further proof do you need, Law-man?' De Nouailles was almost mocking.

Catchpoll's eyes narrowed to slits.

'Much more than you could ever provide,' he snarled. 'Walkelin would blame himself, aye, because he would see that talking to the girl might have put her in peril with the man in Harvington who killed Walter Horsweard. He has a soft heart still. It is not saying he killed her.'

'You will not find Horsweard's killer here.' There was an arrogance to de Nouailles' tone, a bravado, that Bradecote longed to choke from him.

'Nor will you find the maid's killer in Walkelin, de Nouailles. He is the lord Sheriff's man and upon his business.'

'And on my land. You think my peasants will sit by idle as the law protects its own from the penalties for foul misdeeds? We will have justice, one way or another. All it takes is for my steward to swear oath that he found your man upon the girl's poor, innocent body, "stealing her scarf", and I hang him for theft and common assault. It is my right, and simple folk will believe what is told well. I will hang him tomorrow.'

'You use your rights beyond all that the King's Justice permits. Murder, rape, aye, and serious assault, are not crimes covered by your jurisdiction.' Bradecote was outraged. Wrong as it might be, he could see how de Nouailles, coming upon the clerk with his wife, might act in passion, though why he did not simply take his sword to him in her defence and then report the matter to the sheriff he did not see. De Beauchamp would have said the man had the right to defend his lady's person and honour in a trice. He remembered how close he had been to killing a man who had thought to molest his Christina, when he had not yet right to call her his. Here again de Nouailles was seeking to use seigneurial rights to deal with a case that belonged to the higher authority. 'You are deciding guilt without evidence or indeed a real confession, without defence. It means all you have to do is accuse a man of a crime you can hang him for, whether he has committed a crime or not.'

De Nouailles said nothing, but his eyes glittered.

'You no more think him guilty than we do,' growled Catchpoll.

'No?' De Nouailles smiled, triumphantly. 'But you cannot prove me wrong, nor him innocent.'

Catchpoll was so tensed that Bradecote thought he might lunge at de Nouailles' throat. He put out a restraining hand, and looked de Nouailles in the eye.

'Walkelin is the lord Sheriff's man, and de Beauchamp knows him well by character. He would no more believe in his guilt than we do. If you hang, or harm, him, then William de Beauchamp will see you keep no yard of this manor, and when truth is known of all these things, there will be no mercy.'

'Mercy is for the weak. I am not weak.' De Nouailles climbed back upon his horse, wheeled about and cantered away.

'My lord.' Catchpoll's voice had an edge of worry Bradecote had never heard before.

'Yes, Catchpoll. How fast and far can you run?'

'You lead, I'll follow, my lord.'

In truth, Catchpoll, limited by length of leg and by age, did very well, but staggered into the village a good hundred and fifty yards behind the undersheriff. Bradecote made for the priest's house and flung open the door without ceremony. Father Paulinus was within, and turned in surprise to see Bradecote, chest heaving, and leaning against the doorpost for support.

'Father, I bring grim news, but I need your help swiftly if one tragedy is not to be followed by another.'

'What is it?'

Briefly, and between gasps, Bradecote told him of the cruel murder of one of his parishioners, and the threat to Walkelin. Father Paulinus went pale and crossed himself.

'Walkelin is innocent. He spoke to the girl at my command, and then he came to you in the field. I am surprised you were not called from there to the scene.'

'A child came for me, almost as Walkelin left. He was heading south of the manor and I went to the north. A babe was born early this morning, before its time, I think, for it is a small scrap of life. The parents feared it might die without baptism and the chance of heaven, so I did not linger. I gave the sacrament and left all in the disposition of God.'

'I would you had taken the other route, for Walkelin's sake, and found him before the steward did so.'

'Leofwine found him? How odd. I saw Leofwine as I went to the wheat field. He was going into the manor, looking thoughtful. I asked him if all was well, and he said the lord de Nouailles was in a foul temper and no doubt he would spend the better part of the afternoon keeping him from flaying the hide of one who ought to know better than approach him in his ire. I did not think he would be outside the walls again today.'

Catchpoll, now arrived and with head bent and hands on knees, heard the last phrases. He grunted, but was incapable of words.

'That might be significant later, Father, but de Nouailles is prepared to have the steward swear an oath that Walkelin was caught in the act of theft, and will hang him, without a shred of evidence, to make himself look authoritative, and perhaps even conceal the real culprit. The wench is in God's hands alone now, Walkelin may yet be in yours.'

'In mine, my lord?'

'If Walkelin is held in the manor, where would he be kept?'

'Beneath the hall itself. There are storerooms there and the lord de Nouailles has kept prisoners there before, briefly.'

'Is it barred and guarded?'

'Barred outside, yes, but previously there was only a guard when he held one of the village men for what was a small theft, and then took his hand. It was not popular.'

'We need . . . to get into the bailey first . . . my lord, and . . . you can be assured . . . the gatekeeper has been . . . ordered to keep us out.' Catchpoll was breathing heavily through his nose.

'There is a postern gate, my lord. On the north side. It has not been locked in years. I fear the youth of the manor have used it most for trysts in the meadow beyond. There has been no threat to the manor, so it was more use unlocked.'

'But it will not be opened from outside,' Catchpoll managed, still taking great gulps of air.

'It could be opened from within. Father, might you get within the courtyard of the manor and unlatch the gate secretly?' Bradecote was thinking fast. 'I would not ask if I did not think Walkelin innocent of any evil, and in danger now. You have reason to go within, for no doubt the girl's body has been taken there. As for no entry, they will have a struggle keeping out the Undersheriff of Worcester. Whatever de Nouailles wants to claim, there is murder, and that is the sheriff's business.' He turned to Catchpoll. 'If I go in and make bustle, and Father Paulinus can get to the postern gate, you come in, slyly as you can, Catchpoll, and get our Walkelin out of his prison while I create whatever confusion is needed for distraction.'

In less serious circumstances Catchpoll would have smiled at the thought of the undersheriff 'creating confusion'.

'Then what, my lord? Evesham?'

Bradecote had thought of it, of course. It was the safest course, and yet the more he thought about it, the more he wanted to remain in Harvington, for crime was set upon crime now, for certain, and he did not want the perpetrator to feel they would evade the law by throwing blame upon its minions.

'No. Put Walkelin in sanctuary within the church, and tell him to claim it formally. Then you guard it until Father Paulinus can return. If de Nouailles makes his accusation known as truth, the villagers will take some persuading not to act.'

'Can you not simply claim Walkelin by right?' asked Father Paulinus. 'Since you are the law.'

'Not if de Nouailles convinces others of his guilt, and if you but shout loudly enough and confidently enough you will be believed by many, Father. We need to get him out secretly, and then we find who violated and murdered the girl. There are too many deaths here, and I will have it cease.' Hugh Bradecote was unusually grim.

'If it is just, then I will help, and I see that it is so. Come, my lord, and let us free your "dove" from the clutches of the "hawk".'

Walkelin sat in the blackness of the windowless store, his brain reeling, and feeling rather sick. Everything had happened so fast. He had barely had the time to kneel and confirm that there was no life in the poor girl when the lanky steward and another man leading a Roman-nosed bay horse had arrived, and suddenly Walkelin found himself declaimed as a foul rapist and killer and hit so hard upon the head he had no recollection of what happened next, until he was in the darkness. His head still swam from the blow, and in the swirling images within his head, the maid's bulging eyes accused. He felt responsible for her death. Whilst it was possible that it had been the act of some lecherous man, perhaps even one she knew, he had a feeling she had been killed for speaking with him. He knew he ought to be trying to work out what she might have told him of importance, but he could not think beyond the fact that Brian de Nouailles liked his 'justice' swift and summary.

Hugh Bradecote concealed his anger and his concern well. It was vital that he did so, for ranting at the lord of Harvington would achieve nothing, and might even get Walkelin hung from the battlements as a taunt. Father Paulinus looked grave, but that was perfectly reasonable for a man called to the untimely death of one of his parishioners. That the parish priest would gain admittance to the manor was surely beyond dispute, but whether Brian de Nouailles might bar the undersheriff was open to contention. It was clear that the gatekeeper was undecided, when faced by one whom he was bound to admit and the other who had probably been proscribed. Father Paulinus stared at the man gravely.

'I am come to pray over Hild's body, and since she met a foul end, the undersheriff has the right of law to see the corpse also, Wystan. Let us in.'

'But my lord said—'

'The law is higher even than the instruction of your lord. As the good Father says, I must see the girl's body. The lord Sheriff of the Shire will demand to know of this.'

Wystan the Gatekeeper was secretly impressed that the lord Sheriff himself would be making demands about 'his' manor, and with further remonstrance from Father Paulinus, opened the gate, cautiously. The man of God and man of the law entered sombrely. They had reached halfway across the courtyard before Leofwine the Steward placed himself before them, grim-faced.

'Your calling gives you cause to be here, Father, and glad we are of your presence in this tragedy, but he,' and he pointed at Hugh Bradecote as if he were vermin, 'goes no further.'

'As the officer of the lord Sheriff of this shire I am here to see the body of the girl who has been found violated and murdered. Such a crime is in his remit, and the corpse must be viewed. If you deny me, then I travel to Worcester and bring William de Beauchamp in person, and a very aggrieved William de Beauchamp at that, for he holds his office of the King, and by denying me, you are denying the King's Grace.' Bradecote sounded calm, reasonable. Leofwine, overawed by the concept that he was infringing Royal prerogative, wavered, and then stood aside, but walked at their side to guide them to where the body lay, in an empty stall in the stables, on a board laid over two trestles.

Bradecote wished he had Catchpoll on hand, for those gimlet eyes saw so much that ordinary men missed. He tried to think like his serjeant for a minute. The maid Hild had been comely, and rosy-cheeked. The body was a cruel travesty of that life. Father Paulinus sighed, and went down upon his knees, which creaked slightly. As he closed his eyes in prayer, the undersheriff took up one of the pale hands that lay crossed upon the stilled breast. There was no sign of anything beneath the nails, even dirt. She had been washing that day, so it was not, he thought, surprising they were clean, but she had not fought her attacker. That there had been violence towards her was not evident by anything obvious. Were it not for the lack of colour in her skin, she might have been lying there asleep. Could her attacker have delivered a blow so hard to the skull that it had stunned her so much that she had thereafter offered no resistance? There was no tearing to the bodice of her gown, and her skirts were drawn decorously close about the ankles. Bradecote knew he ought to view the corpse more intimately if the girl was violated, but to do so in the presence of the village priest seemed almost a sin. He contented himself for a minute or two by reaching behind the head and lifting it a little, to feel if her neck was broken. De Nouailles had not disclosed how she had actually been killed. There was the very beginnings of stiffening, but it was clear the neck was intact. Nor were there marks about the throat to indicate strangling.

He spoke softly to Leofwine, as the priest chanted in Latin.

'You found the girl. Was she on her face, on her back . . .'

'On her back, of course. How else would she—' He halted, and coloured. There were things he would not say before the priest.

'And her skirts were . . . disordered?'

The two men were caught, edging round the realities. The steward nodded. Father Paulinus opened his eyes, aware of constraint. He was no fool, and he also had a task to do for the living.

'My lord, I will absent myself a few minutes, if you have need to discuss . . . matters.'

'Thank you, Father.'

He helped the priest to his feet, and with a heavy sigh, the Father brushed the hay from the skirts of his habit, and left the stable. Undersheriff and steward faced each other over the chilling body.

'The law requires that I look at the body for signs of how she died. Are there women who would remove her garments? I would have her treated with respect in death even if in life she received little.'

'At the hands of your man,' growled Leofwine.

'By whoever's hands. I am seeking here not who, but how, that the lord Sheriff might be told of what has happened here, today.' Bradecote kept it very formal.

'I will fetch the cook.' He left the undersheriff alone and went to find the homely dame whom Walkelin had aided but the day before.

As soon as he shut the door behind him, Bradecote took a deep breath and lifted the skirts swiftly. It would actually be less embarrassing than doing so in front of another, and he could make a cursory assessment. To his surprise there seemed no marks at all upon her lower limbs, and, from what he had learnt from Catchpoll, he had thought there would be some signs. He heard a woman's voice and drew the clothing back into position before the cook could see. The woman had damp cheeks.

'My lord, you have need of me?'

'Yes. Would you remove Hild's clothes, and give them to me, then cover her with the blanket? I must see the body to check for any marks. I will turn away while you do so.' He sounded considerate, and not overbearing.

The cook bit her lip and curtseyed her acquiescence. He faced the wall and listened to the sobbing, half of grief and half of exertion. After a few minutes the woman sniffed.

'All's done, my lord. Would you have me leave or stay?'

He turned to face her. She looked a sensible dame.

'Remain. I would have you see that I do my duty and nought else.'

He inspected first the clothing. There was mud upon the back of the skirt where she had lain in the field, but no sign of blood. The front of the bodice and shift were clean, the back of the bodice as dark and muddy as that of the skirt. The shift drew his attention, for on the back there was a small but distinct tear, and blood. He studied the bodice back again and found a small rent in it.

'Good Mother,' he did not know how else to address her, 'you see this?'

The cook frowned, and nodded.

'Poor girl.' She did not think to question why a maid who was announced as raped had a wound to the back.

Bradecote pulled back the blanket and rolled the body away from him to view the back. There, on the left side just below the ribs, was a small puncture wound. He was reminded of the wound in the river-sodden chest of Walter Horsweard.

'Here is the wound itself, and from where it enters I doubt not it was fatal. Some small blade or awl made this. The lord de Nouailles said that the maid had been raped and murdered. That she should have been stabbed from behind is odd if that were so. What man would violate a girl then turn her onto her front and stab her?'

'Does it matter, my lord?'

'Yes. I see no sign that a man took her by force, but that she was indeed murdered, though not for some reason of gratification.'

The cook did not know what gratification meant, and said nothing. Bradecote covered the body with the blanket.

'The man-at-arms who spoke to you yesterday lies in your lord's prison accused of rape and murder. Of this I have no doubt he is innocent. He spoke to her at my command before the midday meal, and his only "crime" was finding her. My duty is to keep the innocent free, and to take the guilty before the law. I do my duty.' He spoke solemnly.

The door opened and Father Paulinus entered, followed by the steward.

'Is all that need be done, done, my lord?'

'It is, Father.'

'Good.' His look was encouraging, and Bradecote prayed that their simple plan might yet work.

'The maid Hild was murdered, but there is no sign that she was taken by force. She was killed by a stab wound from behind, into the heart. Tell me, Master Steward, why you decided to accuse Walkelin, the sheriff's man, of such foul crimes simply because he was kneeling beside the body. The evidence of the innocent victim herself shows the charges as false. I wonder at you making such a charge without cause, unless of course you were close by, knowing she was dead because you killed her and were set upon denouncing whoever found the girl to deflect attention from yourself.'

It was an accusation bound to have Leofwine vehement in his own defence, which was just what Bradecote wanted. It was as feasible an answer as to what happened as any other that presented itself, though it was pure conjecture, but the combination of outrage and fear would create a stir, one which the undersheriff hoped would draw all attention within the bailey from the incarcerated Walkelin.

Father Paulinus pursed his lips and frowned at Leofwine with a mixture of enquiry and disappointment, which made Leofwine realise that he might truly be in a dangerous predicament. The cook, for her part, curled her lip at him.

'Me?' he cried, stepping back as if recoiling from anything so terrible.

'Why not? You are free to range about the manor lands alone, while many of the villagers would be working the fields with kin and neighbour, and if they absented themselves it would be noted. Hild may never have heard or seen the man who killed her, and it was most probably a man, but even if she did, and she was stabbed as she turned away, she made no attempt at defence, so she did not see the man as a threat. Also, she was stabbed in the back, but only the back of her gown is muddied, so she was caught as she fell or collapsed, and laid that way upon the ground. All you needed to do was conceal yourself nearby,' Bradecote was hoping that the scene of the killing provided some form of cover within view, 'and emerge, the figure of outraged authority, when some innocent bystander

163

found her.' He was warming rapidly to the idea as he spoke. It really did fit as a likely sequence of events.

'But why should I want to kill her?' yelled Leofwine, as the door opened, and Brian de Nouailles stood at the threshold.

Hugh Bradecote was relieved that his arrival might mean that he did not to have to come up with an instant answer to that question.

'I gave orders that you were not permitted here,' snarled de Nouailles. 'I would guess you would rush to free your lecherous mongrel from justice. Get out.'

The undersheriff stood his ground.

'Firstly, I am here as the sheriff's officer to see the victim of a crime that is far too serious for manorial justice, and do not repeat the stupid' – and Bradecote gave a sneer of which Catchpoll would have been proud – 'claim that you can accuse Walkelin, the lord Sheriff's man-at-arms, of stealing a scarf and hang him summarily. There is a girl's body here that attests to murder, and it is for murder will there be a hanging. Every man, woman and child of this manor shall know that.'

De Nouailles ground his teeth, and looked murderous himself.

'Secondly, you were loud in claiming the maid had been violated, when there is no sign of any such attack, so I ask myself whether you simply believe anything your steward tells you. She was, assuredly, murdered, but with a stab in the back, not the action of a "lecherous mongrel" but someone who either wanted her to speak no more to the law or was angered by what she might already have revealed. All this proves that Walkelin is falsely accused.'

There was a small note of triumph in Bradecote's voice, but even as the words left his mouth he saw a looming complication. What he said made such sense, de Nouailles might be forced to release his prisoner, and it would then look very suspicious if the prisoner was found to have escaped. He stepped towards the door, towards the fuming de Nouailles, and spoke boldly.

'Come. You have no cause to hold de Beauchamp's man. Let him out, and assist the law in finding who killed your serving wench.'

There was a flicker in the hard eyes of Brian de Nouailles, one which Bradecote recognised from combat; it was a moment of self-doubt, of feeling beaten, and it was the moment to press home an attack. He faced the angry lord, who stepped back into the courtyard before he could be set aside and lose all dignity. Bradecote strode towards the hall, announcing very loudly that the prisoner was to be released, taking charge and also, he hoped, letting Catchpoll know what was happening. As he reached the point where the door in the end of the undercroft came into view, he saw Catchpoll, in the act of unbolting the door, but stopped in mid action. Only for a fleeting second did Serjeant Catchpoll look uncomprehendingly at him. Then he paused, and declared, with a flourish worthy of trumpets, that the lord Undersheriff's command was to be obeyed, and shot back the first of the bolts with a hard clank. Steward and lord were still caught so off balance they did not query how it should be that Serjeant Catchpoll should be already at the storeroom door, when his superior had only just made his demands known in the stable, thirty paces away.

The second bolt clattered back, the door was swung open by Catchpoll, who spared Bradecote a glance, which the undersheriff correctly interpreted as 'keep it up', and the undersheriff called into the gloom.

'Come out, Walkelin. There stands no charge against you.'

Walkelin emerged into the sunlight, blinking both at the brightness and in surprise.

'My lord?'

'Come. We have no time for you to be loitering in storehouses like a mouse. There is the murderer of an innocent maid to hunt down.' Bradecote sounded intentionally impersonal, as he was sure de Nouailles sounded with his own men. Here such a manner would be understood, expected. He then turned to de Nouailles, whose brain was now beginning to function again. 'There is no sign that Hild died because of a man's lust, but if you are wise you will not have your women wander about alone outside the bounds of the manor bailey. I wish to see every man who was out in the fields today. With permission, Father,' he turned to the priest, 'I would speak to them one by one in the church. It is a good place for truth.'

He sounded confident, assertive, and as if, thought Catchpoll wryly, he had been doing the job for years. It was a good performance.

Father Paulinus nodded.

'Good. Then I will commence after the good Father has said Terce. Oh, and your gatekeeper will not keep me standing outside your gates in future. Hild's killer will hang, my lord de Nouailles, and your dislike of the law will not keep her from the justice she deserves.'

It was a speech for the cook, the men-at-arms, the stable boys, the ordinary folk of Harvington. Hugh Bradecote fully expected Brian de Nouailles to revert to his usual obstructive and unpleasant manner, but he wanted the villagers on his side, on the side of the law. There was something that hung in the silence that felt like an unvoiced cheer, and of the many pairs of eyes that watched the three sheriff's men and the parish priest walk out of the manor gates, only two held antagonism.

Chapter Twelve

Walkelin did not think; he just walked. Only when the quartet reached the priest's house did he blink and seem to recognise where he was. The kindly Father pressed him to sit upon a stool, and then went to fetch him a beaker of small beer.

'I . . . She was dead when I found her, staring dead,' he managed, in barely more than a whisper.

Catchpoll looked down at him, and when he spoke, it was in a fatherly tone.

'Just sit and gather your wits, lad. No point in giving us a jumbled half-tale.'

'While he does so, Serjeant, I will tell you what I observed from the body.' Bradecote smiled wryly. 'I doubt not you would have got more, but I tried to look as you would have looked, and to make the same deductions. What I discovered was certainly enough to prove to the world what we know from knowing Walkelin, that he never harmed the maid.'

He proceeded to recount his examination and what was said. Catchpoll furrowed his brow in concentration rather than disapproval, and sucked his teeth, ruminatively.

'The nature of the wound is very like that we found in Walter Horsweard, very like. Of course, it does not have to be the work of the same man, but for there to be two killings in the same place . . . No, the same killer did for them both.'

'And I am very suspicious of this cry of rape. Why raise a clamour over a crime like that when Leofwine could as easily have just cried foul murder? It is strange.'

'It would make the villagers even more inclined to go along with their lord's taking justice into his own hands.'

'My lord.' Walkelin looked from Bradecote to Catchpoll and back. 'When I was taken, it was not just by the steward. There was another man with him, a man about my own age. I do not recall him being named, but they knew each other well, from the way they were together. He was leading a bay horse, one with a big nose. I cannot tell you much about the man, for I was hit, and hit hard, and recall nothing more until I was in the darkness beneath the hall, but he wore a cap.'

'There was a second man, a man in a cap, and yet Leofwine has made no mention of him, nor used him to confirm how he found you with the girl.' Bradecote raised a suspicious eyebrow. 'Catchpoll, I get a prickling feeling over that, don't you?'

'Oh aye, my lord, that is not right at all. If Leofwine was so keen to pin the murder on young Walkelin, adding another witness was an obvious course. So why keep him a secret?' Catchpoll's eyes glittered. 'You know, I think this may have saved us ferreting in Warwickshire, don't you, my lord?'

'I do. Nephew Aelfric seems to have returned, and with a bay horse also. That is not quite the same as us having words with him, but surely the rest of the manor will not be trying to keep his presence hidden. We will find him.' He paused. 'Walkelin, I doubt you will have trouble from the villagers. Your innocence ought to shine clear enough, but I want you to go to Evesham tomorrow, and do what we should have days past; speak with Will Horsweard about the horse. If he says "It was a bay with a big nose" we are far advanced. It might not be quite enough as proof, and if it had any other markings it would help, but if we find it, we can always call Horsweard here to confirm it is the right animal. A horse dealer will know his brother's horse as most people know the faces of their acquaintance.'

'What is more,' Catchpoll added, 'if Aelfric has indeed returned, it is mighty suspicious that as soon as he does so another body turns up with the same kind of wound. The only problem I see is getting more than Aelfric to the noose. Whether he was ordered to deal with the girl, I would not like to say, but I would wager your horse, my lord, that Horsweard was killed upon command of de Nouailles, perhaps by way of the steward. Either way, the lord of Harvington stands in need of neck stretching for it. Proving that is not going to be easy.'

'We get ahead of ourselves, Catchpoll. We need to find out about the horse – Horsweard's, not mine, which you are so keen to stake. If we can find the horse and link it to Aelfric then we can attempt the next step to de Nouailles. I did not note the horses in the stable when I viewed the body, alas. However, for all that our first aim is to take whoever killed Walter Horsweard, the local population will only have an interest in how quickly we discover who killed one of their own.

'Walkelin, can you give us a clear account of all that happened from the time you met Hild with the washing? She was surely killed for what she may have revealed or might reveal. Think of anyone else you saw when you were going to see Father Paulinus, and describe the man with that bay horse. I think you had best remain here for the rest of the afternoon, but Serjeant Catchpoll and I must be seen to be active in our pursuit of the girl's killer, and if we linger, seeming to be skulking in here, it will be said our only interest was in getting you cleared of involvement.'

Walkelin chewed his lip, meditatively, sorting his thoughts. There was a lot in his head, but it still felt as if everything had been tossed about like threshed straw. Father Paulinus returned with a beaker, and after downing the half of it, Walkelin wiped his hand across his mouth and began.

'She did not tell me anything in a way which showed she saw it as important, my lord. Whatever Hild knew, she thought of it as just what she knew of her own place and life.' He paused. He had travelled about in the following of William de Beauchamp as an ordinary man-at-arms, and since being taken on as Catchpoll's 'serjeanting apprentice' he had seen more of his shire in depth, actually looking at it. He suddenly realised how lucky he was to see so much. 'I don't suppose she had ever gone beyond Evesham. Everything she knew was in this village, her little world.'

'Most folk have a small world, young Walkelin, and are content with it. Don't you get maudlin over it.' Catchpoll did not want him wallowing in sympathy for the victim.

'I know, Serjeant, but . . .' Walkelin sighed. 'I was keen to find out about Aelfric, since he looks our likely killer of the horse trader, and she was open enough about him. I suppose that is why she died.' He looked suddenly at the priest. 'So am I not responsible in some way for her death, Father?'

'Assuredly not, my son.' Whatever Father Paulinus did or did not know about the law, he was clear in his mind about right and wrong. 'You were simply a seeker of the truth, and had no thought to put the poor girl in peril. No, the blame, and the sin, lies with the man who killed her, and it will go hard with him in the Higher Judgement, unless his contrition and repentance are total. I took confession of a man once who had killed. He had done so in passion, and in passion Fallen Adam is so often the strongest part of us, but he was truly contrite, and accepted his penalty in this world without any claim for mercy and humbleness to receive the all-important judgement of his Maker. I have always felt that God's mercy would eventually be extended to him, though of course, who am I to judge?'

'Some go calm, some go witless scared, and it is not always as you would think, with hanging.' Catchpoll nodded in agreement with the priest's words.

Bradecote did not think this had aided Walkelin very much. He wanted to get him thinking.

'Aelfric. What exactly did she tell you about him? It was interesting before, but now . . .'

'She told me he was the son of the steward's younger brother, and both his parents are dead. The steward has had him almost as a son and he has been spoilt. He thinks he is the heir to his uncle, and above the other manor inhabitants. It did mean he tried to take liberties, which she said she repulsed.'

'They all likes to say that. No woman declares herself easy to another man,' mumbled Catchpoll.

'In Hild's case she spoke true, I would think,' interposed the priest, still clearly attending. 'She might have given the occasional soft look to a lad, but she was neither foolish nor wanton. And she did not like Aelfric, even before he grew to full manhood. He used to pull her hair before she reached an age to cover it.'

'Well, she said she had held him off, and her eyes flashed angry as she recalled it. She said he had begun to say his uncle was getting too set in his ways and old, behind his back of course, and he was keen to prove himself to the lord de Nouailles.'

'A man like that would take upon himself tasks others would shirk, like getting rid of a troublesome brother-in-law.' Bradecote rubbed his chin. 'But it would be terribly hard to prove he was ordered to do so. De Nouailles need only shake his head, and say "He was too keen by half, and took mere words of frustration as a chance to show his loyalty".'

'And, forgive me, my lord, what threat did Walter Horsweard pose after the second visit when he had made his feelings known? He was spent.' Walkelin frowned.

'Aye, finding a real motive for that killing would be difficult.' Catchpoll sucked his teeth.

Father Paulinus looked troubled.

'You believe the lord de Nouailles was responsible for the death of the horse trader?'

'Yes, Father, for who else would have cause to even dislike

him in this manor? We know that the man who killed him rode a stocky chestnut, and Aelfric rides such an animal. He also left the manor just after Walter Horsweard.'

'But I heard it said he was sent upon the lord's business into Warwickshire.' The priest looked even more unhappy.

'Yes, Father, but what better way to arrange it than telling him to first rid the world of Horsweard and then remain out of the way for a while.' Bradecote smiled, wryly. 'You think the best of people, Father, as a good priest, but we must think as good officers of the King's Peace, and think the worst.'

Catchpoll thought this a good phrase, and committed it to his memory for future use.

'In the case of Aelfric, I admit thinking the best is not easy, my lord. If you were to ask who, if any, of my parishioners could be capable of such a foul deed, then his would be the first and probably only name that I could give.'

'Other than Brian de Nouailles.'

'I still do not believe he killed his lady, but for the rest . . . he is not in charity with the world. I think she was his only hope of truly finding it, and with her death . . . so you are correct. I pray for him, but in my weakness and frailty I know that I do so because the poor lady would wish it. God has granted the beauty of the flesh to many women, and few see it as she did, as a burden. She had such beauty of soul that it far outshone the mere physical.' Father Paulinus sighed. 'She was impossible not to love, and so even a man in whom love would otherwise have been unthinkable, loved her.' He crossed himself.

'Well, at least our lists of suspects is the same, Father.' Bradecote felt sympathy for the kindly cleric.

'None of which so far gives a reason why Aelfric, returning to Harvington, would straight away take it into his head to do away with the girl Hild.' Catchpoll brought them back to the problem in hand.

'Perhaps he saw her and wouldn't take her no for an answer, simple as that,' offered Walkelin.

'Too much of a coincidence to me.' Catchpoll pulled a face that in others would indicate extreme pain.

'But if he saw her, with me, a stranger, talking happily, could jealousy have got the better of him?' Walkelin persisted.

'I still don't like it as a reason to up and kill someone.'

'But if we are correct, he has killed barely more than a week since, and having done so once, he might be far more likely to do so again.' Bradecote was warming to the only explanation that presented itself.

'That is true, my lord, but before we cling to this theory of the frustrated lover with the desperation of a drowning man to a floating branch, let us consider any other options.' Catchpoll ticked off his fingers. 'He sees the girl with a stranger, finds out the sheriff's men have traced Horsweard back to the manor, and thinks she might have something to say that proves his guilt. Perhaps she saw him take the track after him or overheard. He is suspicious and worried and acts in haste.'

It was Hugh Bradecote's turn to look sceptical.

'Or,' continued Catchpoll, 'he knows she has knowledge of him doing away with Horsweard. What if she happened to be as she was today, with washing? He recalls seeing a female figure at the river, with washing. He puts the two things together and sees she may betray him.'

'Better, but if that is the case, why not run for it, since he has no idea whether or not she has already disclosed this to the law?'

'I cannot explain that part, my lord, I admit it, but he might feel angry at her. She is a maid who has resisted him before, and now this. He kills her through anger and fear and then, having found his uncle and either lied that he saw Walkelin here do the deed, or perhaps throwing himself upon his blood kin relationship, gets him to "find" Walkelin and have a handy culprit who might, with luck, be dealt with so that he can turn up again in a day or so having no knowledge of the murder.'

'That would fit.'

'But it does not make it any easier to take Aelfric for the murder or link him to his lord for the first murder, my lord.' Walkelin looked miserable.

'All the more reason for you to discover the details of the bay horse, Walkelin. Even if Aelfric only reappears in a day or so, if he comes on that horse, we have him. Tomorrow you go to Evesham. Now just tell us of any you saw when you went to see Father Paulinus, and Father, could you tell us whom you saw also, that we can discount the many rather than the few from our enquiries this afternoon.'

The priest was the more useful, since he could name the people he saw, and Walkelin had to describe them as best he could for Father Paulinus to give name and direction, but between them they came up with several villagers whom the undersheriff and Serjeant Catchpoll might sensibly speak with before the day's end.

They had little hope that asking their questions would elicit any useful information, and they were quite correct. They were met with shakes of the head, and much complaint that the presence of the law had not brought security but sorrow to their village. The simple peasantry wanted the culprit arrested and hanged, but the sheriff's men had somehow brought this calamity to them. Had the strangers not entered the village, murder would not have followed. Bradecote felt as if he had become a raven, a bird of ill-omen. When he mentioned this to Catchpoll, the grizzled serjeant laughed.

'If that is the worst you get to feel, my lord, you are a lucky man indeed.'

'That last family we spoke with, the wife had her children about her skirts like a mother hen. Had I got closer she would have pecked me. We are wasting our time and becoming more unpopular, and if unpopular we will not receive the aid we need.'

'That is true in part, my lord, but if, as you said, we had hidden away in the priest's house, it would be all over the village, aye, and the Hundred soon enough, that the sheriff's men only care for the safety of the sheriff's men, and justice is for those with influence. This way they know we are seeking the girl's killer.'

'And will be less than pleased when we tell them it was one of their own that did it.'

'The law does not make friends, my lord, it just does the job so thieving, murderous bastards do not have it all their own way. Rarely does anyone come and thank us for doing our duty. Far likelier we are to get a soil bucket tipped over us.'

'That has happened to you, Catchpoll?'

'Once or twice in the early days, my lord. I have learnt to walk more carefully at times since.'

'You never mentioned this to me, Serjeant.'

'No, my lord, but then most would draw the line at throwing filth over a lord.' Catchpoll grinned, fleetingly.

They returned to the priest's house a little before Vespers, with nothing encouraging to report to Walkelin, who was wrestling with an idea which was like the hint of dawn, just below his horizon. Something was niggling at his brain, but as yet it would not develop.

'No need to be downcast. We have not learnt much, except negatives, of how many folk could not possibly be involved, but tomorrow you will follow up our four-legged clue, Walkelin, and everything will seem much brighter.' Bradecote tried to sound positive.

'Come to Vespers and pray for guidance.' Father Paulinus was sincere in his suggestion.

'I think that our presence might be seen as a blight, Father.' Bradecote shook his head.

'Not by God.'

'No, but He will hear us if we offer up our prayers here also.'

'Indeed He will.' Father Paulinus looked more cheered.

When the priest had gone to conduct the office, Walkelin asked if they had heard Aelfric mentioned. They shook their heads.

'Let us just get your description of that horse, lad.' Catchpoll permitted himself his death's head grin, the lips a tight drawn slash in the grey stubble of his close beard.

'We will avoid all mention of him until your return, and

then we will seek him out, Walkelin.' Bradecote appeared as unconcerned, in Walkelin's view.

Whatever problems they faced, both the undersheriff and Serjeant Catchpoll did have great hopes of the link with the horse. After all, Aelfric had not worried about bringing the bay back to Harvington. He would not try to conceal it, and if asked, would no doubt claim it was just a horse from his lord's Warwickshire estate. That could then be refuted by Will Horsweard, and if required, any neighbours in Evesham. Nobody would consider the horse.

They were wrong.

Brian de Nouailles sat at his table, staring with beetled brows at his man Aelfric as his fingers drummed an angry tattoo upon the elm planks. Leofwine guarded the hall doorway, that none might enter, and know of his presence. The steward had foreseen that his nephew's return, with the sheriff's men sniffing about and looking for Walter Horsweard's killer, was neither opportune nor likely to please their lord, and had had the foresight to send the younger man to a dilapidated dwelling in the woods until called for by the lord de Nouailles. Well, he had been called for now, and was not liking it.

'But, my lord, it is a good horse.' Aelfric was not self-assured when confronting his lord, however much he swaggered about the manor. There was a trace of a whine in his voice.

'I am not asking about its stamina and looks, you dolt. I asked why you brought it back here. And what, in the name of God, did you think you were doing returning here before I sent for you?'

'But there is no link between—'

'"But", "but", it is all "buts" with you. There was no link until we had de Beauchamp's men turn up in my manor asking all manner of offensive questions. And just how did you come to the decision that it was the time to come back to Harvington? I sent you away, and I told you to await my command before coming back, a command which you have ignored. Tell me, Aelfric, do you think yourself cleverer than me? Do you know more than I do?'

'No, my lord. Of course not, my lord. I just thought—'

'No, you never thought, you just guessed, and you guessed poorly. At least you had the sense not to bring it into the stables, not that it counts as thought, and the sheriff's hounds have not seen you with it.'

'But—' Aelfric cringed, correctly anticipating the lupine snarl.

'You said "but" again. And now you are going to tell me that you, and the horse, have been seen?'

'Y . . . es, my lord, but only briefly, before my uncle hit him – the red-haired man – in the head and he lost his wits.'

'Oh, that is all right, then, as long as your uncle hit him witless.'

Aelfric looked relieved, but then Aelfric did not comprehend sarcasm. He did understand a jug hurled at his head, and a flood of invective. That the words were foreign to him did not mean he could not understand what they meant, that his life was going to become a trial for the foreseeable future. He shuddered.

That, at least, pleased Brian de Nouailles.

'I doubt he was as witless as you, even laid out unconscious. Get out of my sight. Keep the horse, and your own miserable carcass, back at the hovel where Ketel the Woodsman lived, and lie quiet. I shall call for you again when I have thought what next to do. Go!'

Aelfric withdrew in haste, and with a vague sense of ill-usage.

Chapter Thirteen

Whilst Catchpoll did not think it likely that they would find anything of note at the place where Hild had been found, it seemed a good way of showing that the sheriff's men were working to find her killer, whilst they were in fact awaiting the vital information Walkelin might bring them from Evesham. He was sent off early next morning, once their fast had been broken, although not before he showed them the place where he had found the body, which lay at the far end of one of the big fields, on a cart track that was bordered to the north by scrubby trees and to the south by the tilled earth, just sprouting green. Walkelin was mounted, but his superiors walked. The peasants, working the field furthest away, did not as much as raise their heads from their hoeing of the earliest weeds. When the trio got to within about thirty paces of the spot, Catchpoll made Walkelin dismount and loop the reins over a branch, and lead them on foot.

'There's just a chance we might find signs of a single horse, nice and fresh like, and that would be useful. Even without proof that the bay you saw was Horsweard's, we can confront Leofwine the Steward over his failure to mention that he was accompanied by a horseman when he came across you and the body. Corner him a little and he might just give us information we need about his nephew.'

'We are assuming it was Aelfric on the horse.' The undersheriff did not want them to get as set as they had been in Evesham upon a trail which led nowhere, however tempting.

'Who else would be with the steward and him not make mention of the fact? Especially if he was returning on Horsweard's own animal. If it had been found and brought in after the murder, less a rider, there would have been an outcry at the time, and nobody mentioned a horse of any kind. And there is that cap.' Catchpoll blew on his chilled hands, for there was a bitterness in the breeze even though the sun's warmth was just strong enough to make itself felt when it peeped from behind cloud.

'True enough, but we cannot simply assume. So, off with you, Walkelin, and bring us back a good description of the bay that Walter Horsweard rode, and please tell us it had a big nose.'

'And try for us first at the priest's house, and then the manor,' called Catchpoll, belatedly, at Walkelin's retreating figure.

The serjeant's apprentice raised a hand in acknowledgement.

'A realistic chance of evidence?' Bradecote was now squatting on his haunches where Walkelin had indicated the body had lain.

'We need no evidence she was here. We are looking for whether she died here or was dragged here, my lord.'

'Or was carried here across a horse. Though why bring a body to where it would be found soon enough by any out in the fields? If she was murdered elsewhere, why not leave her hidden, or hide her in the bushes and trees where she might not be found for several days?'

'A fair point, that. If you want a body found, guaranteed, it has to be for a good reason. I would say we have several.'

'You mean that she should be found before Aelfric appears back at the manor, so that he is not a suspect?'

'Indeed, my lord. And the other reason is that if our murderer wants everyone to keep their mouths shut, showing what happens to them that doesn't is no bad thing.'

'And the reasons can both be valid.' Bradecote stared at the ground.

No cart had passed that way recently. It was the sort of track used most when the fields were productive, and the wheel ruts showed the weathering of winter. There had been sufficient showers to keep the earth soft enough to keep the imprint of a horseshoe, and there were none up close, but then the rider would have dismounted to assist in the taking of Walkelin.

'We had dew, of course. But no rain last night. As I see it, my lord, the darkening here is the mark where the girl was laid upon her back and the wound bled a little, but that does not help us move forward, for we know how she died. Walkelin did not say which direction the steward approached from, but it is unlikely it was across the newly sprung crop, and if he was awaiting someone discovering her, then in cover is the

184

only obvious place. Then, if nobody came this way before the day chilled and folk headed homeward, he had but to find her himself. The villagers could not have been working in this field, or what happened would have been obvious to all.' Catchpoll was almost talking to himself. 'The thing is, if they are working the same as yesterday, well the chances of seeing a bundle on the ground over here are quite small, not unless you were looking for it. So it actually looks pretty certain that Leofwine, if he did not do the deed himself, which is a possibility we can at least use to frighten him, was brought here to discover it. Chance came into play and he saw Walkelin about to do that for him, so he pounced on the opportunity to hand over a nice culprit whom none would mind seeing swing for the crime.'

'The thing is, Catchpoll, if she was killed here, why was she here at all? She spoke to Walkelin, up by the manor gateway but an hour before.'

'She could have come to meet someone, already arranged.' Catchpoll lifted a hand before Bradecote could interrupt. 'I know, that seems fanciful, my lord. But what is not is that Walkelin came this way from speaking to Father Paulinus. Might she have not gone to do likewise? Mayhap she had recalled something and felt she ought to speak to the priest about it.'

'But this is not the direct route from the manor to the wheat field. She would have gone straight, along the other field boundary.'

'Ah, but if her killer intercepted her, having seen her talking to Walkelin, or if he came upon her on the way and she told him about the sheriff's men hunting about . . .'

'That bucket holds no water. She disliked the man, if it was Aelfric. The priest said so. She would not walk off with him willingly, especially out the way of folk.'

'Hear me out, my lord. If she dislikes him, she is caught by the fatal female urge to stir things up. She thinks she can make him worry, not thinking he really is the culprit, but that it would be good to see him squirm. She even tells him that Walkelin has asked about him by name, and is more caught up in her tale than where they walk.'

'But if it was Aelfric, going to see the priest must have been about him, so she would be afraid of him.' Bradecote rubbed his hand along his jaw.

Catchpoll paused. What the undersheriff said was true enough. Then he gave a twisted smile.

'Then what she wanted to speak to the priest about was not about Aelfric, but about someone else.'

'The lady de Nouailles!'

'There was some little thing that pricked her, something floated up in her mind, but before telling of it, she wanted to speak to the priest. Pity it is she never got to him, unless she was going to make a confession, which would have left us none the wiser.'

'Catchpoll, that does just about work, you crafty old . . .'

'Serjeant, my lord?'

'Yes. But is it too crafty? That is all I fear.'

'It matters not, as long as we sees how the pieces fit. As proof it is spit in the wind.' Catchpoll matched action to words, and then continued. 'We were chasing after shadows in Evesham, I'll grant you, but there is no doubt in my mind that Walter

186

Horsweard was killed because of this manor. Otherwise not only horse but scrip would have been taken. The killer was not a thief, and thought about the horse simply because it was not a thing he could leave to be found. To be honest, a man used to getting rid of bodies would have killed him somewhere inconspicuous and hidden the body away from the path of travellers and let nature deal with it. A thief would not have known where he came from or when a cry would be made over his absence. He would rely on being long gone and with no connection. The river is as bad as it is good. Yes, a body might just go so far as to never be named, but as likely it does as this one did, and with everyone keen to prove his English blood . . . No, a murdering thief would not have cast him in the Avon, but disposed of him quiet upon the road and hidden the corpse.'

'Unless he was a first-time murdering thief, and threw the body in the water out of fear and then remembered the scrip. You said this before, Catchpoll, and called the murderer a chance-taker, when it might have been in a panic. But that is a slim chance, I agree, and everything points to de Nouailles and his manor, and Aelfric his man. We just need to close the net tight.'

'And here is something that might aid us, my lord.' Catchpoll had continued his survey of the ground by the trees. 'The hoof marks of a good-sized beast, and defined enough to be yesterday's, and footprints from two different sizes of feet.'

'So we bring the steward here?'

'Mmm, I have another idea, my lord. We makes a copy of the print.'

'How?'

187

'Well, if you hand me your nice cloak, my lord, I press the corner over the hoof print and we see it as clear among the mud.'

Bradecote drew his cloak about him tighter. It was a good cloak for riding, not more than hip length, and a fine chestnut-coloured wool.

'I would rather bring the steward here, Catchpoll, both because he could not say it was just any hoof mark used as a ruse, and because I'll be damned if I am going to go cold for the next hour or more, just for you to look clever.'

Catchpoll grinned.

'I only said as it was an idea, my lord.'

'Remind me not to encourage you.'

'I might be forgetful.' The grin grew even broader. 'So, we go back to the manor and speak to Leofwine the Steward.'

'We do. And to Father Paulinus, in case there was anything Hild had hinted to him recently.'

Walkelin did not dawdle into Evesham. The previous day had shaken him to the core. He had found a girl dead within an hour of speaking with her, faced an ignominious death, and then been returned to the hunters rather than the hunted. His head still ached where he had received the blow, but with the resilience of youth, and feeling better for not being still in Harvington, he rode into the town upright in the saddle, secure in the knowledge that he was the sheriff's man, and his questions would get answers, especially since Will Horsweard would be glad to be no longer under suspicion.

What he had forgotten was that those in Evesham had not been told officially that this was the case. The sheriff's men had simply gone. It was hoped they would not return but since it had only been a couple of days, that was not yet certain. Will Horsweard did not, therefore, instantly react with pleasure to Walkelin's appearance. In fact, he looked as if every horse in his stables had just been trotted out lame.

'Back again,' he sniffed, looking coldly at Walkelin. Sheriff's man he might be, but a very junior one, and there need not be the cautious respect given to the lord Undersheriff.

'Yes, Master Horsweard,' responded Walkelin with a cheerful smile that ignored the lack of delight on the horse dealer's face, and was in fact a very good imitation of what Catchpoll would term 'serjeant's thick skin'. 'I am come at the lord Undersheriff's command to ask you about your brother's horse, the one he was riding the day he left.'

'His horse?' Will Horsweard's suspicion turned to interest. 'Has it been found? It is a good animal and worth—'

'We cannot be sure it is found until you give me its description. If that tallies with the animal we have seen, then not only will you have it returned, but we will have a good idea of who murdered your brother.'

'So you no longer think it was me?' The horse dealer wanted the security of confirmation.

'No. We—' Walkelin was about to say they had discovered that Walter had been cast into the Avon from the Offenham bridge, but at the last minute realised this would lead Horsweard to the obvious conclusion that their brother-in-law must be a likely suspect, and vengeful brothers would be a hindrance to the investigation. He could imagine Serjeant Catchpoll's ire, and that was not a good thing to contemplate.

'You what?'

'We think he was killed by someone not from Evesham.' That sounded a bit vague, but it was the best he could do.

'And will you tell me why that is, sheriff's man?'

'I am not at liberty to say, as yet.' Walkelin thought this appropriately official, if not officious. 'But the horse is what I need to know about. Describe it as best you can, Master Horsweard.'

'That is easy enough. You may as well come in.' As hospitality went, it was grudging, but Will Horsweard did open his door and waved Walkelin inside.

'Walter was on the heavy side and liked a horse well up to his weight. He found the bay last year, and chose not to part with him.'

At the mention of the colour Walkelin was instantly hopeful. A small seed of doubt had entered his mind that he would be going back with the disappointing news that the horse was grey or pale chestnut and the best lead they had would be dashed like a broken pitcher. He tried not to look too pleased.

'What manner of bay, and how tall?'

'Between sixteen and seventeen hands it is, and a dark bay. Not the most beautiful of beasts, but with good stamina, and wonderful hindquarters.'

'How does he look, in detail – any marks?'

'He has a big, heavy nose, and a white off-hind.'

'And if you saw him you would identify him?'

'Oh yes, at fifty paces.'

'That is very useful, Master Horsweard.' Walkelin noted that they had not been joined by Walter's widow. He had little doubt she had left, after what had been said. As if reading his thoughts, Will Horsweard smiled, but grimly.

'My brother's "grieving widow" would not know the horse beyond saying it was "big and ugly", and you will not find her here. She is gone to John Pinvin the bridle-maker, and I thought him a man of sense until now. The wagging tongues of Evesham are full of it, though it will be but the gossip of the moment. I am just glad the woman is out of my house, and that, as soon as she can, she will lose the name of Horsweard. She brought bad luck upon us as I see it.'

Walkelin did not comment that their family's bad luck almost certainly stemmed from marrying off his sister to Brian de Nouailles.

'I never thought to inherit the business at all until Walter showed he was not likely to sire sons, and even then . . .' Will Horsweard sighed, and crossed himself. 'Life is never certain. Now it is up to me, and for all that I am crippled, there is no reason why I should not have heirs of my body. What I lack in looks I have now in wealth and position, and I have seen the dangers of a fancy wife. A comfortable woman, a woman who will make this place a proper home as in my mother's day, that is my aim.'

Walkelin did not think it unreasonable, but he was not there to listen to Horsweard's plans. He made vague murmurs of agreement, and made his farewell without haste, but had the horse trader seen the speed to which he urged his mount he would have been surprised, and then laughed, for Walkelin's mount was a natural plodder, and getting it to maintain even a reasonable canter was hard work. It was a pleased, but rather breathless, Walkelin who let his beast slacken to its normal desultory pace as he entered Harvington and dismounted before the priest's house.

His superiors were not within, so he stabled his mount and walked to the manor, where he was grudgingly allowed within but given a darkling look by the gatekeeper.

The priest was not at home or in the church, and so Bradecote and Catchpoll abandoned thoughts of speaking with him for a while and went to corner Leofwine the Steward. Their first desire was to inspect the stables, but they were prevented from doing this by Leofwine himself, for he crossed the bailey as they entered, fully intent that they should not 'keep the lord's servants from their work'.

'Oh, we are not here to do that.' Catchpoll sounded very content for a man hunting a murderer, if not two.

'And the lord de Nouailles is out riding, so you may not speak with him.'

'No matter, for we are here to speak with you, Steward. We would like you to show us where the body was found.' Bradecote echoed his serjeant's tone, which made Leofwine the more suspicious.

The steward's eyes narrowed.

'You know where it was found. Your man will have told you.'

'But it would be better if you came and showed us exactly how it was you came upon it, and him.'

'I cannot come just now, because I am waiting upon my lord's command.' Leofwine sounded a little desperate, which was all to the good.

'Far be it from us to put you in bad odour with your lord,' murmured Bradecote. 'We can wait, but we will speak with you until the lord de Nouailles has given you his instruction.'

'Come into the buttery, then, if you must.'

'I think we must, don't you, my lord?' Catchpoll suppressed a smile, badly.

'Indeed, Serjeant, we must.'

Leofwine glowered at the pair, but led them up the steps into the hall and then turned into the dimness of the shuttered buttery. A mouse scurried behind a tun.

'So, what would you ask of me . . . my lord?' It did not sound as if Leofwine's answers would be willingly given.

'Several things perplex us. The first is what you were doing that led you to find the body, since the villagers were working in the field some distance away, and if you were overseeing them, how came you to be there?'

Leofwine licked his lips, and there was a heavy pause. They could almost hear the man thinking.

'I was not overseeing them. I had been to Lench, upon the lord's business, and was returning.'

'Good.' Catchpoll sounded as though he was glad the problem was cleared up. 'They can confirm that in Lench, then, and give proof you were not on hand when the wench died.'

'When the . . . You think that I killed her?' Leofwine paled. 'No, I cannot have done so. I found your man by the body.'

'Nothing easier than doing the deed and then hiding, on hearing someone approach. There's good enough cover among the trees and bushes. If nobody had come by, you would have either taken a long way back and been surprised when eventually she was found, or played clever and "found" her yourself, much as you did with Walkelin, but without the advantage of a scapegoat.' Catchpoll was matter-of-fact.

'There is also the matter of the charge of rape you made so swiftly and with so little cause against the sheriff's man, Walkelin.' Bradecote pressed home the advantage. 'And it is very odd that you were so vehement that he was the girl's killer and yet did not mention that you were not alone when you discovered him by the body. You would think that you would have both declared the crime, especially if you believed you had the culprit.' Bradecote emphasised the 'if' as though to stress that he knew full well Leofwine had never thought the statement true, and made no mention of the horse, which Catchpoll silently applauded. 'Unless you had an accomplice.'

There was a moment of silence. 'Not alone? You have no cause to suggest that.'

'Not alone, I say, and we do.'

'Nobody saw—' Leofwine choked back his next word, which Catchpoll would have sworn was an 'us'.

'But we have seen that you were there, Master Steward, and with another man, and a horse. There is evidence in the ground, and the good earth does not lie. It is strange that you did not put either the body or the unconscious Walkelin across its back and lead it home. Your lord said the maid's body was brought back on a hurdle, and though you do not look weak, why carry a man as good as dead weight all that way?' Catchpoll was guessing that, in reality, Walkelin had been slung across the beast at least as far as within sight of the manor gates, and then Aelfric had made himself scarce while all the commotion took

194

place. He might even have gone to de Nouailles' nearest holding to lie low again.

Leofwine was breathing fast, and his eyes held fear.

'No need to look worried, Leofwine.' The new voice was cold rather than comforting.

Undersheriff and serjeant turned as one. Brian de Nouailles stood in the doorway, looking vaguely displeased, and very superior.

'The reason he did not mention it was because it was unnecessary. You do not think I go about on foot among the peasantry, do you? The rider on the horse was me.'

Chapter Fourteen

'You?' Bradecote and Catchpoll spoke in unison, and with total surprise in their voices. It was not an option they had considered.

'Yes. Me.' De Nouailles sneered at them. 'I do not expect to be dragged into this mess. I met my steward as I was riding and we took that path back. He saw all that was needful to report. My eyes are no better than his.' He shrugged.

'Interesting then, my lord, that you were crying rape to us when there was no sign of such a crime upon the body, and yet you had seen it close up,' Catchpoll spoke carefully, not quite accusing.

'She was on her back; he was leaning over her. It was a natural assumption.' De Nouailles sounded bored.

'And although he does not recognise many of your villagers, Walkelin does recognise you, de Nouailles, and you were not the man he saw on the horse.' Bradecote made no pretence at believing the lord of Harvington.

'He was rendered senseless and it is his addled wits against the word of my steward, and against mine. Think what you will, Bradecote. I will swear it was me, and you can do nothing to prove it otherwise.'

'Then show us the horse you rode.' The undersheriff's eyes flashed anger.

'If you wish. It is just a horse like any other, four legs, two ears, two eyes . . .' De Nouailles shrugged again and turned to leave his hall, with the sheriff's men following. Leofwine, unsure whether to follow, remained in the buttery and regained his composure before going to the kitchen and making the cook's life a misery.

De Nouailles strode to the stables and yelled for the stable boy, who appeared from a stall.

'Show the lord Undersheriff my horse.'

'Yes, my lord.'

The youth turned immediately to a stall and brought out a big bay horse. This bay had three white stockings and a proud, finely chiselled face with a wide, white blaze down its very straight nose.

'Was this the horse your lord rode yesterday?' Bradecote spoke firmly but without heat.

'Yes, my lord.' The answer was swift.

'Was it the only horse he rode?' Catchpoll asked, quietly.

'It is his favourite horse.'

'That was not what I asked, lad.' There was no increase in volume, but Catchpoll's voice menaced.

It was, thought Bradecote, the horse de Nouailles had been riding when he found them at the mill.

'It was the only horse he rode.'

'Was there a new horse in these stables yesterday at any time?' Bradecote persisted.

The stable lad swallowed convulsively, and could not resist glancing at his lord, unsure what answer he would wish him to give.

'I did not see a new horse in these stables, my lord,' the boy mumbled.

'So that is the end of the matter.' De Nouailles sounded matter-of-fact. 'Now, you can leave my servants alone to get on with their labours.' His tone was dismissive, and Bradecote did not like being dismissed.

'The matter is ended when I say so, de Nouailles, and I promise you that is not yet.' He almost ground his teeth, and de Nouailles laughed.

'Mere words, Bradecote, mere words. You will find nothing. You choose to waste your own time, but do not waste mine.'

There was little more the undersheriff and serjeant could do than stalk out, the laugh ringing in their ears. They saw Walkelin coming towards them, and his mouth opened to speak, but he caught the look on the undersheriff's face and thought better of it, and so turned and fell into step with them. Only when the gates closed behind them did he ask what had happened. He shook his head at what he heard.

'No. For the horse I saw was almost certainly Walter Horsweard's, my lord, a big-nosed bay with a white off-hind and—'

'De Nouailles says it was him on the horse, and his own bay is in the stables, the bay he says he was riding.' Catchpoll growled the words.

Walkelin's jaw dropped.

'But that is a lie.'

'Of course it's a lie. You know that, we know that, and he knows we cannot prove it,' Hugh Bradecote snapped. He was not a man given to outbursts of rage, but his jaw was working and his brows met in an angry line. 'I'll see that bastard hang, because he is as guilty as hell, and he thinks he is beyond the law. Well, the law doesn't agree with him.'

'That's the way of it, my lord,' agreed Catchpoll, just as angry and yet holding back a smile as he realised just how far Bradecote had come. He was thinking like a serjeant, in a grander way, perhaps, but getting the outlook that Catchpoll had long held, and it pleased the older man. 'The cockier he gets, mind you, the likelier to put a step wrong, and we will have him.'

Bradecote's reply was pithy, rude, and much to both his subordinates' taste. It was a threesome in total accord that stopped before the church, where the priest was bending to talk to a lad who must be nearly of an age to be part of the tithing. Father Paulinus looked up.

'You do not look well pleased, my lord.'

'No, Father. We have good evidence that the horse Walter Horsweard was riding when he was killed has been seen about the manor, but no way of proving it in the face of denials. It is a pretty distinctive animal too.'

'Might I have seen it?'

'Probably not, Father. It is a big bay, with a heavy nose and—'

'A white stocking on one hind leg.' The boy looked up, with a mixture of diffidence and confidence. He certainly had their attention. 'I saw a horse like that this morning, tethered by the cottage in the woods where old Ketel lived.'

'How long ago?'

'This morning, when Mother took us out into the field to work. My brother is young, and gets bored. He slipped away into the woods to play, and Mother sent me after him.'

'What exactly did you see?'

'It was just the horse I noticed. I like horses. Father Paulinus lets me groom his mule.' The boy frowned. 'It was a strange place to see it. Nobody has lived there since old Ketel died.' The child crossed himself. 'I wouldn't go close. Some as say he's still there, and . . .' He looked nervously at the priest, who smiled and shook his head.

'That is just a foolishness.'

'But I heard his spirit in torment, Father.' The voice was a trembling whisper now.

'What did you hear, lad?' Catchpoll tried to sound like a kindly oldfather, but the 'kindly' seemed very lacking.

'He screamed.'

'Often?'

'No, once I heard, I ran away, and I did not tell Mother because she would say I was frightening my brother, and it is not a tale. I would not say so before Father Paulinus if it was.'

'The good Father speaks true, boy. What you heard was no spirit, but a living man, or at least living until the scream

200

ended.' Catchpoll's face had hardened into grimness.

'Excuse us, Father. We wish to speak with you, but it must wait. Where exactly did Ketel live?'

The priest described the place.

'But we are committing Hild to the earth. Will you not be present?'

'I am sorry, Father, but this is more urgent, and if as we fear, may bring more work for the gravedigger.'

The three men ran to the stable, unconcerned at the interest this aroused in the few villagers who saw them, and within minutes were galloping up the road that headed northward.

Brian de Nouailles' pleasure at goading the undersheriff did not stop him turning a snarling visage to his steward when he returned to his hall, and ordering the lad who was setting down a basket of wood for the brazier to get out or feel his boot.

Leofwine was morose, in full expectation of feeling his lord's wrath. De Nouailles was scowling as heavy as a thundercloud, and showed no lightening of his features when he began to speak.

'So.'

'My lord?'

'Tell me, Leofwine, what happened yesterday.'

'My lord, I did not kill the maid.'

'Of course you didn't.' He made it sound as if it were a weakness. 'Tell me how you found her.'

'On the ground on her back and—'

'Jesu, give me strength! You sound as lack-wit as Aelfric. How was it that you came upon her at all?'

'Aelfric found me, and said he had come across her, dead.'

'Where did he find you?'

'In my chamber, my lord. He said he came in through the postern, which had been left open a-ways, and none saw him.'

The scowl became a frown.

'Why did he not ride in, telling of his "find"?'

'I did not ask, my lord. He seemed upset – and who would not be? I was just thankful that he had done so, what with sheriff's men about. He said he wanted me to come and be the one to find the body, then he would come home, but I told him how things stood, and said he was best out of sight and mind until the fussing died down. I said at the time it was rash, him—'

'I have no interest in what you said then nor think now. I am only interested in keeping Aelfric from a noose.' De Nouailles' sneer was pronounced. 'So, he persuaded you to go with him?'

'Yes, my lord. Out the postern gate and with none the wiser. Everyone was working the East Field. We was taking a roundabout way so as not be in the view of any as lifted their heads, and then Aelfric sees the sheriff's man-at-arms coming along in the distance. That red hair of his is easy to spot. Aelfric was leading the horse, you understand, so wasn't too likely to have been seen. He half-dragged me into the spinney and said this was even better, if we found a stranger there to blame.'

'Why should he need someone to blame?' De Nouailles was suspicious.

'He said the chances were it was a stranger, anyway, and it could be said the same man had killed Horsweard. I told him that would not work, because the red-haired man was the sheriff's man. Then he laughed and said accusing him would take the law's attention away from Horsweard good and proper, and I thought as you would like the idea, my lord, being as you dislike the undersheriff.'

'You have that, right enough. Sets himself up as righteous and nigh on saintly, and pushes his nose into private matters. He even had the gall to tell me he had lost a wife, knew what grief was. He knows nothing; he was not married to her.' He did not say his wife's name, but his expression became intense, and Leofwine knew that for a moment Brian de Nouailles was not looking at him.

'So we came up through the trees, knowing he would stop by the body, and Aelfric got on the horse, in case he ran, he said, though I thought that unlikely, and we, well, ambushed him, called him murderer and violator for good measure, and I hit him over the head with a stout stick. We put him over the horse's withers in front of Aelfric and came back carefully, as close as we could to the manor gate, then I slung him over my shoulder and staggered in the last hundred paces, and Aelfric slipped away to old Ketel's place.' Leofwine paused. 'If you want to know more, you must ask Aelfric, my lord.'

Brian de Nouailles had good reason to know that Aelfric would give him no answers, and, though a man not prone to regret, wished he had thought to ask certain questions of him whilst he could.

The tumbledown dwelling was slowly being absorbed into the woodland, and was not easy to find, even with the leaves of oak, ash and chestnut only unfurling from bud. From the evidence of the boy, they did not expect to find the horse still tethered by the crumbling walls, and the only proof it had been there was the pile of fresh droppings, roughly scattered, and hoof prints in the soft ground. There was silence, except for a robin singing lustily, and the scrabbling of two squirrels, mere flashes of chestnut red, chasing each other in the upper branches of a gnarled oak. They did not bother to draw steel before entering.

As their eyes adjusted to the gloom, they knew what they were likely to find, but there was no corpse. Catchpoll flung open a shutter, which disintegrated and hung like a torn flag from its hinge. The trio blinked at the sudden light.

'The bastard is still one move ahead of us.' Bradecote kicked a broken pot, viciously.

The other two both knew whom he meant.

'Let us just see if we can be sure Aelfric was here, my lord. You never know, there might be something useful. If de Nouailles came here to get rid of him and the horse, he might have got careless.'

'And to think he was here, even as we were snuffling like hogs in leaf litter where the girl was killed. Are we going to end up handing back a string of bodies to grieving relatives and never wiping the sneer off de Nouailles' face? I so want to do that Catchpoll, even if it is only as the rope tightens about his neck.'

The undersheriff was too aggrieved to search, and Catchpoll did not mind if Bradecote vented his natural ire, while he looked, and looked carefully. That there had been someone in the single chamber was clear from the tell-tale blackening and traces of ash half-rubbed from the long disused hearth, and the detritus of decay upon the floor that was disturbed.

'We know that Aelfric cried out, so we can be pretty sure he died here, and there are scuff marks enough this side to suggest he backed away, if you look. He would have taken whatever blow it was to the front, since he wasn't making for the door.' Catchpoll knelt on the floor and felt, with a surprising delicacy of touch, among the half-rotted rushes, blown in leaves and accumulating earth. 'It is a cool day, and there is dampness here.' He held up his fingers to the light from the gaping window. They showed smears of red.

'But we have no body, we have no horse, we have not even proof it was Aelfric.'

'That part we might, my lord.' Walkelin had been investigating the corner adjacent to the window, and lifted, with every sign of triumph, a woollen cap. 'I would think his uncle Leofwine could identify that.'

Bradecote nodded, but did not look as cheered as Walkelin had anticipated.

'But without his corpse, without Horsweard's bay, we can only say we have reason to believe Aelfric will not be returning to Harvington.' The undersheriff was not in optimistic mood.

'Ah yes, my lord, but since he killed Aelfric this morning and then disposed of him, and the horse, he cannot have gone far with either, not since he got back to the manor in time to rescue Leofwine from the knot he was tying himself into.' Catchpoll was being as positive as he could. 'If we find the horse, we can give something back to Horsweard's brother, and if we find the body, we can say with some certainty the man who killed him and tipped him in the Avon is dead.'

'A few days ago that would have sufficed me, but not any more, Catchpoll, not any more.'

'I know, my lord. Well, we won't find a horse in the rush leavings here, so best we start outside.' Catchpoll brushed the dirt from knees and palms, and headed out into the light. The others followed, Walkelin tucking the discovered cap into his belt.

'Are we looking for tracks to follow, Serjeant?' Walkelin looked to Catchpoll.

'It would be to our advantage, and the horses should have left one easy enough to follow. Even had he wished, de Nouailles could not have left here at speed. Upon the road he might meet another traveller, and explaining a body would not be easy, so he will have kept among the trees. We also know the body cannot be buried, both for time to dig a grave and the fact that I doubt very much if the fancy lord – begging your pardon, my lord – has ever lifted a spade, let alone thought to bring one with him. So, if we follows hoof prints I would say we just needs to keep our eyes open for where the body has been covered or hidden.'

It sounded straightforward enough, and finding the imprints of the two horses' shoes was not difficult, nor following them for the first half-mile. Bradecote was pessimistic, however.

'I grant we are following his path, Catchpoll, but what was to stop him hiding the body away from the horses? Even thirty paces away we would not see signs.'

'Because if that was the case he would have to stop and the horses would not remain stock-still, my lord, but trample about in the one spot, and that we have not seen.'

Bradecote gave himself a mental shake. He wasn't thinking, he was just moping, and moping would not catch Brian de Nouailles.

Catchpoll was a good tracker, Bradecote knew that from previous experience, and he followed the serjeant's lead without question, and thereafter in silence. Walkelin marvelled that a man he considered in advancing years could see the trail even when the obvious imprint of hoof in mud was absent. He thought that when they returned to Worcester, he would ask him to teach him the finer points. After another mile the tracks ceased to be of help, because the two horses joined the main trackway, where there were too many imprints to be sure which was which.

'Will he have crossed straight, Catchpoll?' Bradecote frowned.

'Not if he has any sense, my lord. He would see the way clear a good ways north and south and following the track for even a hundred paces or so would make it the harder to pick him up again. Walkelin, you take that side, and I will take this, and we look for any shoe marks or signs of a horse blundering through the bushes. That will save us time.'

Hugh Bradecote recalled the last time he and Catchpoll had been seeking a trail off a trackway, and it gave him a sense of perspective. Then it had been his Christina's life in peril, and what had clawed at his insides had been fear not anger. She was worthy of being a distraction. De Nouailles was not; the man had got under his skin, and that was a bad thing, because it slewed his focus. As Catchpoll had said, the man might get cocky, and make a mistake. It was his duty to see that mistake, not miss it because of a red mist of anger before his eyes. A shout went up. Walkelin, a few paces ahead of Catchpoll, had found the trail again, on the Avon side of the track.

'He would not leave the cover of the woods and cast him, like Horsweard, into the river, would he, Serjeant?' Walkelin wondered out loud.

'Doubt it. He has seen already how a body comes back to haunt you. If we miss it now, this body may never be found, unless some hound leads a man to it.' Catchpoll pulled his horse up, suddenly. 'Here he stopped, so . . . Scout about, Walkelin.'

Walkelin dismounted and was going to hand his reins to Catchpoll, then realised that the instruction was merely to set him off first. His superiors dismounted without rushing. After all, if the body was here, it was not going anywhere. They tied their mounts securely, and Catchpoll's first foray was ahead, but he returned in scarcely more than moments.

'The marks continue, and I had hoped one set would be clearly the lighter, but I cannot be sure, my lord.'

'Will he have just concealed the corpse in a bramble patch, or covered it with leaves and branches, Catchpoll?'

'Neither, my lord, because he did this.' Catchpoll had hardly gone more than ten paces, and was stood looking down, beside a fallen tree that lay parallel to the tracks of the horses.

Bradecote and Walkelin joined him. On the other side, face to the tree, and lying alongside it as close as a lover in a bed, was a body. The clothing was dark enough not to draw attention and the cotte had been drawn up a little so that it concealed the whiteness of the dead face of Aelfric.

'Simple, and if you was not looking for it, very effective.' Catchpoll remarked, climbing over the fallen trunk and pulling the body onto its back. The eyes were open, the pupils dilated in the surprise of death, the jaw slackened as if to voice complaint. 'Well, we can tell Will Horsweard there is a form of justice, at least.'

'And now we need justice for a murderer, in both senses of the term.' Bradecote looked down, unmoved. 'I take it we need not linger here in the hope of finding anything useful?'

'No, my lord, unless de Nouailles dropped his dagger, or a ring or . . . Ah yes, just for my own peace of mind . . .' Catchpoll knelt and looked at the clothing where it had attracted dirt to the stickiness of the gore. The wound was not made by a narrow blade as had been used on Horsweard and the girl, but a dagger driven, said Catchpoll, most likely to the hilt and about an inch and a half wide at that point. 'Not that I thought he made an end of himself, of course, but it is nice to see it was definitely another weapon. And also, since this is de Nouailles' dagger, we can be assured that it was not de Nouailles who killed the girl. There was always a slight chance he did, and this one in fact found her when trying to keep out of the way with his uncle.'

'I had not even thought of that.' Bradecote shook his head.

'And what is more . . .' Catchpoll reached to the dead man's belt, where a knife was still scabbarded. He withdrew a slim blade no more than six inches long. 'That is the weapon that killed Horsweard and the wench. We cannot get a confession from the dead, but that is as good.'

'Do we take him straight back or hope to find the horse?' asked Walkelin.

'Let us see if the two horses continue together for a while yet or if it was let loose hereabouts. A little delay will not change matters in Harvington.' Bradecote wanted to feel they had tried to find it, at the least. 'He cannot have continued long to the north before turning for home. The body can go across your horse and you can double up behind Serjeant Catchpoll.'

Walkelin and Catchpoll slung the corpse as directed, and led Walkelin's mount. It was not long before the sets of hoof prints returned to the trackway.

'My lord, I would guess that he set off a short distance at pace then spooked the spare horse to gallop on alone, and turned back upon his own tracks. We can try further but . . . I am not sure how far it is to the next village thisaways, and the beast might have turned off anywhere along the way and wandered.'

'Agreed, Catchpoll. Horsweard must go without his horse. Let us take the body back to Harvington and see how de Nouailles reacts.'

Chapter Fifteen

The track that led back to Harvington was straight enough, and by that route it was only about five miles to the manor, so even at no more than a brisk walking pace that would not dislodge the body, it did not take them long to reach the junction in the village. Walkelin dismounted there, and went to see if Father Paulinus was at home or in the church, while undersheriff and serjeant turned up to the manor itself and presented themselves at the gates. With Aelfric's body in view there was no question of their not gaining entry.

A man was sharpening a sickle on a whetstone; a maid was carrying a brace of partridge to the kitchen for the lord's meal. Both stopped and stared, transfixed.

Bradecote and Catchpoll brought the horses to a halt in the middle of the bailey, and dismounted. Bradecote was about to ask for the steward when Leofwine appeared from an outbuilding. He too stood still for a moment, making the bailey a grotesque tableau of shock, then he came forward, his face a grim mask.

'We found him, a little off the northern road, about four miles from here. This is – was – Aelfric?' Bradecote was emotionless.

'Yes, that is my brother's son. How did he die?'

'He was murdered, stabbed.'

'Like the horse trader and Hild.' Leofwine made the connection immediately.

'He died by a knife, but not the same knife, nor the same hand neither,' Catchpoll sought to quash the idea at the start.

'How can you know?'

'Because it's my job to know, and I have been doing it many a year. The blade was quite different, and there are other signs . . .' He left the end of the sentence hanging, cryptic, since his eye caught Brian de Nouailles emerging from his hall, and introducing doubt into that proud skull would be of use.

'What is this?' De Nouailles was not quite shouting, but making it obvious who was in command, and the statement was superfluous; it was perfectly clear what 'this' was.

'De Nouailles, we have found this man dead by violence, off the road to the north, and he was living at sunrise.' Bradecote wanted any suggestion that he might have been dead some time as little as Catchpoll wanted folk to imagine a single killer. If everyone was a little on edge and questioning, it was all to the good.

'You have a nose for corpses, you sheriff's men.' De Nouailles made it sound as if they were a different species. 'Pity you have not the same nose for murderers.'

'Oh, I think you will find that we do, de Nouailles,' riposted Bradecote, with a slow smile. He was consciously not showing the courtesy of calling de Nouailles 'my lord de Nouailles' any more; no longer would he pretend respect. 'It is just that it is not always such an obvious stench to begin with, not quite as clear.'

Catchpoll's thin lips compressed to avoid breaking into a grin at that, especially seeing the lord of Harvington's eyes snap with anger, but he was a man who would not admit defeat easily.

'But it is clear what is going on. You, for all you prance around as the sheriff's officer, have not been able to protect the people of my manor from thieves and murderers. Aelfric was on his way back home from discharging his task at Beaudesert, and must have been set upon by the same men who murdered Horsweard, even if it was a second who did the deed with the knife.'

So he had heard what Catchpoll said about the knife, thought Bradecote. He noticed Walkelin and the priest enter the bailey. Father Paulinus seemed to sag a little, and crossed himself at the sight of the body, still slung across Walkelin's horse.

'There were two, you think? Why?' Bradecote let that sink in. 'Yours is a simple answer, but not one we think right. You see, we found a cap in a broken-down cottage in the woods rather nearer Harvington.' Bradecote looked to Walkelin, who pulled the cap from his belt and handed it to Leofwine. 'Is that your nephew's?'

'Very like, my lord, in size and colour.' Leofwine turned it over in his hands.

'And a horse was seen,' continued Bradecote, 'a horse that

matches the description of Walter Horsweard's bay, with a big nose and white off-hind. It is odd therefore, that the body was found further away.'

'Not at all. One must have kept Aelfric's horse, which is of course my horse. They killed my loyal servant Aelfric, even taking the cap from his poor head, leaving his body to be devoured by animals, caring not that they kept him from hallowed ground, then went to earth in the cottage for the night.'

'There was blood within the cottage, fresh blood.' Catchpoll added to the things to be explained.

'Then there must have been a falling out of thieves at the place in the woods. One man killed the other, and rode away with Aelfric's chestnut cob, which must have been tethered the other side of the building, and also the horse trader's beast. No doubt he is miles away by now, and there is no justice for a man of Harvington.'

This speech was greeted with murmurs of approval among those in the bailey, who, having stared their fill at the body, now regarded the sheriff's men balefully. Leofwine fanned the flames of their discontent, turning upon Bradecote.

'What the lord says is truth. If you, my lord Undersheriff, had done what you said you came to do, find Horsweard's murderer, my nephew, the last of my blood, would be standing beside me now, would be ready to follow me in service as steward, not a poor, lifeless corpse to be dropped into the earth.'

Hugh Bradecote debated whether now was the time to declare Aelfric as the murderer of Walter Horsweard and almost as certainly the maid Hild. He felt de Nouailles looking at him, sensing his frustration, enjoying his discomfort. It was again Catchpoll who spoke up.

'Sounds a good enough story, my lord, but there is no second corpse, and Aelfric has not been dead long enough to stiffen, so he was not killed yesterday.'

De Nouailles ignored the second part of this.

'The surviving brigand took the body of his former companion in crime and cast it away.'

'Now there's a thing. I have been chasing thieves and murderers for a score years and over, and never have I come across a man who kills, in anger, in a place none are likely to find, and then takes the body with him upon a little jaunt.'

'There is always a first time, and since you found the place, perhaps the murderer did not consider it a place nobody would find. It seems he was right about that.'

The undersheriff came to a decision. After all, it was de Nouailles who had just stressed the colour of Aelfric's horse.

'We were given a description of the man, one man, mark you, who killed Walter Horsweard. This was by a man of Offenham, who saw two men and horses upon the bridge, one man distinctively dressed in green, as Horsweard was, at the right time on the day he left here. That was the same day Aelfric was sent on his travels. The man with Horsweard wore a cap, and rode a chestnut cob. Odd that we find a cap and have signs of Horsweard's beast in the same place, and you yourself said Aelfric generally rode a chestnut cob, which belongs to you.' In truth, some horse droppings and hoof prints were not signs it was the big-nosed bay, but the sighting was as good a proof.

'Are you saying my nephew killed the horse trader?' growled Leofwine. There was, thought Catchpoll, no surprise in the question, more a sense of 'prove it'.

'All evidence points to it.'

'What reason might he have, then? He had seen the man but once or twice here and never spoken with him as far as I know, never mentioned him.'

'Personally? None, I suspect, but then he was a loyal servant, was he not, de Nouailles?' Bradecote stared at the lord of Harvington, challenging him.

'He was. I will not say otherwise, and I may have cursed the man Horsweard for reminding me of my lady wife's death when it was a raw wound, but that was no instruction to kill him, and I cannot think it likely Aelfric mistook the matter.'

De Nouailles subtly introduced the idea that if Aelfric was proved beyond doubt to have done the killing, it was not done at his orders. It was clever, and just what Bradecote had feared he might do from the start.

Walkelin was watching the uncle, and there was just a flicker as lord disassociated himself from man. Beside Walkelin, Father Paulinus gave a soft sigh, and closed his eyes in prayer.

'And he had no reason to kill the girl.' Leofwine's voice this time held the hint of an unspoken 'did he?', a wish that it might be true rather than a certainty. He recalled the questions his lord had put to him, the questions he had not asked himself. He asked them now.

'The wound was, almost certainly, from the same knife, that much we know.' Catchpoll did not waver.

'Speculation based upon hope, no more. It would be tidy for you, no doubt,' de Nouailles sneered.

'The man I saw with your steward, before I was hit, was not you, my lord,' declared Walkelin, daring to put himself up against a lordly man, 'and he rode Horsweard's horse and wore a cap.'

There was a murmur among those in the bailey, and by now everyone had come from their tasks to watch, and to listen.

'And yet this morning you told me it was you who was with Steward Leofwine, de Nouailles. Why did you lie?' Bradecote flung the question at him.

De Nouailles growled, and his hand went automatically to his sword hilt at the open insult. Those gathered in the bailey looked at him, with just the faintest of doubts. Then he smiled, though not pleasantly.

'I heard you pressuring my steward, in whom I have absolute faith. I just wanted you off his back.' He paused, and then added, 'Besides, I really do not like you, Bradecote, and I liked the look of disappointment on your face. I had no more reason to think Aelfric killed the wench than any man here.' He shrugged. 'So, I lied. Is telling you a lie a crime I can be flogged for?'

'It is bearing false witness; it is a sin,' announced Father Paulinus, simply.

'Worse are committed every hour, in every manor in the shire, Father. And show me a man who says he does not lie, and I will show you a liar.' De Nouailles did not look penitent.

Some of the servants looked at their feet. What the priest said was true, and they would not speak against him, but they all knew that what their lord said was realistic.

Catchpoll sucked his teeth, and his face contorted in a manner his superior correctly interpreted as 'we get no further this way'. Bradecote knew both his men were as convinced as he was of de Nouailles' guilt when it came to Aelfric, but everything was thrown back at them. He wondered how he might extricate themselves in any semblance of good order. It was the priest who came to their aid.

'My lord, if you will permit, and Master Steward also, may the body be taken straight away to the church and be laid out there? Whatever sins Aelfric died with upon his soul, it is our duty to pray for him and to see him buried decently.' The priest made sure that de Nouailles thought the remark addressed to him, but cast Bradecote a glance of furtive swiftness. It was de Nouailles' bailey, but the corpse 'belonged' to the law as yet.

'I have no objection. Leofwine?'

Leofwine blinked as though his mind had been elsewhere, and he nodded. Father Paulinus stepped forward, took the reins of Walkelin's horse from Serjeant Catchpoll and led the horse so that he might give them to Leofwine.

'Bring him to church, my son.' The priest spoke calmly, and turned to walk slowly towards the still opened gates. Leofwine followed, and Bradecote, gathering his men swiftly with a glance, simply stepped forward and formed a line of three with them and took station behind, as if in some solemn parade. They left the bailey without a word, with de Nouailles staring after them. They did not look back, but might have been cheered had they known that the lord of Harvington was no longer smiling.

Bradecote and Catchpoll did not go as far as following priest and steward into the church. Walkelin helped Leofwine take the body from his horse and carry it inside, but absented himself thereafter and joined his seniors in the priest's house.

'I wish I could say I felt at least some satisfaction over this, but I can't,' complained Hugh Bradecote. 'Two murders are solved in deed, but we have no solid motive, and we know that the murderer was killed by the man who set him upon the path of killing in the first place, and looks like remaining free. What justice is that?'

'Poor justice, my lord, but it clears our path a little. The murder of the maid we can set aside now, for whatever his reason to kill her, it was Aelfric who took her life, and in order to place Aelfric's death at the hands of his lord we need to prove he set Aelfric to kill Horsweard.'

'What chance Leofwine will give us that? He looked as if unpleasant thoughts were in his head.' Walkelin did not sound as if he thought this more than just a hope.

'Possible, but if he now believes his nephew killed the girl, and it was news to him, he might not be swift to point the finger at his lord.' Bradecote shook his head. 'No, we have to try and do this ourselves, not pray for the steward to lose faith in de Nouailles.'

'But he may question whether his lord killed Aelfric, knowing he was absent this morning, and knew where Aelfric was holed up like a rat.' Walkelin looked a little more cheered by this thought. 'Kin are kin, murderous or not.'

'And a man's loyalty can sometimes be beyond kindred.' Bradecote sighed. 'We go back, and back again. Our problem is firstly that however hard we look at it, de Nouailles really does not seem to have murdered his wife. I mean, we agree that de Nouailles did not push the loved-by-all Edith to her death?'

'Physically, my lord?' queried Catchpoll.

'Yes. We will look at whether his actions upset her and led indirectly to that fall, in a minute.'

'She was not pushed, my lord. All who saw agreed about that.' Walkelin spoke with assurance.

'Good. Then do we think she was dead when he found her or did he take advantage of the fall and kill her thereafter? I say she was, and no.'

'I will agree with that, my lord. I have wondered on it, but I agree.' Catchpoll sniffed. 'Which means de Nouailles had no reason to threaten his erstwhile brother-in-law over it. We have been looking at a crime that never happened.'

'Which means Horsweard must have heard something else, my lord, and that surely was about Thomas the Clerk.' Walkelin had his intent look, which his superiors were learning to read as him having a thread that he would tug at until it pulled clear of any muddle. 'And it is unlikely he heard about him in Evesham, so someone here must have spoken to him about the man.'

'A fair thought, young Walkelin. We sort of set that too far out of the way.' The serjeant nodded his approval. 'It also gives us several possibilities. Perhaps the brother heard of the assault and that there was no theft at all, and that it had overset the lady, the hanging of the clerk. He might therefore blame de Nouailles and threaten to say that what had been done was not legal, and thus murder. The lady died indirectly because of her husband's acts and he could not prove anything in law, but with Thomas the Clerk, there was a killing being covered up. There was a murder, but not the one we thought at first.'

'Of itself it might be enough, Catchpoll. De Nouailles clearly does not like de Beauchamp and may think he covets his lands. Being brought before him would stick in his gullet, and he would not worry about removing Horsweard.' Bradecote sat upon a bench and steepled his fingers. 'But if that was his reason, it would be mighty difficult to prove, even if we found who told him of it.'

'That part, surely, is not hard, my lord.' Walkelin looked surprised.

'Go on.'

'Your lady has a tirewoman, yes?'

'Of course.' Bradecote absent-mindedly poured a beaker of cider, and handed it to Catchpoll.

'Then what happened to the lady de Nouailles' tirewoman? Did she assume other duties in the manor? Is she now just one of the villagers?' Walkelin gasped. 'And I take back what I said about Evesham, my lord. She might have wanted to leave after her lady's death and gone away to Evesham and there met Horsweard, which would be why he returned as he did, despite the previous threats.' The last sentence tumbled out in a rush.

'I must be giving you too much time without tasks, lad. You've been doing a rare amount of thinking.' Catchpoll gave Walkelin a wry smile, and took a draught of sweet cider.

'Finding her would be very useful, so I hope she has not left Harvington,' murmured the undersheriff, providing himself with a beaker, 'but if that is the sum of the reason, I am not sure we can arraign de Nouailles. She might be too afraid to state what she said to Horsweard before the law, and it comes down to hearsay and one word against another. She would not expect her word to be taken over de Nouailles'.'

'I had not finished the possibilities, my lord, and the second is more hopeful for us,' continued Catchpoll. 'If Horsweard heard about the clerk and the murder dressed as lawful process, would he not ask himself why? His kinsman is a monk of Evesham. He might have heard about a dispute—'

'Or the tirewoman told him all about it,' Walkelin interjected, 'once she started the tale. Her being female and liking gossip.'

'There are times as I thank the Almighty for gossip,' agreed Catchpoll, 'though it can as easily be a confusion. Bit like having a subordinate butt in while I am a-making of a case.'

'Sorry, Serjeant.' Walkelin did not look very sorry.

'Anyway, where was I? Ah yes, Horsweard hears about the clerk and the lease and does some of his own thinking and threatens de Nouailles with revealing his thoughts to the Abbot of Evesham. That would be a very good reason to get rid of him quick and quiet. And, what is more, if we can lay hands on that lease, we may be able to prove it false, which gives us something solid against de Nouailles. At the very least he would lose that mill he claims.'

'A small victory, but something, yes. You do not read, Catchpoll, and I have to say that although I do, I am not sure I could tell if a document was "wrong".'

'Begging your pardon, my lord, but I did not think you would be the man for that. Father Paulinus might be, or else we take it to Evesham and let their scriptorium brothers read it.'

'Which is all very well, but first we have to . . . er, obtain the document from wherever de Nouailles keeps it. I cannot see him handing it over to me for inspection.'

'No, my lord, nor do I. We will need to get inside his solar when neither he nor his steward are on hand, which means a plan.'

'And have you got one, Catchpoll?'

'Not as yet, my lord, but you may be assured I am working on it.'

'Will you work the better for another beaker of cider?' Bradecote picked up the jug and proffered it.

'That I might, thank you. Too much addles the wits, but the right amount is like oil on a hinge, makes the workings sweeter.'

'I thought you was going to say less noisy, Serjeant.' Walkelin grinned.

'Do you want any cider?' Catchpoll sounded curmudgeonly, but his eyes twinkled.

There was a pleasant air of camaraderie and almost light-heartedness, and the fermented apples had surprisingly little to do with it. Hugh Bradecote set aside his frustration, and the permutations chasing themselves round in his brain. The sheriff's men had, despite no man in custody, solved two deaths, and knew the culprit in the third, or fourth if one counted the clerk's death as an unlawful killing. They had reached the point where to take matters further they needed fresh minds, and it had been a tiring day.

Father Paulinus, coming from the shrouding of the second corpse in his village in as many days, frowned at the three carefree countenances as he entered, and looked pointedly at the jug.

'I am sorry, Father.' Bradecote's smile faded. 'I know you come from contemplating untimely death. We are not merry for drink, nor are we heedless that what we investigate from without is a tragedy to the families within. It is just,' his smile reappeared, though it was twisted, 'we know what is left to be proven, and after a day of chasing about the countryside, we cannot get to grips with it. Better we cast it and gloom aside for the evening, and start afresh on the morrow. I would ask, however, if you think you could tell if a document was a deceit.'

'And can you tell us who was the lady de Nouailles' tirewoman?' Walkelin's tenacious mind still held that as a key fact.

Father Paulinus blinked, and addressed the first question.

'I have never looked at any document distrustingly.'

'Leases can be forged, Father. You know that as well as I do. Over the years, even the Church has "found" some that do not bear study. Answer me true, would your former monk be able to forge a document? Had he the skill?' Bradecote knew the answer, he was sure of it.

'He had worked in the scriptorium, had a good hand, which is why he sold his services as a clerk thereafter, and would have seen old leases. But surely he would not have—'

'A man living hand to mouth, paid for every letter, wandering the shire for work, would be a man less scrupulous.'

'But it is wrong.' The priest's own innocence vibrated in each word.

'Men sin in many ways. And if he did try to molest the lady de Nouailles, he was not above some pretty big sins.' Catchpoll was angling for more details.

'You know, I doubt that he did.' Bradecote was thinking hard, and did not see Catchpoll look aggrieved. 'Doing so, with the wife of a lord, the wife of a man who clearly has a bad temper, it would be reckless in the extreme. If he wanted a wench, there would be easier, and willing no doubt. We saw how de Nouailles was ready to use his rights over theft caught in the act to remove Walkelin, whom he knew to be innocent. I say he has used this ploy before. He employs a clerk to forge his lease, and only he and the clerk know it is forged. The clerk is therefore a risk. He might reveal it when drunk, or might even be rash enough to think of blackmail. No, the safe way is to remove the clerk, and that means murder and stealth, or making it look legal.'

'Murder by stealth would be easy enough, though, my lord.' Catchpoll rubbed his nose. 'An itinerant clerk would have no kin to note his absence if he disappeared sudden like.'

'Yes, but de Nouailles likes to remind people how harsh he is, likes to have people fear his wrath. This way he does that.' Bradecote really did not like the man.

'True enough.'

'Father Paulinus, is there anything you can tell us about how the lady de Nouailles was before she died, that is not completely covered by the sanctity of confession? Lives depend upon it.' Bradecote looked gravely at the priest, whose expression had become distressed.

'I . . . She was troubled.'

'You told us that much, for you said her brother knew she was troubled and her husband the source.' Walkelin reminded him.

'And that she feared God might judge her lord harshly,' added Bradecote. 'If she knew that there had been no assault . . .'

'But I do not understand. I am sure there was. I can tell you she said she wished she had not been burdened with a form that brought men to sin, and how else could that be read?'

'The clerk need only have looked at her lustfully to bring that thought to a pious lady, and could she not have meant that his jealousy about any man looking at her had led her husband to sin and have the man killed?' Catchpoll pressed home the argument, and before the three of them the priest wavered.

'It is possible, and that would—' He stopped, and shook his head. 'I can say no more.'

'Could you tell if a document was forged,' Bradecote repeated his earlier question, 'or if it had been altered in any way?'

'A good forgery would be hard to detect, I am sure. Vellum is expensive, and so there are ways to erase mistakes, of course, made when writing.'

'Ways Thomas would know.' Walkelin spoke almost to himself.

'Yes. But he must have known that the abbey might wish to study the lease, see how it matched their own, so he would have made it as good as possible.'

'If we found it, could you tell if it was altered or forged?'

'I cannot say that I could, my lord. I was not gifted in writing, not a precise enough hand, and did not work in the scriptorium.' The priest gave a small smile. 'God called me to a flock, not a goose feather.'

'What about if we took it to Evesham itself?' Bradecote did not want to give up.

'That is more likely, but then if they denounced it, Brian de Nouailles would say either that they had forged it to discredit him, or were telling a falsehood.'

'But if it was their forgery he need only present the original, and they could go to the lord Sheriff, who employs a scribe, to confirm they were telling true. Our problem lies in getting hold of the document itself from the hall.' Bradecote sighed.

'I do not know how you will manage to get it from the manor, my lord, but what if you were to ask Abbot Reginald to come here and demand to see it in person? It would be very difficult for the lord de Nouailles to refuse the Abbot of Evesham on his doorstep.'

'Father Paulinus, that is inspired.'

'Then the thought is from the Almighty. I am but a simple man, my lord.'

'I will enjoy seeing the look on de Nouailles' face when we prove his fraud, but before we rush to that pleasure, can we avoid him slithering from the noose yet again? He will make no admission of guilt to make things easy for us.'

'He has wriggled free thus far, my lord,' offered Walkelin, 'but each time it was more difficult. This afternoon, in his own bailey, I saw doubt on the faces of his people, aye, even on the face of Leofwine, his most loyal man.' Walkelin felt deep down that justice simply had to win.

'Let us see. We prove the lease a forgery, and with the added evidence that it was a scribe trained in Evesham, it puts beyond all reasonable doubt that Thomas the Clerk was the man who made it for him. That loses de Nouailles the mill. If we speak with the tirewoman, and if – an important "if" – she says that she knows the clerk was hanged without just cause from the words of the lady de Nouailles, and if she told Horsweard of it, we have a case good enough to take before the sheriff and then the Justices. It would be reasonable that he had his man Aelfric do the killing. If he denies it, there is still a chance he avoids a hanging for that. As I see it, our problem then becomes we have no proof it was him that killed Aelfric bar our common sense, and circumstance.' Bradecote was looking at possibilities.

'Yes, and just who was the tirewoman?' Walkelin was now nearly shouting this vital question that kept being overlooked.

'Why, Agatha, the mother of Hild.' Father Paulinus said it as if it must be known the length and breadth of the shire.

There was silence as this sank in. They had been absent from Hild's interment, and had not, it must be said, considered her kinfolk in their questions. The connection made their theory the stronger.

'Well, there you are, my lord. We may only have sense and circumstance, but to my mind we have damning levels of both, surely?' Catchpoll's face contorted in a slow grimace. 'The man was killed this morning. The evidence of the corpse itself, plus the child hearing the scream and his cap in the shack, makes any other reading mere fancy, and the Justices are not fools, well, not often. De Nouailles was from home at that time, and only he and Leofwine knew where Aelfric was hiding. Only he had a motive for silencing him, and the convoluted tale he told of how it must have been the mythical brigands, that did not even convince peasants. We also have a reason why Aelfric might have had cause to silence the maid Hild, if mother spoke to daughter, as is likely. It is even possible that Aelfric, hearing the tale of Thomas the Clerk, might have thought to make his own position more secure by letting de Nouailles know that he knew the full story of why he had been sent to kill Horsweard, and the more fool him if he did. No, in the face of all that, the lord Sheriff would not see any arraignment as foolish, and since they do not like each other, will probably be happy that de Nouailles lingers in chains for a while, even if the case cannot in the end give a hanging. I even think there is a chance he will confess out of anger rather than guilt.'

Father Paulinus looked once again sorrowful, and Hugh Bradecote tried to lessen his misery by repeating what the Abbot of Evesham had said to him about the judgement of the law, and of heaven.

The sheriff's men stood themselves down for the evening with new hope, but the priest returned to his church, heavy of heart, to pray for the dead and, he feared, the doomed.

Chapter Sixteen

Brian de Nouailles sat in his hall, a cup of wine in his hand, and a flagon at his elbow. His expression was grim, but also haunted. The only explanation he could come up with for Aelfric murdering a girl he had known since childhood, if it was not her refusing his advances, was that she knew something, something which connected him to the killing of Walter Horsweard. Oh, how he wished the pestilence had come upon Evesham and the family of Horsweard had ceased to exist, once Edith was his. All they had caused was trouble, making her wistful, and thrusting their noses where they had no right. He had been glad when the hag of a mother had died, but the brothers, the cripple and the blusterer, had stuck to him like goose-grass.

If all the wench had seen was Aelfric and the horse trader no harm was done, for neither would leave the churchyard to tell de Beauchamp's law-hounds any of it. He had no qualms about killing Aelfric, for it was the man's own fault for returning without permission, and besides, he had killed the girl. The thought niggled, however, that what the girl knew lay deeper in the tale, for Hild's mother had been Edith's tirewoman, and women talked together, especially with Edith not so used to keeping her distance, and often deprived of female company. That he had kept her in semi-isolation had been to protect her from the sharp tongues of the more aristocratic dames who would have looked down their noses at her, and spoken barbed words that would have hurt her. He did not care if he withdrew from his neighbours; most he cordially disliked anyway, and for love of his wife he would have eschewed all mortal company for the rest of his days.

The haunted look grew more pronounced. He would have given every drop of his blood for her, and yet he had not been able to save her. Even his last words to her had been harsh, trying to argue her from her misery, which had come over her like a November fog after that snivelling clerk had dangled from a rope. The toad had tried first to blackmail him, and then made a lewd suggestion to his virtuous wife, and mere dangling was too good for him. From choice he would have strung him up by other than his neck, but to keep it lawful-looking, that is how it had had to be. How could he have guessed Edith would be so overset by it all?

He emptied the flagon. The sound of her cry as she fell, the ripping of the sleeve as he caught at it, flooded bright and sharp in his mind, and the memory of her limp in his arms, the eyes that had bewitched him, staring and unseeing, twisted in him like a knife. He groaned, picked up the flagon, and threw it with force to smash near the hearth. He cried out, an anguished animal cry, howling her name into the emptiness of his hall.

For a while his mind was empty, an aching void, and then he picked up the threads of thought. The only real threat to him was if the truth about the mill lease came to light. He would deny any deaths, but that would cost him the mill, which was not only lucrative, but the starting point for all his woes, and he would be damned if he would let some peasant's bleating see it given back to the grasping Benedictines.

He would speak with Agatha. That he should see her following the murder of her daughter was not beyond belief, since they had been household servants. If there was any suspicion that she knew too much, then he would make the necessary arrangements. He called, without thinking, for Leofwine, but the steward was still in the church. An underling entered, nervously, from the buttery.

'My lord?'

'Where is Leofwine?'

'He has not come back from Father Paulinus yet, my lord.'

'Fa—Ah yes. Fetch me the woman Agatha. I would speak with her?'

'Now, my lord?'

'Of course now. Why else would I order it?'

'Yes, my lord, at once.'

Brian de Nouailles was not sober, but he did not care. He was sober enough to out-think peasants, and that was all he needed to do. And when he had finished out-thinking this peasant he would drink until his beloved, beautiful ghost left his head, and he had oblivion.

* * *

The servant sent to fetch Agatha found a woman in turmoil. The loss of her daughter was now made the worse by the thought that her killer had grown up with her, was one of the village own. She had not been in the manor when Aelfric's body had been brought in, but had emerged from her seclusion in her cott as he had been carried to the church, and a neighbour had told her the tale. She recoiled from it at first, another death, another life snuffed out young, and with her daughter laid in the earth but that afternoon. Now another corpse would lie where her Hild had lain last night, and to think it was her murderer was beyond contemplating. She jumped at the insistent knock, and opened the door with a trembling hand. If she was relieved to see only Ansculf, his words made her pale once more.

'Now?'

'He is in no mood to be refused, if ever he has been. Best come and come quick. Sorry I am to disturb you, though.' Ansculf looked shamefaced.

'No fault of yours, friend.' She reached out a hand and patted his, and took a deep breath. 'Best to get it done, then.'

They arrived suitably short of breath to show that the lord de Nouailles' command had been obeyed with speed, and just before Leofwine made his way back to the manor, head hung low, and in deep thought. De Nouailles looked up from gazing into the dregs of his wine, and grunted, then pulled himself up from the half-slumped position in which he had been sat.

'You, get out,' he spat at Ansculf, who began to withdraw in haste, but then demanded that he bring more wine. Turning his attention to Agatha, he sniffed. 'Your daughter's death, it was a waste.'

She nodded, not knowing whether this was his idea of commiseration or, in some strange way, a complaint that it had happened.

'It was not my fault,' he grumbled, and Agatha said nothing at all, for why should she think otherwise. 'You will miss her.'

'Yes, my l—'

'Sometimes the dead are so real again you could almost touch them, and yet you know that if you do they will be as the air, and the dream of them gone.' He was not talking to her, but to himself.

The peasant woman knew what a man looked like when maudlin with drink, and Brian de Nouailles was a fair way there. She also realised he was not thinking of her daughter at all, but the sweet soul whom she had served. She kept a respectful silence, and wondered why she had been brought to him. Perhaps he wanted to talk about his lady to one who knew her. When he spoke again, she almost gasped.

'If Aelfric did not want her for her body, why might he have had cause to kill her?'

It took a fraction of a moment to realise he was now back to thinking of Hild.

'My lord?'

'You heard me, woman. You are not deaf. Indeed, I wonder if your ears have been too keen.' There was an edge of threat in the tone, but he did not say more.

'I . . . My Hild was a good girl, my lord. She did not give in to sweet words from lustful youths.'

'I care not about her virtuousness-ness,' he slurred his speech, but the eyes were alert, like a hawk upon a sparrow.

234

'I want to know why Aelfric put a knife in her back.'

At this Agatha stifled a sob, and put her hand to her mouth. He watched, unmoved, and even began to drum his fingers upon his table. It was never a good sign, and Agatha knew it of old. How many times had her poor lady been cast into panic when he had been displeased and started to drum with his fingers. She watched, mesmerised, and fought down the tears. Ansculf returned with more wine, cast her a look of sympathy, and retired without receiving any acknowledgement.

'Is it so certain it was him, my lord?'

'The sheriff's hounds seem to think so, and . . . reluctantly I agree with them. It seems that my hot words about Horsweard had him leaping off to cast him dead into the Avon. Why he got that in his head we will never know. However, I was wondering if your girl, or perhaps you, were washing by the river that day, and saw something. If she knew and . . . teased Aelfric with that knowledge, that might have given him cause enough for a killing.'

Agatha blinked. So Aelfric had killed twice? She crossed herself.

'I am not even sure which day it is you mean, my lord, but I can say for sure I never saw nobody harmed near the river, and my Hild never said aught to me of witnessing anything, and she would have told me. We had no secrets between us.'

She thought he would be pleased with the answer, but had to repress a shudder as he looked at her with gimlet eyes.

'No secrets. Of course.' There was silence for a minute or so. She dared not speak, and the lord kept on staring at her as if he could see into her thoughts. 'Did you see Horsweard the last time he came here to rant at me?'

235

'I . . . He wished me good morrow as he passed upon his horse, my lord. He knew me because I had been my la—He had seen me before.'

'And as he departed?'

'Ah, then my lord, I but raised a hand and did not speak to him.'

'So, you spoke when he arrived?'

'Just a few words, my lord.' Agatha was a very poor liar. Even wine-sodden, Brian de Nouailles could see the pitiful attempt at concealment, but for her part she clung to the hope that he was deceived. This grew as he poured himself another cup of wine, and did not even look at her.

'You may go.' The dismissal was sudden.

Agatha bobbed an obeisance and hurried from his presence. She was a worried woman, and would have been even more so had she seen the sneering smile spread across de Nouailles' face.

Nobody was surprised that Leofwine was monosyllabic at the evening meal. The cook, shaking her head over what had been revealed even as she stirred the pottage, remarked as how Aelfric had been treated like the son he never saw reach an age even to walk.

'Not that Aelfric deserved such regard. Right cruel he was, at times, about his uncle, and him that good to him. You mark my words, he did them bad things thinking to get advancement from the lord, and supplant Leofwine before he was much older. Wickedness and waste, that is all as has come of it.'

The girl who had replaced Hild as her aide made suitable 'agreeing' noises.

So Leofwine sat at the head of the rough table with the household, and looked into his bowl as if it might give comfort for the soul rather than just the stomach. He was not known as a cheerful man, but this evening everyone followed his lead and spoke in hushed tones and only out of necessity. He took bread with barely a murmur, refused a second helping with a shake of the head, and when he had drained his beaker of ale, wiped a hand across his mouth and left in silence. As he closed the door behind him, he heard the murmur of voices begin. They would be talking about Aelfric, about him. Let them talk.

He stalked to his chamber above the gatehouse, where the barest needs of his existence made the room little more than a monk's cell. There was a narrow bed, a stool, a small chest in which he kept a change of raiment from mouse and moth, a rush light and a soil bucket. In the absence now of a lady of the manor, the keys to the stores hung upon a hook. He sat upon the hard bed and slumped forward, his head in his hands. He was subject to grief, and a growing sense that he was adrift in a situation he did not comprehend.

Until his lord had raised the issue, he had not considered why it was that Aelfric had come to him when he had found the body of Hild. He had assumed it was because he had been shocked and come to the man he trusted most for guidance, his father figure. Whatever he thought about Walter Horsweard, and it was not much, he was not particularly horrified if Aelfric, in the impetuosity of youth, had charged off to implement his lord's wish that the man never darken his door again. If the horse trader was such a benighted fool that he did not heed the warnings of a man as irascible and aggressive as Brian de

Nouailles, then the more fool him. He had been warned clearly enough, and if his lord had called Leofwine in and told him to do away with the unwelcome reminder of his beloved wife's origins, Leofwine would have done the deed, and hoped it gave his lord ease, even if he got no thanks for it.

Leofwine the Steward was a similar age to his lord, had grown up alongside him, if a few paces behind. In his father's tenure of the stewardship he had railed as the youthful lordling had done against the 'inactivity' of the older generation, and used him as a model for a time, until marriage softened him and took his focus, right the way up until the day he buried wife and child, and with them he vowed to bury his heart. He looked to Brian de Nouailles again, cold, aloof, masterful, and itching to succeed to land and title, and whilst master would never stoop so low as to show friendship to one of peasant birth, yet there had been forged an understanding. As soon as he took seisin of the manor, Brian de Nouailles had placed Leofwine in his father's position, using his steward as his conduit, relying upon him to implement his wishes and impose his harsh rule over his peasantry. They had learnt fast enough that the new steward would never stand up for his neighbours against the lord, but was not otherwise unfair, just unsmiling and unsympathetic. Having no choice, they learnt to live with it.

When Brian de Nouailles had wed, not just for an heir, but besotted by a beautiful face, Leofwine had been disappointed, even vaguely jealous, but the lady had charmed him as she had her lord, and seeing the depth and rawness of loss at her death, Leofwine understood, remembered, and would do almost anything to ease it. If that had included killing Horsweard himself, for the crime of rubbing salt into the unbearable wound, he would have done so, just as he had been happy enough to accuse the interfering sheriff's man, just to please de Nouailles. He had not thought it likely any sentence would have been carried out, but if it had, then so be it.

That was a very different thing to murdering Hild, daughter of widow Agatha, with whom Leofwine had worked more closely in the years of her service to the lady de Nouailles. Never by so much as a look had the woman shown less than total respect for the lady, never mentioned her origins. Leofwine understood loyalty. If Aelfric had killed the girl, then it was fitting that their lord had dealt out justice, and in his own way, though it pained the steward that it should be needful for him to do so, for Aelfric was – had been – his hope for the future. The lord of Harvington had never believed in the King's Justice, only de Nouailles' Justice.

But . . . There was a 'but' worming itself, unbidden and unwelcome, into Leofwine the Steward's mind. Since his lord knew of his loyalty, why had he not spoken to him, knowing he would be grieved at the necessity, when he had gone to deal his justice? Why had he made up so complicated a tale about brigands and caps and horses? He need only have said that he had confronted Aelfric with his guilt already, guilt the undersheriff already suspected, and dealt with him as the law would have done, but to show his own people there was justice, not some distant code. Surely he would not have feared repercussions from merely acting precipitately? But he had gone out of his way to distance himself from anything to do with Aelfric.

The 'but' grew, and like the maggot in the apple, changed, so that it became a 'what if', and that what if made Leofwine go cold. What if his lord had simply decided that Aelfric was a liability, and had no idea whether he had killed Hild, but did not want him found by the sheriff's men? It would have been easy enough to meet him, send him away not just to one of his manors, but perhaps to lie low in a town like Coventry or Warwick. He did not need to kill him, unless there was something more, something he had never trusted his steward to know. That lack of faith, of trust, was a betrayal after so many years. Was that why he had not given him the task of removing Horsweard? Had he actively ordered that killing, after all? And if not just an angry outburst, why?

There were too many questions, and no good answers. Leofwine lay upon his bed, eyes open, and his mind in the dark.

It was a trembling Agatha who headed not for her own hearth, but for the church, and there she flung herself upon the cold stone of the chancel step, despite the clear sight of the shrouded form that had been Aelfric. She prayed devoutly for forgiveness and for aid. Her tears fell in sorrow, in guilt and in fear, and she did not hear the soft footfalls of the priest as he entered his church to pray once more for the soul of one he feared was in great need of prayers. He was not surprised at Agatha's weeping, but her penitential position made him frown and step forward to lift her to her feet. She cried out in alarm at his touch upon her shoulder.

'Agatha, it is only me. What cause have you to prostrate yourself in this way?' His voice was very gentle. He suddenly thought of her seeing the shrouded body on the bier. 'If you have uncharitable thoughts over Aelfric, God will understand, even as He wants you to be forgiving. With your loss so very fresh—'

He did not finish the sentence. The woman took his arm in a vice-like grip, and raised a face that was all desolation. It shocked him.

'You do not understand, Father, you cannot even guess. It is my fault my girl is dead, my fault all three are dead. God Almighty has shown me I will pay for the sin, but if I die unshriven, what hope have I of ever gaining absolution and escaping the Fires of Damnation?'

The priest blinked in consternation.

'These are but the wild imaginings of grief. You are overwrought. Let us sit quietly, and—'

'Let us sit, yes, Father, but oh, you must hear my confession, lest I die in such sin.'

'You did not kill the poor souls who have passed from this life, Agatha. It is known how they died and by whose hands.' He caught himself up upon the last point, since only the sheriff's men had knowledge of who killed Aelfric. 'At least the last might be guessed and it was certainly not yours.'

'There is blood upon my hands and my soul.' Agatha was becoming even more hysterical.

Father Paulinus was tempted to find Nesta or another sensible village woman to aid her, but neither wished to leave her alone in such a state, nor have another present since she wished to ease her mind by confession, though it was but the confession of a nightmare. He took her hands.

'Softly now. I will hear your confession, my daughter, but do not confess to things you cannot have done.'

'And if I am cast into the Pit, if the Agent of Satan kills me, you must say, you must reveal it to all.'

'Yes, yes, but your sins are—'

'I have killed them with my tongue, like the Serpent.'

Father Paulinus now thought her raving.

'Agatha, Agatha, please, you—'

'I know I did not wield the knife, but if I had but kept my tongue stilled, and not spoken, none of this would have happened.'

The priest had been about to speak, but halted.

'If you need to speak to the lord Undersheriff, I will come with you.'

'No, for if I say . . . It will end me. I must make confession, Father. Please, hear it now and give me my penance.'

Reluctantly, Father Paulinus nodded his acceptance.

It was a troubled priest who returned to his home, though the sheriff's men assumed his silence and demeanour were due to the likelihood of seeing another of his flock meet a bad end. His only consolation was that he had not only given penance, but a piece of advice, advice he hoped Agatha would follow.

Chapter Seventeen

Brian de Nouailles woke unrested, his head throbbing, his mouth foul, and his stomach rebelling. It was not therefore a lord in even the slightest of good humours who rose late, and pondered long whether to yell for a servant and risk his head exploding, or leave his solar very gingerly and seek someone in the buttery for himself. He opted for the latter, and growled in so low and sinister a fashion as he entered, that the maid filling a bowl for the cook dropped bowl and contents and screamed. The sound tore through his skull like an axe blade, and his growl became a roar of pain. He lashed out at the hapless girl, striking her about the ear, and her wails added to his misery. A lad carrying an armful of rushes up the hall steps promptly turned about and withdrew, but wisely thought to go and find Leofwine the Steward, who might face his lord with less likelihood of violence.

Leofwine was not hungover, but he was even more morose than normal. He had cause, thought the lad, and went to warn his fellows that if they valued their skins they would keep out of the hall as long as possible during the morning.

The steward entered the hall with a calm deliberation. De Nouailles demanded respect, but despised cringing. The servant girl was snivelling in the buttery, and the lord was sat in his chair in the hall, a heavy cloak about him, his arms folded upon the table and his head bowed to rest upon them. Leofwine drew close enough that he need not raise his voice.

'You have need of me, my lord.' It was more an assertion of fact than a question.

Brian de Nouailles groaned, and lifted his face. He did not look good.

'Yes,' he grumbled, as if it was reluctantly that he admitted it. 'I do. First, keep anything shrill and female from this hall until after noon.'

'Of course, my lord.'

'Then I have a problem I wish you to deal with for me.'

'As you command, my lord.'

'Agatha.'

'Agatha?'

'Yes. There is only one in Harvington, when last I knew.'

'Mother of Hild.'

'Yes. Do I have to repeat myself?'

'No, my lord. What is the problem with Agatha?'

'Her existence.'

There was a short silence, which in normal circumstances de Nouailles would have found annoying, but this morning he actually welcomed. Leofwine the Steward felt a chill within him, and when he did speak it was very deliberate.

'You wish me to . . . dispose of Agatha.'

'Yes. Was I not clear?'

'Upon such a matter, my lord, I felt I ought to check.' There was nothing in his voice to suggest that inside he was recoiling.

'Good. Well, I trust you to deal with it. Only you, faithful Leofwine, of all my servants, can be trusted to do as you are told. The others . . . they whine, or they pretend not to understand, or they try and think for themselves like Aelfric, and look what that led to.' The lord of Harvington sounded as if he were beneficent but ill-served.

Just for an instant, Leofwine felt the old pride. His lord trusted him and no other when it came to anything important.

'How would you suggest I deal with her?'

'I don't care how you do it, but make sure it is out of the way so that those bastards of de Beauchamp's do not smell blood and set up their howling. I want rid of them from my manor. And while I think of it, upon your return, go to the priest and tell him, if he values his roof above his head, he will cast the sheriff's men from under it before sunset.'

'My lord. Might I just ask why Agatha's existence is a problem?'

'You may ask, but you have no reason to know the answer. Suffice to say that her tongue has cost lives and I would not have her cost this manor any more. Now see it done, and tell the cook I will have meat and ale at mid morning.'

'Yes, my lord.' Leofwine, his face impassive, withdrew from de Nouailles' presence, and fulfilled the last command straight away. He then went to his chamber, and clasped his dagger belt about his waist, but before departing knelt upon the floor and prayed. His orisons complete, he set off to the home of the Widow Agatha, close by the junction of trackways in the middle of the village. He looked to left and right, to see if anyone was about and likely to see him, and then opened the door, speaking her name.

It was not only inside the manor that the night had not passed well. Within the priest's house Father Paulinus rose to his early prayers heavy-eyed and heavy-hearted. If the priest looked as if he had slept badly, then by contrast, however, the sheriff's men looked rejuvenated. Bradecote eyed the priest with some concern, but hoped that the day's events would cheer him, since there was every reason to think that Evesham Abbey would see its mill returned to it. He also hoped beyond hope that the day would see Brian de Nouailles not only taken into custody for the fraud but facing a capital charge. That would not give the poor man ease, but there was nothing to be done about it.

As soon as they had broken their fast, Bradecote sent Walkelin to Abbot Reginald, with an instruction that short of him being on his deathbed, Walkelin was to get him to Harvington well before noon. In the meantime, he and Serjeant Catchpoll would go through every permutation of events they could think of that de Nouailles might use to escape justice, and ensure every way was closed, and speak with the erstwhile tirewoman.

Even as Walkelin rode off at speed, and on Catchpoll's horse, which was better than his own, undersheriff and serjeant trod, in a more leisurely fashion, to the dwelling that was pointed out to them as that of Agatha, mother of the late Hild. They knocked upon her door, but there was no answer.

'Must be out early in the fields, I suppose,' muttered Catchpoll.

'Yes, but . . . We check within, Catchpoll. In our delight at finding a connection between Hild and Agatha, we did not consider one worrying thought. What if Hild revealed to Aelfric that her source of information was her mother, or he guessed, and passed on that information to de Nouailles, by choice or under threat?'

Catchpoll's answer was to fling the door wide open, and step smartly within. The room was as bare as any peasant's abode, but with the marks of a housewife about it that a dwelling of men only would lack.

'Well, she is not here, and if she left, it was willingly, for there is no sign of any struggle. Yet if she had not been here for the burying of her daughter, the good Father would have mentioned it, surely? If she was away, then she would have been called home, and in this cool weather there would be no harm in delaying the covering of a corpse.'

'So she left after the funeral rites yesterday, or this morning. One wonders why?' Bradecote frowned. 'Possibly, remaining was too hard upon her with the death fresh, but then her friends and neighbours would be about her to give comfort. So perhaps she herself has realised she is in danger.'

'Which means we are looking and not knowing where to start.'

'Come on, Catchpoll, we do. If she was at the funeral, which person of all men would she entrust such knowledge to?'

'Her priest!'

'Exactly. Let us return to the good Father Paulinus.'

The priest, when asked about Agatha, coloured.

'Ah.' His expression was slightly guilty.

247

'Father?' Bradecote tried to imagine why.

'She came to me yesterday evening, for confession.'

'And?'

'I took it.'

'And?'

'Then I suggested to her that it would be a good thing if she went away for a little while. She has a sister in Lench.'

'Was this simply because of her grief, Father?' Bradecote was watching him closely.

'In part, for she was much inclined to bring down all blame for the misfortune on herself, and that was mistaken. However, I cannot deny that what she told me made me think, and my thoughts were that staying here might put her in the path of danger, and incline another to sin.'

'You mean, Father, you thought de Nouailles would want to kill her.' Catchpoll was not going to step gently about this.

'The thought occurred to me. After what you had said, if it is true, then . . . Yes.'

'But you cannot tell us what she revealed,' continued Catchpoll, weary of the rules that governed priests.

'I am sorry. I asked her to come to you, but she would have it as confession. Though she did say that if evil should take her, then I was to tell you everything.'

'Small comfort, that, since it would mean another death.'

'Where else would we find her?'

'That I do not know, my lord, if she is not with the sister. She had a kinswoman in Fladbury, but she died two years back, and there's a nephew of her husband's in Cleeve, and another in Evesham.'

'Which gives us more places to hunt than hunters.'

'Let me ask her friends. They may know which is the most likely. If she had fallen out with one or other it means you can both visit the other two and be sure of her.'

'Thank you, Father. We are hoping that Abbot Reginald will be here before noon, so it would assist us if we were not running about the manor when he arrives. Walkelin alone cannot deal with de Nouailles on the lease.'

Fired by the urgency of his mission, Walkelin was soon clattering through the northern gate of Evesham as if the hounds of hell were on his heels, and with Catchpoll's horse sweated up. The flow of people and animals in the street curtailed his pace to a trot, but he soon reached the abbey gate, and rang insistently for Brother Porter, into whose care he gave the horse, and from whom he discovered that Abbot Reginald had been seen entering his lodging only a few minutes previously after Chapter. Walkelin did not think running within the enclave looked seemly, but he walked fast, and only halted at the oaken door to the abbot's lodgings. He paused then. He, as a mere man-at-arms, and latterly serjeant's apprentice, had not spoken with many important people, and the Abbot of Evesham was certainly an important man in the shire. He had got used to the lord Bradecote, of course, and was now able to face being addressed by, and speaking to, the lord Sheriff, without his knees knocking, but this was different. He told himself he was upon the lord Undersheriff's business, and that gave him the right to knock firmly upon the door and request speech with Abbot Reginald in a manner which was not supplicating, but assertive whilst still respectful. He had heard that in the lord Bradecote's voice. He was given admittance, and ushered in to where Abbot Reginald sat with a document before him. Walkelin made his obeisance, but began to speak even as he straightened.

'My lord Abbot, I have a request from the lord Bradecote, and it is urgent.'

'I see from your demeanour this is so, my son.' Abbot Reginald heard the mixture of excitement, nervousness and tinge of pride in Walkelin's voice, and hid a smile; the enthusiasm of the young was a magical thing. 'Yet unless you intend to run from me within moments, might I ask you to be seated. It is more restful.' He indicated a short bench with his hand.

Walkelin was not used to sitting in the presence of his betters, and blushed. He half-lowered himself, hovered, and finally sat, rather gingerly, upon the edge of the bench so as not to be too comfortable.

'The lord of Harvington says he has a lease from this abbey that gives him tenure of the mill across from Offenham for a hundred years, my lord.'

'He does, but it cannot be so.'

'The lord Undersheriff is in no doubt about it, and believes he knows who falsified the writing. However, getting the lease from the lord de Nouailles might be . . .'

'Nigh on impossible?' The cleric did not laugh at Walkelin trying to be diplomatic.

'Yes, my lord, and so the lord Bradecote asks that you yourself come to Harvington with all haste and demand to see it, since it would be hard to refuse you admittance, however little the lord of Harvington likes it, then you can tell if it has been altered, or is new or . . . whatever makes it not true.' His rushed words, almost falling over each other, were in sharp contrast to the abbot's measured tones.

'I am glad he trusts in our veracity.'

Walkelin did not know what veracity was, but he nodded anyway.

'It is most urgent, my lord Abbot.'

'Yes, so you have said. Forgive me, but why is that so? If the document is at risk, why, its loss would scarce be a problem.'

'Ah no, it is not to prove your ownership of the mill alone. We—I mean my lord Bradecote, believes it may prove vital in the case against Brian de Nouailles.'

'Against . . .' The abbot frowned, and Walkelin wondered if he was wrong to have revealed this fact. 'It is thought that he killed Walter Horsweard?'

'Not by his own hand, but this may show why he directed the deed to be done, my lord.'

'Ah, I see. Then we must see to it that justice is done both over life and land.' He rang a small bell, and a desiccated-looking brother entered, and was sent to bring Brother Albanus from the scriptorium.

Brother Albanus had a slight stoop, ink so deep ingrained into his fingers that it was stained into the flesh permanently, and etched creases at the corners of his eyes from squinting over his work.

'You called for me, Father. I am here.'

'We have need of your knowledge, Brother Albanus. There is a document at Harvington, and we would have it looked at by one expert in such things. You are relieved of duties in the scriptorium, Brother, and must accompany me as soon as we may to Harvington.'

'Immediately, Father?' The monk looked most surprised.

'Yes. At the best pace we may make. You will go and inform Brother Columbanus that you will be absent until, perhaps, Vespers. Meet us at the stable.'

Thus dismissed, Brother Albanus hurried away. Abbot Reginald requested his cloak to be brought, and in a noticeably more sedate manner. Walkelin controlled the urge to shout at the churchman to make haste.

The abbot, Walkelin was glad to see, did not ride a mule but a horse that seemed alert. Brother Albanus, however, did not actually ride at all. He clambered onto a mule with every sign that only divine intervention would see him survive the few miles to Harvington. Any hopes that Walkelin had of returning at the pace at which he had arrived were dashed. Even at a sluggish trot, the poor scribe bounced in a most precarious fashion, his fingers trying to simultaneously wind into the beast's mane and link together in prayer for safe deliverance. Walkelin prayed also, but his prayers were that he would not be blamed for their tardy arrival.

The sun was not at its zenith, however, when they reached Harvington, and he bade the monks wait whilst he collected his superiors from the priest's house. Father Paulinus was not yet returned from his mission, and they were alone.

Hugh Bradecote was secure enough in his status that he did not feel that it demanded that he enter the manor mounted beside the Abbot of Evesham. He was content to walk beside Abbot Reginald's horse, and his carefully chosen words showed that he did not want to prejudice the assessment of the document that was to be inspected.

'It is hard to see how you could be forbidden to see a lease made by your own brothers, but that does not mean you can expect to receive a joyous welcome, Father.'

'I am not going to quake at loud words, nor blanch at foul epithets, my lord Bradecote. We will do what must be done, and calmly.' His eyes conveyed the message that he understood that the judgement of the vellum must be upon its own merits, or lack of them.

At the manor gates, the gatekeeper, overawed by the arrival of an obviously senior cleric, made no demur at their entrance. Bradecote expected to be met by the steward, but he was not forthcoming, so as soon as the Evesham party had dismounted, he led them across the bailey, and up the steps into Brian de Nouailles' hall.

Brian de Nouailles had eaten. It did not make him feel much the better. He slouched over his table and gave in to the desire that he might shut his eyes and thereby shut out the world. The swift tread of his steward made him raise himself, reluctantly.

'That was quickly done.'

'My lord, Agatha has gone.'

'Gone? Where?'

'I do not yet know, my lord, but William, Wulnoth's lad, said she left early, just after sunrise, for he saw her leave the church and Father Paulinus watched her go.'

'Did he? Interfering priest.' For a moment de Nouailles stared into space, then frowned at Leofwine. 'Why are you still here?'

'My lord?'

'You are meant to be finding Agatha. Go on. She cannot have gone far.'

Leofwine had been gone only a few minutes when de Nouailles was disturbed again.

'What this time?' he growled, and then scowled, for the footsteps were more than simply those of one man.

Hugh Bradecote flung open the door as though by right, and was followed by his minions, and two Benedictines, one a timorous-looking individual who hung back, and the other a recognised figure, whom de Nouailles would not have invited in under any circumstances.

The arrival of the loathed Abbot of Evesham and the sheriff's trio was the final straw.

He let out a groan through gritted teeth.

'Is there no peace to be had from interfering officials and conniving clerics? Go away and . . .' He wanted to suggest something offensive but humanly possible, but his brain was not up to the task.

'The lord Abbot of Evesham is here, de Nouailles,' declared Bradecote confidently, and loudly, seeing as the man clearly had a sore head and winced at even the first word, 'to see this vellum of yours, which says the mill you had from his abbey is upon a hundred year lease.'

'He can't see it.'

'But if you do not present it, my lord, why should anyone believe in its existence?' Abbot Reginald was not a man to raise his voice, but it was firm.

'Because I say so.'

'Forgive me, but that is . . . insufficient proof.'

'Do not try my patience, monk.' De Nouailles' eyes narrowed in anger.

'And do not try mine, de Nouailles.' Bradecote was cold, implacable.

'I do not know where it is.'

'No? A document so valuable? That is hard to believe.'

'Believe it.'

'No. I rather think that instead we will turn out every coffer, every box, in this manor until we find it.'

'You have no power, no ri—'

'I am Undersheriff of Worcester, and my power and my right come from the lord King. Catchpoll, go into the solar and bring anything that might contain documents. No need to be tidy about it.'

At this de Nouailles stood, grabbing the table lest he sway.

'Wait. I don't want that dog fouling my lady's possessions. I will fetch it.'

Bradecote felt one single shaft of pity. He had kept his dead wife's belongings, had he? So he could not bear to let go. De Nouailles, sobering by the minute now, disappeared into his solar and returned with a linen bag, in which was the folded vellum.

'There, see it if you must, but it bears the Evesham seal, and shows the mill mine still.' He pushed it across the table, roughly.

'Does it so?' By not a flicker of a muscle did the Abbot Reginald show that this was something he had long wished to view. He took the bag with as much care as if it had contained a relic, removed the document and called forward Brother Albanus, who had been lingering unhappily in the background, unused to such heat and unpleasantness. The sight of the parchment eased him, like finding an ally. He sighed, and took it up, tenderly.

He began to read it, his face bearing the trace of a smile, which turned to a frown. He looked up suddenly as if to exclaim, but his abbot nodded at him to continue. The frown of concentration became more questioning. The vellum was taken nearer to one of the narrow windows and the shutter opened to cast a better light upon it. The stained fingers turned it over, the myopic eyes peered so closely it was as if he was smelling the parchment.

'I am a little confused, Father. This hand is an Evesham hand, I have no doubt of that, and the seal is our seal, and yet it deceives. Why would a brother in our House create this thing?'

'Brother, that much I can explain to you. We have reason to think it was written by a scribe by the name of Thomas, who had once been a Brother of Evesham.' Catchpoll offered the answer.

'Thomas . . . Yes, I recall a brother lost to us of that name, years back.' He shook his head. 'He has done a bad thing here, though with some skill, and should do penance for it.'

'Too late to do any in this world, Brother, for he is dead these four months.'

The Benedictines crossed themselves. Brother Albanus looked pained.

'God have mercy upon him.'

'Indeed, Brother, but tell me what you see.' Bradecote did not want to rush the man, but time was pressing.

'This claims to be a lease dated 1108, but patently it is not. The vellum is not new; that would be too obvious. It is reused vellum, which is not unusual, even for leases. You can see where it was scraped clean, and where vestiges of its old existence remain. That too is perfectly in order, but not only are there old and faded lines, there are the ghosts of words, ghosts that show the lie. Here.' He pointed to a vague mark upon the vellum. The undersheriff squinted and Serjeant Catchpoll screwed up his face. Even had he been lettered, he thought he would not have been able to interpret it. 'That says "in the twentieth year of Henry the King", which gives a date of 1119 to 1120, and means the original words were set down about a dozen years later than those seemingly written over them, thus declaring them false.'

Hugh Bradecote could have danced a little jig in jubilation, but contented himself with a slow smile. Abbot Reginald folded his hands in a prayer of thanksgiving, and permitted himself a smile so discreet that it was barely visible.

'Thank you, Albanus. The words of truth shine forth even through the ink of deceit. Now, my lord de Nouailles, this proves that you have played us false. The mill is ours as of now.'

'No. It is your seal. You do not contest that. I say the monk lies, lies because you wish it. This is no fair scrutiny.'

'A seal may be removed and—'

'This seal belongs to this parchment, my lord,' interrupted Brother Albanus.

'See.' De Nouailles sounded confident once more.

'It does?' Bradecote cast the brother a questioning look.

'Oh yes, but then that is in order. You see, now I look again at what remains beneath, I see something I recognise.

This is, or rather was, a document I wrote, when I was barely more than a novice. I can see a little quirk that I have always had with the letter M. This was something that pertained to some dealing with the lord of Harvington, and must have been here for years.'

'This is but the word of one Benedictine obeying the instructions of his superior.' De Nouailles was repeating himself but with less conviction.

'But it can also come with us to Worcester, and the lord Sheriff's scribe will be able to see the forgery, even if he cannot identify where the forger learnt his letters. Explain it to de Beauchamp.' Bradecote was in the ascendant once more. 'It also gives you a reason to see that the forger never revealed his deed. Was that why you hanged him, de Nouailles, to keep him quiet?'

'He paid the price of theft, from the very person of my wife.'

'He paid the price, but was it owing, is what we wants to know?' Catchpoll ranged himself beside the undersheriff.

'You seek to find reasons, but are casting about and will follow the wildest of scents.' De Nouailles waved away the suggestion with more bravado than assurance. Then his expression changed to one of weary resignation. 'All right. I concede. The mill is clearly yours, Abbot, though may it rot and give you nothing but expense in the years to come. But you cannot lay the deception at my door. I do not write, nor read, and employed the thieving clerk to tell me its contents. Why should I doubt them? What was written was obviously set down at my father's instruction, when I was a mere youth. What son does not believe his father?'

Bradecote and Catchpoll glanced at each other in growing disbelief. That Brian de Nouailles would wriggle out of even the charge of keeping Evesham's mill by deception had not occurred to them, yet here he was, foisting all blame upon his own father, who could not refute the charge.

'But—' Catchpoll wanted to press further.

'But nothing. I give back the mill. It is more than enough. You make me sick, the lot of you, the law, the Church. And priests are the worst of it, acting so holy.'

With which he got up and stalked from his hall, leaving his accusers staring after him.

Catchpoll swore under his breath, volubly. Bradecote wanted to break something, preferably de Nouailles' neck.

'I fear that whilst we have been blessed with success, the proving of the lease has not given you what you needed, my lord. I am sorry for it, for there walks a man who has turned from God.' Abbot Reginald spoke in as measured a tone as ever, but there was a tinge of regret to it.

'Not your fault, Father Abbot,' murmured Bradecote, still staring at the closed door. 'I had you brought in haste that proved unnecessary and—'

'My lord.' Walkelin's eyes had widened, as two unpalatable thoughts hit him, and he interrupted, ignoring the frown from Serjeant Catchpoll.

'What?'

'Why did the lord de Nouailles leave his hall, with us in possession of it, rather than withdraw into his solar and order us out as he slammed the door?'

'Mayhap he wanted fresh air,' grumbled Catchpoll.

'Holy Mary, there is still that one way to prove his guilt. If the tirewoman declares what she knows, with the evidence of the false lease . . . He has gone to silence the woman Agatha.' Bradecote cursed himself for not seeing the wider scope.

'But she is not in the village, so all we have to do is find out—' Catchpoll began but was interrupted yet again by Walkelin, who was suddenly moving towards the door.

'But his last words were about priests. He could have said "monks", but he said "priests".'

'Father Paulinus!' Bradecote leapt like a horse under spur. 'Apologies . . . Cannot offer escort back . . . Keep lease.'

The three sheriff's men were running, charging through the door and bustling down the steps, leaving the Evesham Benedictines standing alone in the silent hall.

'Father Abbot, do you think he meant we should keep the document or that he should?'

'It is not entirely clear, but if we do, then he will know where to find it, and I think we are likely to be in the way if we remain.'

'We do not have to return to Evesham in such haste as we came, do we?' There was pleading in Brother Albanus's voice.

'No, Brother Albanus, we may take it gently.'

'Thanks be to God!'

Chapter Eighteen

Agatha was sat in the single chamber that was her brother-in-law's home, kneading dough upon a flat-stone. If she was adding to the mouths he must feed, it seemed right she should take on tasks her sister used to do, and free her niece, barely old enough to keep house, to work in the field. When there came a knock on the door she jumped, and said nothing, her hands stilled. The knock was repeated, and then the door opened. Leofwine the Steward bent his head to step over the low threshold.

'So here you are. I've been looking for you, Agatha.' His voice was very quiet.

'Here I am, Master Steward, and my sister's husband knows why.' She tried to look confident, but failed.

'Does he? Well, the lord wants you back in Harvington, so perhaps you could also tell me why on our way back.' He patently did not believe her.

'I don't have to go. I am a free woman, Leofwine son of Osbert, as well you know.'

'True, but disobeying the lord goes hard with folk.'

'Aye, and obeying also. Only look at your Aelfric,' she retorted. Leofwine looked grim, and her face suddenly crumpled. 'It's sorry I am, so sorry that all this has happened.'

Leofwine recalled his lord's words; 'her tongue has cost lives' he had said. Was it true after all?

'You could not have changed what happened.'

'Ah yes, but it all started with me.'

'What did?' He looked genuinely perplexed now, and came forward to sit opposite her, and leant forward. It was not a threatening pose. 'We go back a long time, Aggie.'

'We do.'

'He wants you dead.' Leofwine did not need to say de Nouailles' name.

'Yesterday I was afeared by that thought. Today,' she sighed, 'as I walked here, I seem to have lost some of that fear. What will be will be, as I found out with my poor girl. I never thought . . .' Agatha dabbed at her eyes with her skirt.

'What is it you know? What is it she knew and told Aelfric?'

'I thought it was right, when I told him, never thinking what would happen after.'

'Told who?'

'Her brother.'

'Aggie, give me the tale from the start, I beg you. I cannot unravel riddles.'

'It all goes back to the mill.'

'The mill?'

'Yes, the one the old lord had of Evesham. Well, the lord got that nasty pinch-faced clerk, didn't he.'

'Aye, to read the lease.'

'Read it, ha! He wrote it. I saw him, and I told my poor dear lady. How I wish I had not, for it distressed her something terrible, but she dare not say aught to her lord for he was in one of those tempers of his. Then she spoke to the clerk, and he . . . he made a comment. He must have heard who she was before she wed, and . . . it was unseemly. She told the lord, when he found her weeping, and then he was so angry I thought he would take his sword and fillet the man, and, whatever the law says, I would understand that. But he didn't. He waited, then made the claim about the attack and the brooch and hanged the clerk for theft with the goods upon him. That was a lie. I thought about it, and he wanted him dead because of the work he had done. My poor mistress, it broke her heart, and good as killed her. That morning, when she fell, I was in the hall when the lord was shouting at her to forget it all, and she could not, good soul as she was. Weeping and shaking, no wonder she slipped, and then and there the life was out of her, and she was gone.' Agatha crossed herself.

'And a bad day for all it was.'

'But then her brother came, and the first time he was grieving too but was treated harsh.'

'The lord has forgotten all but harshness. I know, grief can take a man that way.'

'I sometimes thought it took you, Leofwine, but then there was some glimmer of what you was when . . . She was a good woman, and right for you. I said as it was best I said no, and I was right.'

263

'You were, but you had said yes before that.'

Agatha blushed.

'That were the blood rising like the grass in spring, and thanks be that none was ever the wiser, for we were foolish.'

The memories of youth before trials intruded for a moment, then passed.

'So you told the horse trader about what ailed her.'

'I did, and as how the clerk died not for any theft. He must have flung that in the lord's face and brought him to a killing rage. I saw the poor man ride out, and I saw Aelfric upon the chestnut take the other road, but he was watching very careful. I have no doubt he doubled back down the track that meets before the bridge and—'

'Yes. I would have done as much if asked, but was not asked.'

'Kill a man in cold blood?'

'Not so cold. You see I saw the pain, recalled it. Bitter it is. If the fool had made the lord dwell on his loss, goaded him with it, then I would have been in hot blood for my lord, but hear me true, never would I have taken your Hild from breath as Aelfric did. There would have been another way, but he was hot-headed, not hot-blooded. The lord made him pay, and though it breaks me to see the last of mine laid in earth as with yours, there was a right to it, law or not. But you see, the lord did not kill him for the debt owing, but as with the clerk, to ensure silence, as he would with you. It goes beyond. I am de Nouailles' man, always have been, but it goes beyond, Aggie.'

'I'll take no harm from you, Leofwine?'

'No, none.'

'So what happens now? If you fail him, disobey? It is you

who said it goes hard with folks, and none more so than you who he sees as all his own. Would you say I could not be found?'

'He would have me out again to hunt for you and under command not to return until the task was done, and with bruises to remind me of my duty, so it would be but a delay.'

'But if I did not return?'

'No harm from me, I said, Aggie, and I stick to it.'

'But I could be "lost" to the world. What if you help me on my way to the nuns at Wroxall? I have no dower to offer them, but a lay sister to do the menial tasks might not be rejected, and if they knew I was escaping being done away with . . . See me safe the first day to Alcester. I could walk there in three or four days and would be no threat to the lord, so as good as dead. It would be both a lie and true, and none ever the wiser.'

'Would you wish it?'

'I don't think my wishes are very important any more. I will miss Harvington, for it is all I have ever known, and its people are my people, blood kin or not, but if I served the godly Sisters of Wroxall, I would be doing what God would see was good, and my prayers for the departed might be heard the better.'

Leofwine frowned, and said nothing for so long that Agatha resumed her kneading, not wanting the dough surface to dry. It was a very restful, homely action. She glanced up several times, but said nothing, for what was going on in his mind was a very private struggle, and so she kept a respectful silence. Eventually he spoke, in a whisper wrung out of him, and one that trembled.

'The thing is, Aggie, I am not so sure the Almighty wants all the evil that has gone on in our village to be ignored, aye, and continue. There is right and wrong, and for far too many

265

years I have ignored the wrong and even persuaded myself there was simply a balance of it to maintain. But this morning, when the lord sent me for you, I prayed, prayed as I have not for many years, determined to listen. I heard nothing, but the answer came here, with you. I understand why the lady was so distressed, for all she wanted was to please her lord, care for him, protect him, even. I have wanted that, done that as best I can, but . . . The sheriff's men will still be with Father Paulinus. If I can get you safe to them . . .' He paused, and shut his eyes for a moment. 'There's harsh, and there's unlawful, and I would look away from that out of loyalty, but these last few months, all the misery has come from wrong. He killed, however it was dressed up, from greed, and it brought about the death of as near an angel as could tread the good earth. He got my nephew to kill, and showed him once done it was easier to do again; and that cost your Hild her life. Then he killed Aelfric for his silence and would have me do the same with you. I will take you to Alcester if you say so, Aggie, but if it is God's will you want to do, I think we take the shorter road, and go back to Harvington, and God have mercy on Brian de Nouailles.'

It was her turn to think, but she did not take long. She twisted her floury hands together for a minute, and bit her lip, then looked Leofwine the Steward straight in the eye. She crossed herself.

'God's will be done.'

Brian de Nouailles did not knock. Knocking was for those without right, and in Harvington he had right over everything. He threw the door open wide, so that it banged back upon its

266

hinges, and stepped into the priest's simple home. The Widow Nesta, laying a fresh fire in the little hearth, looked up and was afraid. De Nouailles said nothing, turned, and left. The woman shuddered, and offered up a prayer for the well-being of Father Paulinus, for the look upon the lord's face had been murderous.

Father Paulinus was on his knees, lost in quiet prayer for the soul of the shrouded Aelfric, who awaited burial. The sight of the priestly Benedictine in this position fuelled Brian de Nouailles' anger all the more. He advanced up the short nave towards the chancel step, the acoustics amplifying every heavy tread. The priest continued on his knees, perhaps expecting that his orisons would be respected, and the visitor await their conclusion, but as the footfalls grew close, he sighed.

'Can I assist you, my son?' He did not look round.

The appellation drew a low, animal growl in response. In a dog it would signal an imminent attack, and Father Paulinus crossed himself and rose from his knees, slowly, deliberately, and turned to face the incensed lord.

'I offer what help I can.' His voice was gentle, but he knew he stood in danger, for the man in front of him was tensed, a muscle working in his jaw, the pulse throbbing in his neck, his eyes narrowed to flashing slits, his mouth a hard line.

'"What help you can". Such lies! You help yourselves, you black monks, and cloak it all in "holiness". But I am not deceived. I do not listen to your honeyed words and let them clog my mind. All you really want is power, power over this life by saying you have power to influence the life to come.'

'Each person has that power within them, if they listen to God's word. I make no claim for myself, nor for any priest.'

'No? Yet it is up to you to grant absolution, to set penance. How often have I heard it suggested that if one takes a certain course, one which gives money, land, goods, to the Church, then it will weigh in favour at Judgement.'

Father Paulinus was too honest a man not to admit that some clergy had been known to say such things, though he deplored it.

'You have never heard such claims from me.'

'No, because you know I would not believe them. Did you try them with my wife? Did you make her unhappy that she had come to wealth and position? Were you hoping for largesse, thinking she would influence me where you could not?'

'No, my lord de Nouailles, I did not. I prayed for her happiness, and acknowledged her as an example of goodness, which I can only aspire to copy. Her spirit was more pure than any woman I have ever met, and her sweetness and goodness made her unhappy when she felt the human failings of those she loved as wounds upon her heart.'

'You mean me. She loved me.'

'She loved everyone, seeing them in God's image as a Christian should do, but yes, above all others, she loved you.'

'So you blame me, me who would do anything for her. You see how you work against us, priest, loading us with guilt so we "need" you the more?'

Father Paulinus could not help the hint of a sad smile at the man's self-deception. His devotion had been real enough, but he had never given his lady what she truly wanted, which was for him to think of others, not reserve the only softness in him for her. De Nouailles saw the smile, and something in him snapped. The priest took a sudden step back out of instinct, and as instinctively sought to defend himself in the only way he could; he made the sign of the cross.

De Nouailles grabbed at him, taking him a handful of cowl and twisting it so that it half-strangled the cleric, and pulling upwards so that he was forced onto his toes. As the door of the church was flung wide he did what even he had previously been unable to do within a church, let alone 'his' church, to which his grandsire had added the short bell tower, and drew steel, his dagger catching the light from one of the little round-arched windows.

'De Nouailles!' Bradecote's shout filled the stone enclosed space.

Brian de Nouailles looked down the aisle, and sneered.

'Always one step behind, aren't you, sheriff's man? Well, you can halt your steps right there, unless you want to see me prove monks are as frail and human as the rest of us.'

'He is a priest. He is your priest, and he has done you no harm.'

'He's still a black monk, and they scheme together, still flock like rooks, sticking their beaks where they are not wanted. Who told the Evesham Abbot about Thomas and the lease, priest?'

'I did.' Walkelin spoke up. 'That you used a clerk who had been at Evesham was no secret. And we suspected that what he did was not just read for you. You are seeing what does not exist.'

'You? You could not work out which end of a horse to face.' De Nouailles sneered, but his attention was distracted a little.

Catchpoll, who had arrived a couple of yards behind the younger men, leant a little forward and whispered in Walkelin's ear.

'That's it lad, focus him on you, and edge to the left. I will see if I can get near enough on the right to make a rush at him.'

Walkelin obeyed, speaking with a swagger and confidence that were at variance with his normal self-effacing manner.

'Not only can I work that out without being told by some high-and-mighty lord, I can tell one horse from another, even when the same colour.'

Bradecote was quite surprised at how cocksure Catchpoll's protégé could pretend to be; at least he presumed it was all an act. It certainly seemed to be working on de Nouailles, whose sneer became a snarl.

'Insolent dog. When I've taught the clergy a lesson, I have one for you too.'

'Rank doesn't mean you fight better, just with a prettier dagger.' Walkelin was warming to his task. There was something dangerously liberating about speaking back at a puissant lord.

Catchpoll had manoeuvred himself a little closer up the side of the church in light shadow, taking things very steadily. Father Paulinus saw, and studiously avoided watching, but he tensed, and that was all that it took. De Nouailles turned his head, for Catchpoll had almost been in a blind spot.

'Nice try, you old fox, but I am not to be taken that easily. Get back, now.'

Catchpoll did not wait to confirm his action with Bradecote but stepped back, hands raised in a gesture of compliance.

'Why continue this, de Nouailles? At some point you have to give in.' Bradecote kept any note of triumph out of his voice.

'At some point, aye, but that point is of my choosing, Bradecote, and when I have all I want from this interfering snake. You see, not only do I still think he is behind Evesham clawing back what was mine, but he spoke to the woman Agatha. What chance you told her to make herself scarce?'

'All I did was take away the risk of another mortal sin.'

'Thoughtful of you, but is it not also a mortal sin for a priest to break the seal of the confessional?'

'It is, and I have not broken it.' Father Paulinus, who had, at the prick of the knife at his throat, suffered a moment of very human weakness and not desired an early meeting with his Maker, had now regained his composure.

'With this lot about your hearth every eventide? I do not know whether to account that another lie or a jest, but you had better hope the former, for if I laugh, my hand will shake, and your throat will feel steel.'

'I have not broken the sanctity of confession, anyone's confession.' He stressed the penultimate word, and de Nouailles stiffened.

'What have the godly to confess?' he growled.

'Only the saints no longer sin. Even the godly fail, though it might be because they are placed in so difficult a position that they are complicit with sin.'

'You think I dragged her down? No, you made her dwell on things not her fault, and for that you will—'

The church door, not more than half-closed from when the sheriff's men had entered, swung wide again. Agatha stood upon the threshold, Leofwine at her back.

'For God's sake, I told you to get rid of her, not bring her back, you mindless bull's pizzle,' yelled de Nouailles.

Agatha, calm as if she were coming to Mass, walked up the

aisle, even past the sheriff's men. Leofwine followed, but hung back a step.

'Well you see, my lord, we had a little talk about that, Leofwine and me, and decided there had been enough deaths hereabouts these last weeks, and all unnatural as they were. So I am back, and if you thinks harming the good Father will clear your path, then you are mighty mistaken. I know what I must do, and what I must say, and so it will be, even if you try to make an end of me for it.'

'Then be wise, woman, and step back out of reach,' murmured Catchpoll, suddenly nervous that their star witness, who could make all the pieces fit together, was putting herself into danger.

Agatha ignored him.

'You thinks you wants our priest, but it is me, Agatha, daughter of Cuthwin the Deaf, who will denounce you to the law.'

'And you are nothing. Denounce away, woman. Any jury will be as deaf to your words as your father was.'

'You forget we have witnesses who have seen you threaten the priest, and admit that you commanded your man to kill this woman.' Bradecote wanted this stand-off over. There was, as the woman said, no sense in harming Father Paulinus, but he was not sure that de Nouailles was thinking with sense, just gut anger. His next words confirmed that.

'And you think that worries me? You want me, you will have to take me by force. I am Brian de Nouailles and ashamed of nothing I have done.'

'Ashamed? How can you stand there and say such a thing?'

Agatha was so indignant that she pressed forward, shaking off even Leofwine's restraining hand.

'Nothing, woman.'

'Not ashamed that you killed that . . . angel?'

The disdain on his visage changed to black wrath, and he let Father Paulinus go, almost throwing him from him. The priest staggered, putting out his hands to prevent him falling flat on his face upon the floor. Bradecote and his men stepped closer, ready for a concerted attempt to grapple with de Nouailles.

'A black lie, and I shall take your tongue for it, you old bitch.'

'A truth, a truth you cannot face! You killed her as sure as if you had broke her neck with your bare hands. Murderer!' Agatha was screaming, and pointed at him, making the accusation a curse. 'You broke her heart with your lies and your killing, and she was sore tormented by it, for she could no more turn upon you than I could turn upon her. Death released my poor lady from you, from your evil, and if ever there was one upon whom the Good Lord will have mercy it is she. You killed her, you killed my lady!'

Bradecote tensed, ready to throw himself between the man and the near hysterical woman as he pounced. Brian de Nouailles' eyes widened, his nostrils flared, yet even as the undersheriff leapt forward, the lord of Harvington looked heavenwards and howled 'No' like a wolf in the night. The dagger clattered to the ground and he was sinking to his knees before the three men grabbed hold of him, and pinioned him. He was convulsed by wracking sobs, and his colour drained so much that had the blade not been clear upon the stone at his feet, Bradecote would have sworn he had severed some vital vessel.

Leofwine took the trembling Agatha, sobbing even louder, and held her, soothing her with words even as he looked over her head at his lord, and Walkelin was struck by the thought that the words were for him also. Father Paulinus, shaken as much in mind as in body by what had passed, covered his eyes for a moment and intoned familiar phrases of liturgical Latin which gave him calm and strength. Then, not sure whether the broken de Nouailles would yet be open to accepting even his own forgiveness, he went to the steward and laid his hand upon the man's shoulder, for he could see, as perhaps few others could, how desolated the man was by the fall of a man to whom he had looked up to for decades. The words that sprang to the good priest's tongue, were those of his Saviour upon the Cross.

'It is finished.'

Brian de Nouailles had 'given up the ghost', but 'the ghost' had not yet given up on him.

Chapter Nineteen

The funeral of Aelfric was an odd affair, not only because it was known that he had killed the girl the villagers had seen laid to rest only the day previously, but because all knew that their lord faced a capital charge, and there was worry over who might come to them in his stead. Nothing was said but much was conjectured, and from more guessing than knowledge. The future of the village was in all minds, even Leofwine the Steward's. Some questioned how it could be that Agatha stood beside him, and made her responses as firmly as any, when his nephew had killed her daughter, or how she could hold his hands in her own and weep with him at the conclusion. They did not know as she did, that he was mourning not only his kin but the man he had served, almost blindly, from boyhood.

Brian de Nouailles had been taken by the sheriff's men and locked in his own 'cell' beneath his hall, and there Walkelin took the first watch over him, with the promise that he would be relieved after the evening meal, and that plenty would be kept hot for him. Hugh Bradecote also told him that he faced the first watch through the eating hour to remind him 'this particular "high-and-mighty lord"' would continue to tell him what to do, but as Walkelin began to stammer that his disrespect had all been an act, Bradecote's lips twitched, and he patted his worried underling on the back.

'There was a time for it, Walkelin, and you did well. Just remember to keep it like a best cotte, to be brought out rarely.'

When undersheriff and serjeant sat in the priest's house, watching the bubbling pot from which came the enticing smell of fish and barley stew with herbs, only Serjeant Catchpoll showed any interest in it. Father Paulinus sat upon the edge of his narrow bed, deep in his own thoughts, and Hugh Bradecote stared at the simmering liquid dolefully, without seeing it.

'Have we been successful here, Catchpoll?' His voice had a dullness to it.

'Yes, my lord. How can you doubt it? We are taking a murderer twice over for justice, and the other is dead and left to the judgement of heaven. All we have missed is restoring a stolen horse.'

'But since we started there have been two more deaths.'

'Which we could not have avoided, as far as I can see.'

'And if we had not stirred up the hornet's nest, would not the latter two not have been stung, and died.' Bradecote felt a sudden wave of guilt.

'Ah, now that is no way to think, my lord. If the law did not seek out the breakers of law then in short shrift there would be mayhem. Do you think that de Nouailles would have been all mild and biddable in the future? Or that Aelfric would have sat upon his hands and waited for his uncle to hand over the reins of stewardship? Well, before you answer, I will tell you, and the answer is "no" to both things. It is unfortunate, I grant you, but suggesting that "leave well alone" should be our watchword is like suggesting not disturbing a fox in your henhouse lest he wreak more havoc.'

'I suppose so.' The undersheriff did not look much cheered, however sensible the advice.

'Forgive me, my lord. I would not say this with young Walkelin in earshot, but we all of us have faults, even me,' Catchpoll made this sound as if the revelation would be a surprise to all who knew him, 'and yours is a tendency to over-think, and to lay blame upon yourself where no blame should be.'

'You told me last time we hunted together, that you must not get too involved because that clouds thinking. Well, I let my dislike of de Nouailles lie over everything like a blanket.'

'And yet it did not lead you astray, my lord. It was you who was at first so sure he did not kill his lady, whatever you thought of him, and when you got angry, well, you used that anger to show that the office of undersheriff sets you apart from being the simple equal of a manor lord, and that such a one cannot refuse you entrance or speech. I call that using the anger well, my lord, like using the power of the Avon to drive a waterwheel.'

Even this did not seem to raise his superior's spirits, and he made a poor meal, which, Catchpoll commented, would please young Walkelin, since it left him an even more generous portion. Thanking the priest, Catchpoll rose and went to relieve his 'serjeanting apprentice'.

Father Paulinus, whose own meal had been abstemious, looked at the undersheriff and frowned.

'Your serjeant has the right of it, I am sure, my lord. That becoming involved hastens evil deeds must be so at times, but does not mean one stands back. Without law the highest power is . . . power itself, regardless of right.'

'I know, Father. It is.' Bradecote sighed. 'I think my guilt is as much over the fact that however much I loathe the man, Brian de Nouailles truly loved his wife.'

'And this makes you guilty? Do you not love your lady wife?'

'I do, with every fibre of my heart.'

'Then . . .'

'Father, my first wife died before Michaelmas last, giving me a son, and though I was fond of her, I never loved her, never had a passion for her as de Nouailles had for his Edith.'

'Tell me, my son, did you make her unhappy by lacking passion for her?'

'I . . . I do not think so, Father. She loved me, at least she was driven almost to panic to try and fulfil what she thought might be my wishes. I was never cold, not harsh with her, beyond what any man says on occasion when women fuss too much about them.'

'Then consider your lady, and then the lady de Nouailles, who loved her lord, and was indeed adored. Your lady departed this life having triumphed in presenting you with a son. The lady of Harvington died wracked with worry and fear and guilt. His passion for her did not give her joy, because he is a man in whom all passions are excessive, be they love or hate, devotion or greed. What was your late wife's name?'

'Ela.'

'And the lady who holds your heart now, she loves your son?'

'My Christina? As if he were sprung from our union.'

'I shall pray for them both at Compline, and for you also, my son. Come to church with me and lay your thoughts before God, and let him take away the burden of guilt that should not lie upon you.'

Walkelin came in, rubbing his hands together to take off the chill of an April evening, and in anticipation of a good meal. He had no cares, nor did he study his superior and wonder at his. When he joined the undersheriff in the little church, his prayers were the simple ones of thanks for a full belly and a safe and peaceful night for his mother.

In the undercroft of his own hall, Brian de Nouailles sat in the dark, and his cheeks were wet. He felt no remorse for Thomas the Clerk, for Walter Horsweard, or for Aelfric, but Agatha's accusation rang in his ears like the interminable toll of a passing bell. 'You killed her as sure as if you had broke her neck with your bare hands.' He had denied it so vehemently to himself these weeks, but could not avoid facing it now, and had he his dagger he would not have attempted escape but self-slaughter. He whispered her name, over and over, seeing her face before him, the grey eyes large with sorrow, so real to him that eventually, long after Hugh Bradecote had taken up his own watch outside, and he passed from full wakefulness into the half-sleep before oblivion, he felt her hand upon his cheek, wiping away his tears, and her own falling upon his clasped hands.

* * *

The dawn saw Walkelin yawning over his second watch even as a grubby pink smudge grew upon the eastern horizon. It was well past full dawn when his superiors roused themselves, and found that Father Paulinus had slipped out to his orisons without waking them. They waited for his return before completing their preparations for departure.

'I am sorry that we have been the harbingers of turmoil, if nothing else, Father.' Hugh Bradecote's smile was twisted.

'I think, my lord, the turmoil was already here, seething like a pot about to boil over. You doused the fire.'

'You have given us not only shelter but good company and wise words. Thank you.'

'The shelter was built before my time, and the words, if wise, are from God, but thank you for the compliment about the company. You will have it a mite longer for I shall accompany you to the manor, to offer what I can to your prisoner, and to say farewell to your serjeant-in-training. If his appetite for the truth matches his appetite for food, he will be a great asset to you. The women who cook for me will be holding him up as an example to me, when I do not finish the portions they provide me, for weeks to come.'

Bradecote laughed, and Catchpoll remarked that perhaps red hair made for a greater capacity for food.

Their mood became more sombre when they entered the bailey, unchallenged by the gatekeeper. The most incongruous thing was that everything seemed so very ordinary and normal. Leofwine the Steward emerged from the stable, as unsmiling as ever, but more melancholy than challenging.

'I have had the lad saddle the lord's horse. He will at least ride to Worcester on his own beast, even if his wrists are bound.'

Bradecote raised no objection. After all, dragging a prisoner behind them all the way on foot would simply make the journey twice as long.

'All seems quiet here, Master Steward.'

'What sense would there be in aught else? The manor is the manor, whether there is a lord in residence or not. The fields still need tending, the meals still need to be prepared. No, we continue as if . . .' Leofwine could not quite bring himself to say 'as if nothing had happened'.

There was nothing the undersheriff could say that would improve matters, so he nodded, dismounted and went to see Walkelin.

'Any trouble?'

'Not a murmur, my lord.'

For a moment Bradecote wondered if de Nouailles had managed to find some way to end his own life, but when the door was unbolted and the shaft of light penetrated within, he was there, sat against the wall, a little dishevelled, but breathing still. Yet it was as if he were but the ghost of Brian de Nouailles. He appeared shrunken, his cheeks were hollow as if he had fasted for a week, and there was nothing of the anger, the pride, or the malevolence that had been part of him only yesterday. When Father Paulinus stepped forward to offer him confession, the sheriff's men thought he would cast the offer back with foul words, but he nodded, and the priest, waving away the offer of a presence in case he might be assaulted, entered the gloom and pulled the door closed behind him. What passed between them was for none to know, but the priest emerged some time later, his face a blend of regret and wonder.

'Of a certainty the good can do good from beyond this life,' he murmured, and sighed. 'Take your prisoner, my lord. You will have no trouble from him.' With which he made them a benediction, and walked unhurriedly to the gate, but as he reached it, he had to step aside as a man entered on horseback, a man leading a large-boned bay horse with a big Roman nose and a white off-hind.

Walkelin simply pointed, his jaw dropped.

'Aye, lad, we can see it too.' Catchpoll mumbled.

'The lord Undersheriff?' The rider, who spoke with a distinct lilt to his voice, looked at Bradecote, being the best garbed and with the finest sword.

'Yes, I am he.'

'My name is Rhodri the Welshman, and I live a little short of Bevington. This horse I found grazing just beyond my tilth for vegetables, yesterday afternoon. I feared some soul had met with accident or wickedness, and went to my lord. He said as the sheriff's men were in Harvington as he had heard, and I should bring it to you, lest, look you, it be thought I stole it.'

'Your honesty is commendable, my friend. The man who rode it did indeed meet with wickedness, but we can return it to its rightful owner for whom it will be some consolation.'

'And I did not steal it.'

'No, we are assured of that for we know already who did.'

Rhodri looked most relieved, and handed the reins to Walkelin, who still gazed at the horse as if it were an apparition. Catchpoll went to bind de Nouailles and lead him out to his horse. The man blinked in the daylight, and the more so at the sight of Horsweard's bay, but he said not a word, even as Leofwine, in a last act of service, made his hands into a step so that he could mount. Once in the saddle he looked down at the man who had served him so well, and whose one act of disobedience had cost him so much, but there was no emotion on his face. As he rode out of his manor, knowing he would not see it again, he did not look back. Leofwine the Steward crossed himself.

'He's dead already,' he murmured.

They took the Evesham road, and as they neared the gate Bradecote glanced at his prisoner. He had wanted so much to see him defeated, broken, and yet now it was done it gave him no pleasure at all. At heart he knew this was because what had broken him was not the evidence of the law, but the crumbling of self-deception that had prevented him blaming himself for his wife's death. A beautiful and godly woman had torn him apart, without ever intending it.

De Nouailles' horse was led, and that would remain, but Bradecote felt a sudden reluctance to put the man on show. He unclasped his riding cloak and threw it across the withers of the prisoner's horse, hiding the bound wrists. De Nouailles did not bat an eyelid.

'Walkelin, I want you to take Will Horsweard his property, and tell him justice for his brother has been done. And leave my compliments with the abbot and tell him . . . that all is concluded.'

'I will, my lord.'

'We will cross the river at the Hampton ferry and should meet not far beyond that, for I doubt Horsweard will want a long tale.'

'Very good, my lord.'

Walkelin trotted ahead and turned to the abbey gates as captors and captive made their way through the town without drawing attention to themselves. Brother Porter opened the gate with alacrity

283

and a smile of recognition. The message for Abbot Reginald was discharged swiftly, for Walkelin was admitted straight away into his presence. The Benedictine was relieved to know that no harm had come to Father Paulinus, and said that all, including Brian de Nouailles, would be in his personal prayers. Thereafter Walkelin headed to the messuage of Will Horsweard, with its stable to its side. As he dismounted, he heard the cry of surprise.

'By the saints, you have it after all!' Will Horsweard limped from within the stable, and looked at the horse with as great amazement as Walkelin had earlier.

'We have, Master Horsweard. And I am to tell you from the lord Undersheriff, that your brother has justice. The man who killed him is himself dead, and he who set that man to kill is to be tried for not only that but murders of his own. The murderer was the lord of Harvington's man, and the lord will not see his manor again.'

'But why? What could . . . Did he make away with my sister?'

'No,' Walkelin was not going to try and explain how he was responsible for her death but not guilty of it, or was that the other way about, and the image of the broken man from the cell made him add, 'whatever ill he did, and it was much, the lord of Harvington loved your sister more than anything on earth.'

Horsweard seemed contented with that, and asked no difficult questions. He had come to terms with his losses, and they were consigned to his prayers, not crowding his thoughts. He was delighted to get back both horse and saddlery, and only as he patted the big velvety nose when he tied the horse in its stall did he know, beyond all doubt, that he would sell the beast, at a good price, of course, as soon as he might. There was something in the limpid eyes that was a little reproachful, and he would always think of his brother when he saw it.

Walkelin trotted out of Evesham, and saw his companions disembarking from the ferry upon the further shore. Catchpoll, turning to speak to the ferryman, saw him waving, and so the shrieval party waited until he had made the crossing, and then trotted briskly towards the bridge at Pershore, with the loop of the Avon to their north, and the brooding presence of Bredon Hill to their south.

It was mid afternoon when they finally entered Worcester Castle. Catchpoll and Walkelin took their silent prisoner to the cells, and Hugh Bradecote went, with an injunction for the others to follow when all was done, to make his report to William de Beauchamp.

The lord Sheriff of Worcester did not like to find his own class shown up as criminal. He thought it made a bad impression. In de Nouailles' case he was prepared to make an exception, and rubbed his hands together.

'Well, well. He was ever a hard bastard, and I for one won't be sad to see the back of him. What did you think of him?'

'Much as you, except . . .' Bradecote paused, 'I was looking forward to seeing him hang, but now . . . If you go to the cells, my lord, you would scarce recognise the man from the one who thought himself above the law, cleverer than the law, but yesterday. He is pitiful.'

'Sounds as if you are going soft, to me.'

Bradecote shook his head.

'He was cleverer than the law for a while, and, by heaven, he rubbed that in and I came close to drawing steel upon him out of pure rage, but now . . . As I said, see for yourself, my lord, and you will believe me.'

'But the law caught up with him in the end, and broke him.'

'No, my lord. I could say that, but it would be a lie. What caught up with him, aye, and broke him too, was a ghost.'

William de Beauchamp raised a sceptical eyebrow, and made a derogatory noise in his throat. He expected Catchpoll to be more pragmatic, and said as much when he and his serjeant watched Hugh Bradecote mount up ready to leave.

'You and I do not believe in ghosts, Catchpoll.'

'No, my lord, but I know that if one believes in something hard enough it can be real. The lord of Harvington could not let go of his wife, even buried, and so she kept a reality. You might say that is a sort of ghost, my lord, and my lord Bradecote was right. It was the thought of her, the sight of her in his mind, as took him in the end.'

Bradecote gave a nod, which was both to his lord, and to Catchpoll. He looked thoughtful, but no longer miserable, for he was going home to his Christina and his son, and he knew he would receive a joyous greeting. As the castle gate was opened for him, a slow smile spread across his face. The lady de Nouailles had been described as like an angel, and saintly. His Christina was a good woman, but he doubted she was angel or saint, since he had never heard of either being as seductive as she was when the solar door kept all others out. A bed kept warm, she had promised. She was a woman who kept her promises.

The grey horse trotted under the arch of the gateway and headed for home.

SARAH HAWKSWOOD describes herself as a 'wordsmith' who is only really happy when writing. She read Modern History at Oxford and first published a non-fiction book on the Royal Marines in the First World War before moving on to mediaeval mysteries set in Worcestershire.

bradecoteandcatchpoll.com